# A Murder
# in Passing

## Books by Mark de Castrique

The Buryin' Barry Series
*Dangerous Undertaking*
*Grave Undertaking*
*Foolish Undertaking*
*Final Undertaking*
*Fatal Undertaking*

The Sam Blackman Series
*Blackman's Coffin*
*The Fitzgerald Ruse*
*The Sandburg Connection*
*A Murder in Passing*

Other Novels
*The 13th Target*
*Double Cross of Time*

Young Adult Novels
*A Conspiracy of Genes*
*Death on a Southern Breeze*

# A Murder
# in Passing

## A Sam Blackman Mystery

## Mark de Castrique

Poisoned Pen Press

First Edition 2013

10 9 8 7 6 5 4 3 2 1

Library of Congress Catalog Card Number: 2012954698

ISBN: 9781464201493     Hardcover
      9781464201516     Trade Paperback

Poisoned Pen Press
6962 E. First Ave., Ste. 103
Scottsdale, AZ 85251
www.poisonedpenpress.com
info@poisonedpenpress.com

Printed in the United States of America

*For my new grandson Charlie*
*May you always have a book close at hand*

# Chapter One

"So, where are we going?" I asked the question as Nakayla tossed her backpack in the rear of my Honda CR-V and then climbed into the front passenger's seat.

"I'll know in a few minutes." She pulled her cellphone out of a belt pouch and held it in front of her like a divining rod.

I shook my head with disbelief. "We don't go through such elaborate secrecy on a stakeout. You'd think we were hunting international spies, not mushrooms."

Nakayla laughed. "Mushrooming is serious business." Her phone beeped. "They're early."

I started the engine and backed down the driveway of Nakayla's bungalow in West Asheville. "You're telling me. Seven o'clock on a Saturday morning is way too early."

"You wanted a hobby, Sam." She held the phone closer to her face and read the email. "Great choice. And I won't have to hear you argue with the GPS lady."

"We don't argue. The woman just can't make up her mind. Always recalculating. Now, back to my original question. Where are we going?"

"The Kingdom of the Happy Land."

I gave her a sideways glance. "You're kidding. What the hell's that?"

"The only place in North Carolina ruled by a king."

"What about King George?"

"Touché. I mean after the revolution. It was a commune formed by ex-slaves. I didn't know anything about it until several years ago when I investigated a fraudulent insurance claim against the owners of a neighboring summer camp. We got to be friends and they told me about the Kingdom. I've always wanted to see it."

"And it's still functioning?"

"No. I think it disbanded around the late eighteen-hundreds." She looked at her phone again. "But our club president says the land is supposed to have mushrooms galore, and it's private property. So, we'll get a history lesson, some exercise, and I'll fix whatever we find for dinner tonight. Much easier than cleaning a deer."

"Good point. And I can probably leave my gun in the car."

Nakayla arched her eyebrows. "You brought your pistol to a mushroom club field trip?"

"Hey, you're the one who said there might be claim jumpers."

"No. I said if we announce the location in advance, other people figure we know what we're talking about and immediately search the site."

"It's hard to believe."

"That people would immediately search the site?"

"That you know what you're talking about."

She gave me a jab in the ribs. "I'm the one standing between you and a poisonous toadstool. What do you say about that?"

"Recalculating."

Nakayla dropped the phone back in the pouch. "Smart man." She reclined the seat a few degrees. "The site's a couple miles below Flat Rock. We should be there in about forty minutes."

The previous year we'd solved a mystery involving Carl Sandburg's farm in Flat Rock so the route was familiar. Since then, our detective agency had investigated only a handful of cases, mostly missing persons who turned out to be either runaway teens or husbands with midlife crises who left to find themselves.

Our scarcity of business wasn't a financial concern. Nakayla and I each had offshore accounts funded by acquisitions better left off the books. The Blackman and Robertson Detective Agency gave us a method for converting some of that money into reportable income. Neither of us had a desire for an extravagant lifestyle, but we did enjoy an active one. The dearth of cases had prompted my comment to Nakayla that I needed a challenge, even if it was only a hobby.

And so, on a Saturday morning in May, I found myself hot on the trail of wild mushrooms, not exactly the challenge I had in mind.

Nakayla had been a member of the Blue Ridge Mushroom Club since her first job out of college. She'd gone inactive when we'd formed the detective agency and our business and personal lives intertwined. As a native of western North Carolina, she'd shown me her favorite mountain haunts and introduced me to many of her friends. I'd grown up in central North Carolina, the section known as the piedmont, and only came to the Appalachians for short vacations as a child when the summer heat drove my family into the hills.

A rocket grenade in Iraq had taken my left leg, ended my military career as a CID Chief Warrant Officer, and transported me to the V.A. hospital in Asheville for rehabilitation. The murder of Nakayla's sister had brought us together and I found in her a kindred spirit, a partner who made me whole in a way the doctors and prosthetic devices couldn't. Although we teased and kidded, there was no doubt she and I would stand in the line of fire for each other. I knew because it had happened more than once.

"Aside from the gun, did you bring what I asked?"

I ran down my mental checklist before speaking. "Compass, bug spray, water, knife, trowel, wax paper, a basket, a cooler with ice, and Chardonnay."

"Chardonnay?"

"Yes. I always have wine with mushrooms."

"Good. If you eat the wrong species, the alcohol will accelerate the toxins. Drink all you want. I paid the premium on your life insurance yesterday."

I didn't have a comeback. As far as mushrooms went, I was a babe in the woods and Nakayla ruled the day.

Soon after we passed through the tiny town of Tuxedo, Nakayla instructed me to turn onto a one-lane dirt road that was not much more than a logging trail. The CR-V negotiated the steady climb for what seemed like a mile until we came to an open pasture on a rounded hilltop. Seven vehicles were parked in a loosely formed arc. I pulled to a stop at one end and we got out.

A small group of enthusiasts gathered at the pasture's edge. Some checked their gear; others gathered around a map spread across the hood of a Jeep.

Everyone waved at Nakayla. She was like the prodigal daughter returning from a distant land. There must have been eight or ten of them, a variety of ages and roughly balanced by gender. All were white, not that it mattered to Nakayla. Being the only African-American in the club wouldn't have bothered her in the least.

They eyed me with curiosity. Several glanced at my legs, and I knew they'd been forewarned I was an amputee. I wore the prosthesis I called my "Land Rover." It was stiffer and better suited for hiking. My other device was designed for regular wear and I dubbed it the "Cadillac" for its soft, cushy feel.

A tall man with curly gray hair stepped forward and offered his hand. "Welcome, Sam. I'm Donnie Nettles and the president of this dubious organization."

The others formed a semicircle behind him and I wondered if some initiation was about to occur.

Nettles cleared his throat. "As a paid member of the Blue Ridge Mushroom Club, you are entitled to all rights and privileges."

"Paid member?" I whispered.

"Happy birthday six months early," Nakayla said.

Nettles nodded. "And as soon as we get some rights and privileges, we'll tell you what they are."

The others laughed and I relaxed. The group had a sense of humor.

"But we do have a coveted item that's awarded to each member." He reached in the chest pocket of his khaki shirt and withdrew what looked like a box for a ring. He flipped open the lid, and on a velvet cushion rested a silver police whistle. "You'll notice the letters BRMC for Blue Ridge Mushroom Club have been carefully engraved along the mouthpiece. The chain and pocket clip are designed to loop through a button hole so the whistle will always be within reach."

He stepped forward and affixed the chain to my shirt pocket. "We only have the one box so it stays with me. Wear the whistle proudly. We all do, and it comes in handy in case you ever get lost in the woods. That's happened to more than one of us. Or you can use it if you come across a treasure trove of morels and want to share them with other club members. That's never happened."

The group laughed and broke up. The initiation was over.

"Come with me," Nettles said. "As the newcomer, we'll give you first choice on the happy hunting grounds of the Kingdom of the Happy Land."

He turned back to the hood of the Jeep and I noticed the four corners of the topographical map were weighed down with small, flat stones. A hand-drawn circle inscribed most of the terrain and lines cut the encompassed area into wedges like pieces of a pie. The slices grew wider as the distance increased from the center that marked the pasture.

"I've divided the site into ten areas. Ed Bell, the property owner, assures me each should yield equal opportunity. This time of year we'll most likely find Laetiporus Sulphureus and Pleurotus. There should be plenty of fallen logs to support both species."

"Laetiporus Sulphureus." I confidently repeated the name like I ate it for breakfast every morning.

"It's Sam's favorite," Nakayla said. "They share the same nickname."

Nettles laughed and I knew I was the butt of some joke.

"Sulfur Shelf's an odd nickname," he said.

Nakayla shook her head. "Try again."

"Play nice," I said. "Don't make me blow my new whistle."

Whatever it was, Donnie Nettles didn't want to say it.

"Chicken of the Woods," Nakayla said gleefully. "But don't worry, Sam. That's too many words to engrave on your whistle."

I pointed to the map. "We'll see who's chicken. Give us the area that has the most bears."

"I don't know about the bears, but this southern section is the most interesting. Ed Bell says it's the site of the original palace, as he calls it." Nettles hesitated, and then added, "The terrain is pretty manageable. I hiked it as a kid."

Nakayla didn't say anything, and I knew she was letting me make the call. Rightly or wrongly, I took Nettles' statement as a personal message that he didn't know if a man with one leg could handle some of the other areas. My pride prompted me to ask for the toughest terrain, but I also knew Nakayla was interested in seeing the remains of this nineteenth-century commune.

"Sounds good," I said.

He nodded. "Then let's get the other sections assigned and start. We'll need to meet back here in two hours." He turned to Nakayla. "I promised Ed Bell I'd make sure everyone was accounted for."

"We'll wait with you," Nakayla said. "Assuming we're not the ones who are lost."

"Not two detectives," Nettles said.

"Right," I said. "That's us. We know exactly where we are at all times. Even when we haven't got a clue."

"Which is most of the time," Nakayla added. "We'll just follow a stream, right, Sam?"

"Good advice," Nettles said. "Water will lead you to people."

I laughed. "Nakayla's ribbing me because I once told her I followed a river during night maneuvers. It was survival training over terrain similar to this. I was alone, hacking through underbrush about thirty yards from the river when suddenly a car drove by on top of the water. A car or a pickup. All I saw were headlights."

"The river was frozen?" Nettles asked.

"The river was a paved road. The reflected moonlight on the patches of asphalt I saw through the brush had looked like water. I'd spent thirty minutes being scratched and tripped when I could have been walking along the shoulder of a road."

"We don't mention that story in our brochure," Nakayla said.

Nettles gave me a sympathetic smile. "Hey, I got lost more than once in Vietnam. That was a good way to wind up dead. Here, you're a little safer. Water or a road, either one will bring you to civilization, or in this case, South Carolina, which isn't necessarily the same thing."

"I'll make sure he has a compass," Nakayla said. "And his whistle."

Nettles called the group together. The remaining sections of the map were assigned and we agreed to return to base at ten. I thought the day was shaping up nicely. Take a leisurely hike in the woods, find a couple of mushrooms, finish early enough to grab lunch in nearby Hendersonville, and then drive back to Asheville where Nakayla could prepare our harvest to be eaten atop a cut of grass-fed beef I'd cook on the grill. Maybe a new hobby revolving around food wasn't such a bad idea.

Nakayla and I hiked for about ten minutes before she saw an old log lying diagonally across the slope.

"Here we go. This is what we're looking for." She pointed to orange fungi clinging to the rotten wood like misshapen plates. "Chicken of the Woods."

"The same thing as Sulfur Shelf?"

"Yes. See how it grows in layers? Like shelves on a wall. Get your trowel and basket. We'll wrap the fruit body in wax paper and then you can take it with you."

"What do you mean? Aren't we going together?"

Nakayla bent over the log and started cutting the mushrooms free. "No. If we split up, we'll cover twice the territory. You've got your compass. Remember your bearings and we'll meet back here no later than quarter to ten. I'm giving you these to use as a reference." She gently laid one of the orange mushrooms in a sheet of wax paper, loosely folded it closed, and then dropped the future menu item into my basket. "Most will be this orange color, although older ones might have gone more salmon. If you're lucky, you'll find them on hardwoods. The ones growing on dead pines are a little strong for my taste."

"Okay. Which way do you want me to go?"

She pointed with her trowel. "Head up at a forty-five-degree angle to the right and I'll do the same to the left. Watch your compass and remember landmarks. Daniel Boone you're not."

I lifted the basket. "No. I feel more like Little Red Riding Hood."

I set off across the slope, my tools in my backpack, basket in my right hand, and shiny new whistle bouncing against my chest. The morning sunlight streamed through the canopy in slanted rays. Squirrels chattered, clearly sizing me up as a harmless vagabond. The air warmed and the scent of pine floated on a gentle breeze.

After about ten minutes, I intersected a small creek. I pulled some pebbles from the bed and stacked them as a marker where I should turn downhill on my return. Then I hiked along the stream's edge, thinking the moisture evaporating off the running water might be conducive to mushroom growth. I kept my eyes downward, looking for fallen logs or the base of a dead tree.

My methods weren't without results, but none of the fungi resembled the mushrooms in my basket. A few looked like the cute ones dancing around in Walt Disney's *Fantasia*, but I didn't know if they were edible. I wasn't taking any chances. Maybe I was Chicken of the Woods after all.

Then, across the stream and on a slight rise, a shaft of sunlight illuminated a patch of orange, its brilliance sharp against the muted greens and browns of the forest. An end of a large log nearly three feet in diameter was covered in mushrooms identical to the ones Nakayla had picked. If I were in a movie, the soundtrack would have swelled with an angelic chorus.

Without bothering to seek a shallower crossing, I splashed through the creek, never taking my eyes from the treasure trove. Part of me thought how ridiculous I was to be racing to a rotten log. The mushrooms weren't going anywhere. But the competitive side of me already envisioned the envious stares of the club members when I showed up in the pasture with my overflowing basket. And then there was Nakayla. As student, I wanted to best my teacher, and the sooner I harvested these, the sooner I could press on in search of more.

But, I forgot my world was different since Iraq. I'd grown so comfortable with my prosthesis that I bounded up the hill as if on my own two legs. Now only one had feeling all the way to the soles of my feet. So, I didn't sense the toe of my left boot catch under a surface root. I stumbled like a running back tripped by a defender's shoestring tackle. My momentum pitched me forward, and, instinctively, I dropped the basket and thrust out my arms to break my fall. My hands mauled the bounteous layers of orange and then broke through the log until my arms plunged into its hollow interior up to my shoulders.

For a second, I lay stunned amid the mushroom carnage. My first thought was, "Did anybody see me?" Chicken of the Woods would be a label of honor compared to the new nicknames my tumble could inspire.

I pushed down, trying to get some leverage to lift myself up. Both hands pushed against something hard, like a stick buried within the log. I rose enough to be able to turn on my left side and wrench my right arm free. Then I used that arm as a brace against a more solid section of the log and pulled the left free.

I rolled over, my back to the log, and looked at the front of my chest. The remains of Sulfur Shelf were smeared across my shirt, its spongy mass now the consistency of day-old road kill. In a mushroom handbook, I'd be the chapter entitled "What to Eat and How to Wear It."

I caught my breath a moment and then turned around to see if anything was worth saving. My attack on the log left a gaping hole. The fallen tree had withstood heat, cold, rain, snow, insects, and even mushrooms, but it was no match for Sam Blackman.

I started to get up when I noticed my whistle had torn free from my buttonhole. I checked the ground at the base of the log. Nothing. The whistle had probably been stripped off when I crashed through the outer shell of wood.

I approached the hole from an angle so as not to block the narrow shaft of sunlight. Sure enough, the silver whistle gleamed in the dark hollow of the log where it had come to rest. Come to rest in the chest cavity of a human skeleton.

In the Kingdom of the Happy Land, someone had not lived happily ever after.

# Chapter Two

Nakayla and I watched Henderson County Deputy Sidney Overcash poke his flashlight into the recesses of the hollow log. He made a clucking sound with his tongue.

"The lab boys are going to love this." He reached inside with his empty hand.

"Shouldn't we wait?" I asked. "You're disturbing the scene."

Overcash looked over his shoulder. "I ain't touching the remains. I want to look at the wood." He pulled up a section of the log I'd knocked free. "Hmmmm." He held the chunk close to his eyes, making a show of his detecting skills.

Nakayla and I had crossed paths with Deputy Overcash before when we'd been drawn into an investigation of a woman's death on Carl Sandburg's farm. In that case, jurisdiction fell to the National Park Rangers since Sandburg's home was a national park site. Overcash resented being shut out. I was sure he thought he would have unmasked the killer. The fact that Nakayla and I had broken the case rubbed salt in his wounded ego.

"Interesting," Overcash said.

I refused to bite. Nakayla looked at me and smiled. She understood the deputy's little game.

"What is it?" The question came from the slim man standing behind us. Ed Bell, the owner of the property.

After I'd extricated myself from the log, I'd hurried back to Nakayla's rendezvous spot, blowing my whistle with every

exhalation. We returned to the pasture and found club president Donnie Nettles. He notified the Sheriff's Department and
property owner Bell.

Then he whistled in the mushroom hunters and told them
I'd discovered a skeleton many years old and the authorities had
been summoned. There was no cause for alarm, but in light of
the developments, the outing was cancelled.

Ed Bell arrived a few minutes ahead of Deputy Overcash. I
pegged him for a youthful sixty-five. His pale face signaled he was
clearly shaken by the prospect that someone died on his property.

With Overcash's permission, Bell had joined us as I led the
deputy to the scene. Donnie Nettles had wanted to accompany
us, but the deputy insisted everyone except Bell, Nakayla, and
me should leave the location.

"May I see?" Ed Bell asked his second question, tentatively
stepping closer to the log.

"Stay back." Overcash raised his hand like he was halting
traffic. "Mr. Blackman's correct about not contaminating the
crime scene." He gave me a pointed stare. "Although I have
jurisdiction here."

"I don't know about that." Bell made the statement with such
authority that even Overcash was surprised.

"What do you mean? I think this man was murdered." He
held up the piece of wood. "It's charred on the inside. Someone
could have burned him alive." Overcash seemed giddy at the
prospect.

Bell waved his hand dismissively. "That's probably from the
lightning that killed the tree over seventy years ago. Before I was
born. Red cedar with the top blown out of it. It was dead and
blackened when I was a boy. Didn't topple over till 1954 when
Hurricane Hazel hit the state. Even up here we felt her wrath."

Deputy Overcash looked at his now worthless evidence and
dropped it on the ground. "Well, I don't care if this guy got
stuck in the log trying to get out of the rain, until we know for
sure, I'm treating it as a homicide." Overcash turned to me as
if expecting a rebuttal.

I nodded in agreement. "The deputy's right, Mr. Bell. It is a crime scene."

"I understand." He pointed to a tree alongside us. "See those markings?"

For the first time, I noticed broad swipes of red paint tagging the trunk of a nearby oak.

"That's the state line," Bell said. "Deputy Overcash is standing in South Carolina with his jurisdiction on the other side of that tree."

The deputy's mouth dropped open. He stared down at the broken surface of the hollow log and then at the paint-smeared trunk. "But the base of the log's in North Carolina."

"I don't think our mystery victim crawled into the tree while it was still standing," I said. "Otherwise he'd be closer to the roots."

"Maybe he used the hollow part at the top for a deer stand," Overcash said.

"Interesting hunting style," Nakayla said. "He'd have been hanging upside down."

I couldn't stifle a laugh. Overcash's face went as red as the tree paint.

Ed Bell paced off the distance from the skeleton to the state line. "We're only twelve feet over. And the easiest access is from North Carolina." He turned to Overcash. "Frankly, if people are going to be traipsing across my property, I'd rather deal with the Henderson County Sheriff's Department."

Overcash looked at me. I understood his problem and felt a small degree of sympathy. Jurisdiction had to be established so that if a prosecution case was ever mounted, there would be no confusion as to which state's laws had been violated.

"You're an officer of the court," I said.

Overcash nodded. He knew once Bell had pointed out the border he couldn't pretend otherwise. "I'll radio it in and they'll contact the Greenville County Sheriff's Department."

"Hold up a second," I said. "Have you got gloves?"

"Yeah."

"Maybe you should at least look for an ID. Might be a North Carolina resident." I looked to Bell. "You said this was the easier way in."

"That's right."

"So, the deceased might be a relative of someone Deputy Overcash is sworn to serve and would have to notify."

"That's right," the deputy said. "I would. And how accurate is that tree-marking anyway?"

Bell shrugged. "Can't say. It's not like they staked off the boundary. The tree was probably the sturdiest structure near it."

"Okay." The arrogance disappeared from Overcash's voice.

I stepped forward. "I'll hold the flashlight so you'll have both hands free. Less likely you'll knock something amiss."

Overcash smiled. "I couldn't do any worse than you did."

"Touché," Nakayla chimed in.

While Overcash gloved, I knelt on the opposite side of the log and played the light over the interior. Water had long since rotted or mildewed any clothing away. I didn't see any leather remains near the pelvic bones, although a small billfold might be beneath a hip. If the log hadn't rolled over during some time in the past, then the deceased had crawled in on his back. Or he'd been pushed inside by a person or persons unknown. I angled the beam toward the skull. I couldn't see any hair. Perhaps it had been too short for remains to be visible or some woodland creature had carried the hair away for a nest.

"See anything?" Overcash asked.

I moved back to give him room. "No. I was looking for jewelry or rings that might have identifiable engravings."

"Could you have pushed anything into the rotten wood underneath?"

"I don't think so. My hands landed on a thigh bone. Felt like a stick. The only other thing I touched was my whistle. It landed at the base of the rib cage."

"Okay." Overcash knelt across from me. "I'm just going to do a pass along each side without moving anything. Maybe we'll get lucky."

I slid toward the lower extremities and shot the beam up the length of the skeleton. Overcash's arms blocked most of the light, and I knew he was navigating by sense of touch more than sight.

A few minutes passed accompanied only by the sound of our breathing.

Then Overcash froze. "Hello. What's this?" He pulled his arms out carefully.

In the broad, grimy palm of his gloved left hand lay a small mushroom-shaped mound. It wasn't edible and it wasn't in any of our guidebooks. Even through the coating of dirt I recognized the deformed slug of a high-powered rifle.

He and I both turned our heads to look at the paint-sprayed tree.

"I guess you'd better notify the Greenville Sheriff," I said.

I wasn't sure whether we were in North Carolina or South Carolina, but I was certain the deputy and I knelt at the scene of a murder.

Nakayla and I drove along I-26 back to Asheville. The sun hung high overhead after the morning had been sacrificed to the consequences of my discovery. Deputy Overcash had insisted I remain at the scene to give my statement to his South Carolina counterparts. Maybe losing his jurisdictional squabble during our last encounter made him more conciliatory to other law enforcement agencies. Maybe the respect I showed him softened his tough-ass attitude.

I'd dealt with plenty of his kind in the army. Mid-career officers in their thirties who thought they knew more than they did. At some point, their arrogance tripped them up. To Overcash's credit, he'd stepped back and put the case first.

Two Greenville County deputies had examined the log. They agreed the victim probably came from the North Carolina side and, given the uncertainty of the state line, the three deputies decided the initial phase would be a joint investigation until their respective sheriffs worked out a more official approach. Meanwhile, the forensic team was coming from South Carolina.

I'd given my statement, left contact information with both law enforcement agencies, and wished them good luck. The case was colder than a glacier in the last Ice Age.

Nakayla patted my thigh. "I knew we were in trouble as soon as you asked Overcash if he had gloves."

"What do you mean?"

"I mean we've gone four miles and you haven't said a word. You're driving on autopilot and your mind's back at the log." She laughed. "Remember, curiosity killed the cat."

"I know. I couldn't help myself. I wasn't concerned about the cat. I wanted to know what killed our new friend Mr. Bones."

"So, what do you think about the bullet?"

I shrugged. "Looked like it hit a rib or clavicle. Probably soft-point. A hollow-point would have been more mangled. I'd say it was from a thirty-thirty or thirty-aught-six."

"Deer rifle?"

"Most likely. The lab might get some rifling marks if the slug's not too damaged. But, unless the gun was used in another crime, there won't be any ballistics record."

"It comes down to identifying the victim."

I thought about Ed Bell's history of the lightning-damaged tree. "Yeah. Both departments should search through missing person reports from 1954 to the last year the Medical Examiner estimates the body had to begin decomposition in order to reach its present skeletal state."

"You ever work a case like this in the army?"

"Not really. I was present when we uncovered some of the mass graves of Saddam Hussein's victims. There was nothing for me to solve."

Neither Nakayla nor I spoke for a few minutes. She must have been thinking how the shock of finding one skeleton compared to viewing hundreds of bones from men, women, and children slaughtered by a ruthless tyrant.

I tried to lighten the mood. "So, other than falling face first into human remains, I'd say I did quite well as a mushroom hunter."

"You certainly made an impression on the rest of the club."

I took my right hand off the wheel and returned the pat on her thigh. "Did you expect anything less, partner?"

"I wish I could say yes, but I'd be lying." She squeezed my hand. "You wish you were working the case, don't you?"

"I wish I could say no, but I'd be lying."

"Maybe Deputy Overcash will hire us as consultants."

"And maybe Duke and Carolina fans will join hands and sing Kumbaya at their next basketball game."

"Stranger things have happened."

I took my eyes of the road and stared at her. "Oh, yeah? Name one."

She scowled. "Okay. Maybe the Carolina-Duke Kumbaya comes right after we're asked to investigate Mr. Bones."

I turned my attention back to the highway. "Take my word for it, neither one will ever happen."

# Chapter Three

The Blackman and Robertson Detective Agency occupied an office suite in the Addison Court building three stories above Asheville's historic Pack Square. We had no employees. What with cellphones and sophisticated answering and call-forwarding services, we could work efficiently and effectively in and out of the office. So, with business slow, I'd gotten into the habit of drifting into the office whenever I felt like it.

I'd begun volunteering at the V.A. hospital several hours a week, and some mornings I dropped by for coffee with wounded vets from Afghanistan and Iraq. I'd appreciated the outside companionship when I underwent physical therapy, and I felt a duty to show there was life after a debilitating injury.

On the Monday morning after my mushroom adventure, I left my apartment near Biltmore Village and took the back way around Beaucatcher Mountain to the Charles George V.A. Medical Center on Tunnel Road. A cup of black coffee and a blueberry muffin would be my ticket to a cafeteria discussion where I would contribute by listening, by simply being a presence in the midst of the turmoil and uncertainty facing our wounded vets.

As I pulled into the visitors' lot, my cellphone rang. Nakayla's ID flashed on the screen.

"What's up?" I asked.

"Are you with your buddies?"

"No. Just got here. Still in the car."

"We have a client." Nakayla's words sparkled with excitement.

"Who?"

"A Marsha Montgomery."

"Is she there?"

"No. I set an appointment for eleven."

"Well, I hope it's not tracking some two-timing husband. Did you tell her that's not our specialty?"

"She said it's about a burglary and she wants to meet in person."

I glanced at my watch. Nine-thirty. A burglary case was more interesting than anything else we had going at the moment.

"I'll take the meeting," Nakayla said. "Just wanted you to know."

"I'll be there, but I'm going to drop something off at the hospital first. See you no later than ten-thirty."

The something I had to drop off were two of Lee Child's Jack Reacher novels I'd promised a young special ops soldier named Jason Fretwell. I found him sitting alone in the cafeteria, and from the clench of his jaw, I saw he wasn't having a good morning. A couple of guys a few tables away waved for me to join them. I waved back and then nodded toward Jason. They understood he needed my attention more than they did.

"Hey, Hotshot." I dropped the books by his tray. "Here's just the thing to take your mind out of here."

He looked up without smiling. "Hi, Sam."

A half-eaten bowl of granola sat in front of him. I saw dribbles of milk splattered on the front of his shirt. He gripped a spoon awkwardly in his left hand. From his right sleeve projected the mechanical fingers of a prosthetic device that attached to the stump of his lower arm. Shrapnel from a roadside bomb had shredded the exposed portion of his body as he rode in the passenger's seat of an armored personnel vehicle. A sniper by training, Jason Fretwell now couldn't hit his own mouth with a spoon.

I slid into the seat across from him. "How's it going?"

"Down the toilet." He pounded his artificial hand on the table in frustration. "I can't get this piece of crap to work right."

I pushed the books closer to him. "Then I guess you'll have to spear these pages to turn them."

Anger flared in his dark brown eyes. His pale skin flushed and he reached out and grabbed my forearm with his artificial fingers.

The pressure felt like a vise squeezing flesh against bone, but I held his gaze without flinching. "Go pick on someone who has two good legs."

Jason's mouth dropped open. He stared at the alien fingers digging into my skin. Confusion swept over his face and then amazement as he marveled at the precise manipulation he'd unconsciously made. He looked like a kid whose basketball shot just swished through the net from half court. Hell, he was a kid, barely in his twenties.

"Sorry." He released his grip, but he wasn't sorry. Suddenly, he was alive.

I shrugged. "No problem. For three weeks, I kept kicking people because I didn't know where my new leg ended."

"And now you chase down bad guys."

"Maybe, if they're eighty-years-old and on a walker." I rapped his prosthetic hand with my knuckles. "Look, this device isn't ever going to be as good as your own flesh and blood. If you make that the standard, you're going to go through life bemoaning what you can't do instead of pushing yourself for what you can. I know. I've been at that crossroads and I came close to taking the path to self-pity."

"Why didn't you?"

"Because a woman without an arm yanked my chain." I didn't tell him the woman was Marine veteran Tikima Robertson, Nakayla's sister, and that her interest in me was part of the actions that led to her murder. "She bluntly told me to get off my ass and on with life."

Jason nodded. He studied the curve of his prosthetic fingers. "I'll never be able to shoot again."

"Yeah, and you'll probably never be able to salute without knocking yourself in the head."

He straightened his mechanical fingers, brought his hand just above his eyebrow in one smooth movement, and shouted, "Yes, sir!"

A smattering of applause broke out from adjacent tables. Evidently, our exchange had drawn an audience.

Jason held the salute but he couldn't hold back the broad grin.

A victory is a victory, whether solving a case or helping a young soldier through a crisis of hopelessness. So, my encounter with Jason Fretwell did as much for me as for him.

I entered the offices of Blackman and Robertson light of heart and ready to impress our potential client with my deductive skills. Maybe I'd solve the case from an armchair in our conference room, besting Sherlock Holmes and even his smarter brother Mycroft.

"Good morning, my love." I stepped across the threshold into a room not unlike Mycroft Holmes' Diogenes gentlemen's club. An Oriental rug covered most of the hardwood floor. Two brown leather armchairs sat opposite a matching sofa. We'd designed the decor to project the air of stability and trust. Like we'd been in business over a hundred years. At least that's what I told Nakayla. Actually, I pushed for the purchase because we could get the furniture for a huge discount off the showroom floor and the sofa was long and comfortable enough for me to lie down and nap.

The conference room was the first area a visitor entered. A door to the left led to my office, a door to the right went to Nakayla's. I found her at her computer, staring at an online newspaper.

"I said, 'Good morning, my love.'"

She swiveled her chair to face me. "You have to be more specific as to who you are. So many men love me I didn't know what to say."

"How about 'Sorry, I'm taken.'"

"Okay. As long as I'm not taken for granted."

"Never." I leaned over and kissed her on the lips.

She kissed me back, and then looked at me quizzically. "No alcohol on your breath. I would have sworn you and the boys had been passing a bottle."

"I'm drunk on life."

"So that's why you fell on your face Saturday."

"Way to rain on a guy's parade."

She laughed. "The rain was going to fall sooner or later." She gestured to her computer monitor. "I forwarded you the updated stories about Mr. Bones that ran in this morning's Asheville and Hendersonville newspapers."

Sunday's papers only reported that a human skeleton had been found on the North Carolina–South Carolina border, probably because newspaper staffs on Saturday and Sunday were skeletal themselves. Even the Internet had been quiet last night as the law enforcement agencies from the two states must have agreed to limit details so early in the investigation.

"Has Mr. Bones got a name?"

"Not yet. The remains are staying in Greenville, South Carolina. That county's population is about four times the size of Henderson County and they have more lab resources."

"They'll probably keep the case unless circumstances bring the investigation back across the state line."

"You made the papers."

"I did?" Suddenly I was more interested in the journalistic quality of the reporting. "No one ever called me."

"That's because the person who locked up Friday forgot to forward the phones. There are five messages on the machine from reporters wanting to talk with you."

"Oh." Of course, I was the person who neglected to forward the phones. I waited for Nakayla to rub my nose in it, but she gave me a pass.

"Actually good publicity," she said. "Both articles describe you as Asheville's most famous detective. They make it sound like you went looking for the body."

"Who am I to argue with the press?"

"Who are you to argue with anybody? Just go read your clippings. The mysterious Marsha Montgomery will be here in less than thirty minutes."

I did as I was told and closed the door to my office. Not that I had a need for privacy but because my office was always a mess and we shielded it from a client's curious eyes.

I rolled my chair away from the cluttered desk to the side credenza where I kept my computer. I'd forgotten to turn that off as well and the screen glowed to life as soon as I moved the mouse.

I first followed Nakayla's link to the Asheville newspaper story. It was in the regional section and simply stated that skeletal remains of an unidentified man had been discovered in the woods near Tuxedo on the North Carolina–South Carolina border. The report said the preliminary forensic analysis conducted in Greenville, South Carolina, determined the deceased had been an adult male who may have died between twenty and forty years ago. No law enforcement authorities were quoted.

The article touted me as the man who found the remains. I was described as one of the top private investigators in the state with a reference to the successful solution of the high-profile murders of Tikima Robertson and Asheville police detective Roy Peters, the case that brought Nakayla and me together. The reporter speculated I might have uncovered the remains as part of an investigation, but that I had been unavailable for comment. Just as well, I thought, since it saved me detailing the headfirst plunge into the rotten log.

The article in the *Hendersonville Times-News* landed on the front page below the fold and offered more details. Deputy Overcash was quoted saying, "The investigation will be jointly conducted by the Henderson County and Greenville County Sheriff Departments, given the skeletal remains were found within a few feet of what might be an inaccurate marking of the state boundary. We are particularly concerned if the deceased turns out to have been a Henderson County resident." To my relief the deputy downplayed my role saying, "Mr. Blackman happened upon the remains while on an outing with the Blue Ridge Mushroom Club. The discovery was accidental and Mr. Blackman isn't involved in the investigation."

However, despite Overcash's accurate statement, the newspaper article went on to give a one-paragraph profile of me, highlighting the case Nakayla and I solved the previous year that was triggered by a death on the mountain behind the historic farm of poet Carl Sandburg. I was again lauded, this time as one of the top private detectives in the South, a statement Nakayla saw as good publicity and Deputy Overcash probably saw as an incentive to run me over with his patrol car.

Both the Hendersonville and Asheville stories had one glaring omission: neither mentioned the discovery of the slug. That wasn't bad reporting, it was withheld information. I understood the play. Why tip someone off that the police were looking at a homicide?

At the scene, Nakayla and I had been advised by one of the Greenville deputies not to give any details to the press, but no one had specifically mentioned the bullet. I suspected the decision to leave the nature of the investigation vague had been made at a higher level than Deputy Overcash and his counterparts from South Carolina. ID the remains first and then look for suspects and motives before the public, and thereby the guilty, realizes the case is a full-blown murder case. That's the way I'd have played it.

A single rap sounded on my door. I clicked out of the article. "Be right there."

"Keep your seat." The door swung open and Hewitt Donaldson entered. He held his ever-present mug of coffee in one hand and a curled newspaper in the other. "I just came to bask in the glow of the best detective in the friggin' galaxy."

Hewitt was Asheville's top defense attorney and his offices were next door. In his sixties and a product of the Sixties, the former hippie-turned-Perry Mason relished any case that went up against the system. He'd championed so many underdogs he could have started a kennel club.

"You're the one to talk about glow. You're hurting my eyes."

Hewitt's orange and red flowered Hawaiian shirt looked like it was powered by a nuclear generator. I was surprised he wasn't followed by a swarm of honeybees.

"You can borrow it. I hear mushrooms grow in the dark. With this shirt, none of them will be safe from your amazing detecting skills."

"Can it, Hewitt. If you must know, I tripped and found the skeleton by accident."

He looked at his newspaper. "So, the story's correct? I thought surely the mushroom gig was a cover to get you on the property."

"Nope. The galaxy's greatest detective is also the galaxy's greatest klutz."

"That's much more believable." He took a sip of coffee, clearly relieved the world order had been re-established. "Still, your fungi knowledge could come in handy. I have this case of athlete's foot needs investigating."

"As often as your foot lands in your mouth, it's probably spread to your tongue."

Hewitt laughed, and I knew for once I got the best of him.

A knock sounded, not from my door but the one to the hall. Hewitt turned around and stepped to the side. I saw the door open slowly, and a pretty African-American woman stepped inside. She stopped at the sight of Hewitt. Maybe she thought she was interrupting a luau.

"Mr. Blackman?" She spoke my name like an affirmative answer would be her worst nightmare.

I expected Hewitt to make some sarcastic remark at my expense, but he either respected we had a possible client or sensed the woman's timidity.

I stood. "I'm Sam Blackman. Please come in."

The woman hesitated, and then Nakayla appeared in her doorway.

"Ms. Montgomery?"

"Yes."

"I'm Nakayla Robertson. We spoke on the phone."

The woman smiled. She appeared to be at least fifteen or twenty years older than Nakayla. Probably around forty-five. Her skin was a shade lighter and she wore her hair cropped closer to her head. She was taller, and as she walked forward, she carried herself with an ease of movement that reminded me of a dancer. She wore a smartly tailored, dark blue business suit that identified her as someone who took pride in a professional appearance.

She and Nakayla shook hands.

Hewitt stepped forward. "I'm Hewitt Donaldson. I was just leaving."

The woman's eyes widened. "You're the lawyer?"

"I'm a lawyer. And my office is right next door." He left, closing the door behind him.

Nakayla gestured for Marsha Montgomery to take a seat. "Would you like coffee or some water?"

"No, thank you." She crossed the room and chose the leather chair on the right.

I took the matching one to the left, and Nakayla sat on the end of the sofa closest to our potential client. Neither one of us pulled out a notepad. At this point, we were simply having a conversation. I waited for Nakayla to take the lead.

"You said this was about a burglary."

Marsha Montgomery nodded.

"Have you notified the police?"

"They were notified."

I caught that Ms. Montgomery didn't specify she had notified the police. My partner was also as attentive.

"Who notified them?" Nakayla asked.

"My mother. Lucille Montgomery."

"Was she the one who was burglarized?"

"Yes, ma'am."

"Where does she live?"

"At the Golden Oaks Retirement Center."

Nakayla flashed me a quick look. We were both familiar with the site and knew some of the residents. "That's a surprise. The security there is excellent."

"It didn't happen there. It happened in her home."

"So she still owns her home?"

Marsha Montgomery shook her head. "No. I live there now."

"You were burglarized?" Nakayla asked.

"No." She looked at me and then back to Nakayla. "My mother was the victim."

Again, Nakayla zeroed in on the question I wanted to ask. "When did this happen?"

"In 1967."

"1967?" I blurted out the year, unable to contain my frustration at the prospect of a case with zero chance of a solution.

"I know," she admitted. "It was a long time ago. But it was the summer, if that's helpful."

"The summer," I repeated. "What did they steal? Bathing suits?"

"A photograph, Mr. Blackman." The ice in her voice was as cold as the glare Nakayla gave me. "A photograph I've just learned might be very valuable."

"Okay." I ratcheted down my exasperation. "That's helpful. Do you have a way to prove ownership?"

"I do. You see my mother is in it. The photograph was taken at the Kingdom of the Happy Land. Ever heard of it?"

I looked at Nakayla. Our world had just taken a very interesting turn.

# Chapter Four

Nakayla leaned forward on the sofa. "Ms. Montgomery, didn't the Kingdom of the Happy Land disappear over a hundred years ago?"

"Please call me Marsha. And yes, it did. Then the property was sold for back taxes in the mid-teens."

"Then how old is your mother?"

"She's eighty-five. She never lived in the Kingdom. That's just where the picture was taken."

"The one that was stolen?" I asked.

"Yes. I know it sounds complicated, but it's really not."

"Maybe you'd better take us back to the beginning," Nakayla said. "Assume we know nothing about the Kingdom."

Marsha Montgomery nodded. "All right, but my knowledge is limited to what my mother knows. She said her mother's mother, my great grandmother was born on the Kingdom sometime in the eighteen-seventies. There weren't any real records kept so we're talking oral tradition. My mother says the Kingdom was founded by a former slave owner from Mississippi a few years after the Civil War."

"Slave owner?" Nakayla asked. "I thought they were freed slaves."

"They were. Led by their former master, the first king. My mother says he was the son of a white plantation owner and young slave woman. The plantation owner freed the woman

before the birth and the mulatto child was born as his acknowledged progeny. The boy was educated and given his own farm
and slaves." She looked at Nakayla and shook her head. "Seems
strange he would own his own people."

"Sounds like he didn't abandon them," Nakayla said.

"No. At the end of the war, Mississippi was in ruins. The
plantation house and land had been razed. He gathered the now
freed but destitute slaves together and they set off for greener
pastures. They trekked across Mississippi, Alabama, Georgia,
and South Carolina till they came to the wall of mountains."

"Moses leading the children of Israel through the wilder-
ness," I said.

"Definitely. They were searching for the Promised Land. In
this case, the Happy Land. And they found it when they met
the widow of Confederate Colonel John Davis. Her plantation,
Oakland, was on the North Carolina–South Carolina border. In
exchange for housing and food, the king and his band of freed
slaves farmed the land. They also earned money doing work for
neighbors. Everything was given to the king to hold in common.
He purchased mountain land from Mrs. Davis and the commune
members began building cabins. More freed slaves joined the
group and an itinerant preacher traveled through South Carolina
encouraging others to migrate."

"How many people are you talking about?" Nakayla asked.

"No one knows for sure. Estimates for that first group range
from fifty to two hundred. My grandmother says the wanderers
attracted more during the journey. The free men and women
were no longer slaves to the masters, now they were slaves to
abject poverty. The king promised a fresh start for all who joined
him."

"Why did the Kingdom disappear?" I asked. "Did the king
die without an heir?"

"My mother was told the first king died not too many years
after arriving. A natural leader had joined the group whom
everyone turned to. Robert Montgomery."

"You're his descendant?" Nakayla asked.

"Not blood kin. But babies were named for him. My great grandmother Loretta was born during his reign."

Her comment sounded so strange. His reign. Like we were sitting in some castle in England discussing the royal lineage of Queen Elizabeth.

"That's why there's a lot of Montgomery folk in these parts." She sighed. "But two things killed the Kingdom. Jim Crow and the railroad."

"How?" Nakayla asked.

"Jim Crow laws were designed to squash any Black independence or upward mobility. They were passed in the eighteen-nineties and had the effect of creating economic slavery with white-only this and white-only that." She shot me a glance as if daring me to challenge her.

I nodded. "Self-sufficiency would be a threat. And you don't get any more uppity than to call yourself king."

Marsha Montgomery couldn't help smiling. "You got that right."

"What about the railroad?" Nakayla asked. "Weren't they allowed to ride the trains?"

"Riding wasn't a problem, if you sat in the back or in a Negro car. The railroad brought a faster and cheaper way to move goods and livestock between the mountains and the low-country. Before then everything came up the drovers' road that went right by the Kingdom. Extra hands and carts were used for the steep ascent. Stagecoaches stopped at nearby inns where servants were needed. The commune took in cash from the innkeepers or bartered for supplies from the drovers. When the railroad passed them by, the Kingdom passed away as well. People wandered off to find work elsewhere."

"So how did your mother come to be photographed there?" Nakayla asked.

"She said Miss Julia Peterkin brought a photographer friend to see what was left of the Kingdom. Miss Julia knew my great grandmother Loretta was one of the few remaining survivors and the photographer wanted to hear the story from her."

"And then he took her picture?" Nakayla asked.

"The photographer was a woman. Doris Ulmann."

Nakayla's eyes widened. "I've heard of her. She was friends with Julia Peterkin?"

I made a T with my hands. "Time out. I admit it. I don't have a clue who you're talking about."

Marsha Montgomery turned to me. "Julia Peterkin is the only South Carolinian to win the Pulitzer Prize in Fiction. This is going back to 1929. Her novels portrayed black plantation workers as fully developed characters, not stereotypes. No one had done that before."

"An African-American writer?"

"No. She was the mistress of a cotton plantation called Lang Syne near Orangeburg. But she learned to speak Gullah before she learned English."

"Gullah?"

"The lowland dialect. Actually more its own language. A hybrid of English and West African tongues that originated on the Sea Islands off South Carolina and Georgia. You've heard of the Gullah people, haven't you?"

"Yes." I didn't want Marsha Montgomery to think I was totally stupid. I'd heard of them like I'd heard of the Navajo and Eskimos. But growing up in the piedmont of North Carolina three hundred miles from the South Carolina coast and joining the army right out of high school had limited my exposure to the cultural diversity of the region.

"I need to take him on a field trip to Charleston." Nakayla gave me a sympathetic smile. "And Doris Ulmann was a famous New York photographer in the twenties and thirties who packed up her chauffeur-driven limousine every summer and drove down the spine of the Appalachians to photograph the mountain people."

"She also came to the lowlands," Marsha added. "She and Julia Peterkin worked on a book of photographs and text called *Roll, Jordan, Roll.* That's when she came to the Kingdom with Miss Julia."

"And that's why you think the photograph is valuable?" I asked.

"That's correct."

"Did you ever see it?"

"Yes. It was on a bureau in my mother's bedroom."

"Do you mind if I ask how old you were when it was stolen?"

"I was five."

"And you remember this one photograph?" I couldn't keep the skepticism out of my voice.

"Yes. My mother and I would look at it together. I was five and in the picture she was five. Her mother and her grandmother were in the photograph as well. It made an impression on me. That my mother was once a little girl like me."

"Her grandmother, that would be your great grandmother Loretta, the one born on the Kingdom."

"That's right. Miss Ulmann wanted to meet her."

"Did she and Julia Peterkin use the photograph in their book?"

"No. And I only learned about Doris Ulmann being the photographer a few weeks ago. I'd taken a copy of *Roll, Jordan, Roll* from the library and thought my mother might find it interesting. That's when she told me she knew both women."

Nakayla leaned forward, her brow knitted in concentration. "What do you expect us to do after more than forty-five years?"

"I thought your investigations might have established connections to art dealers who would keep records if a signed Ulmann photograph came into their possession."

"Aren't there duplicate prints?" Nakayla asked.

"Maybe. I've looked through the online catalogue at the Getty Museum but I didn't see it. There are several colleges that have her work but those prints came from her estate. I think whoever took this would have tried to sell it."

"Just your mother being in the picture doesn't prove ownership."

"She still has the letter Julia Peterkin wrote when she mailed the print."

"That's good," I said. "Any other witnesses see the picture in the house? Is your father still alive?"

Marsha Montgomery's jaw tightened. "I didn't really know my father."

I looked at Nakayla, hesitant to venture into sensitive territory.

She spoke softly. "I'm sorry if we're getting too personal, but we're only trying to determine if we can help. Did your mother and father divorce? Is there a chance he could have removed the picture?"

"No. My mother says that wouldn't have happened. And there was no divorce. They were never married."

"Oh. I understand."

Marsha Montgomery gave Nakayla a sharp glance. "I don't think you do. My father was white. Back then, they couldn't have married. It was against the law. But he loved my mother and he loved me."

"Then what happened to him?" Nakayla asked.

The older woman shrugged. "One day he just went away. Mother said he did it to protect us. There were people who didn't like seeing a white man and a black woman together." She looked at me. "I suspect you get too far out of Asheville and you find things haven't changed all that much."

"Do you have any idea what the photograph's worth?" Nakayla asked.

"No."

"Then our fee might be more than the value of the photograph."

"I've looked at some recent auction prices. They've ranged from ten to thirty thousand dollars."

I whistled softly. "Wow. Doris Ulmann must have been good."

"She chose good subjects. Each photograph was like a story frozen in time."

"And what was the story of your mother's photograph?"

"The end of the Kingdom. My mother, grandmother, and great grandmother were standing in front of one of the few remaining stone chimneys left from the cabins. The light streamed through the pine boughs like beams from the Kingdom above. Their faces were radiant. She captured a very striking image. My mother looked like an angel. They all did."

The end of the Kingdom, I thought. The cachet of the setting would probably add value to the print. And if it were the only one. "Who would have known the value of that print back in 1967?"

"Nobody. It was just an old photograph."

"Then was anything else taken? Something that might be easier to trace?"

"Some jewelry. We didn't have a TV or record player. And they took my father's gun."

From the corner of my eye, I saw Nakayla tense.

"What kind of gun was it?" she asked.

"I don't know. He used it for hunting and left it with Mother for protection. I remember he taught her how to use it."

"Shotgun?" I asked.

"No. He had a shotgun but he kept it at the cabin on his family's property. I'm pretty sure it was a rifle. Mother said he used it during deer season." She looked from me to Nakayla. "You think someone might have pawned it?"

"Maybe," Nakayla said.

I knew Nakayla was thinking of another possibility. The same one that took hold of my mind. Maybe a missing rifle, a missing father, and a skeleton in a hollow log were linked together.

One thing was certain. Marsha Montgomery's arrival was no coincidence. We were being played. And I wanted to know why.

# Chapter Five

"Well, that was interesting." Nakayla made the understatement of the day as she stepped back into the office after walking Marsha Montgomery to the elevator.

We'd told the woman we wanted to look at possible avenues for a productive investigation before committing to take her case. Then we could give her an estimate of expenses and an assessment of potential success. In reality, Nakayla and I were signaling each other that neither of us took Marsha Montgomery at face value. It's not that uncommon for clients to tell you half truths or outright lies in an attempt to cast themselves in the most favorable light. Particularly if they know uncovered circumstances could lead to a "he said—she said" outcome.

But Marsha Montgomery's story was in a category all its own. Two events involving the Kingdom of the Happy Land don't appear within a two-day period without some connection. Something brought Marsha Montgomery to our door and that something had once been a living, breathing human being who wound up entombed in a hollow log. If we got involved in the case, it would have to be with eyes wide open that our client sought us out for reasons yet to be revealed. Those reasons could be to keep something hidden rather than bring it to light.

I leaned back in the leather chair. "Interesting, disingenuous, deceitful. Pick a word."

Nakayla slipped her shoes off and sat on the sofa with her bare feet tucked under her. "You want to walk away?"

"Not until I know what I'm walking away from."

"I think it's about the rifle."

"I agree. I think if we hadn't asked what else was stolen, she would have worked it in. But the way it played, she mentioned it in response to a question."

"Why mention it at all?"

I thought for a moment. "She's setting the stage for something yet to happen. Another shoe's going to drop."

"The skeleton's got to be her father and she's protecting her mother."

"That's my guess. Get the rifle out of the house before the date of death."

Nakayla frowned. "Why not get the body out of the log? Bury it in those woods? There were probably root cellars left from the Kingdom. Dig a hole at the bottom of one of them and no one would ever find it."

"And why fabricate such an elaborate story about this Doris Ulmann and Julia Peterkin? The best lie is the simplest lie."

"Maybe it was the simplest lie," Nakayla said. "Marsha had to have a reason to resurrect a forty-five-year-old burglary. She's right about the value of those photographs increasing."

I looked past Nakayla to the door our visitor had exited. "So, you believe her?"

"I believe she's in trouble. Or thinks she is."

I nodded. "I agree. I'm prone to accept her as a client."

"You sure?"

"What else are we going to do? The phone's not exactly ringing off the hook."

"You're right. And we know it's not forwarded."

"Smartass." I stood. "You can start checking into Marsha Montgomery's background. Find out what's fact and what's fiction. Meanwhile, we'll hold off deciding to take the case until I get back."

"Where are you going?"

"To surprise Lucille Montgomery. Let's see how well the mother's story corroborates the daughter's."

◇◇◇

I drove up to the unmanned guardhouse and stopped just short of the red and white crossbar. The entry to the Golden Oaks Retirement Center had been strategically installed at the base of a mountain in Arden, a small town about ten miles outside of Asheville. It was better to turn a car away there before it had to negotiate the winding switchbacks to the summit. Golden Oaks brought senior citizens closer to heaven in more ways than one.

I rolled down my window and pushed a silver button beside a speaker in the guardhouse wall.

"Welcome to Golden Oaks. How can I help you?" The woman's voice was friendly but officious.

"I'm here to see Ron Kline."

"Is Mr. Kline expecting you?"

"Tell the Captain that Sam Blackman is on his trail."

The woman laughed. "Sam, why didn't you say so?"

The crossbar rose.

"Come on up. Do you want me to warn him? He's with his bevy of beauties."

"No. Better not disturb a sultan when he's with his harem."

She laughed again. "You think you're joking? You'll find him in the TV room."

Ron Kline, aka Captain, had to be in his late eighties or early nineties. Nakayla and I met him during the course of our first case when circumstances led us to one of the residents of Golden Oaks. Captain had actually risen to the rank of Colonel, and as a former Chief Warrant Officer myself, we shared the common bond of military service. He'd been a captain in World War Two and he said that had been the most meaningful time of his army career. He'd been closest to his men and the phrase "Band of Brothers" didn't do justice to the unwavering loyalty forged in battle. Now Captain was the unofficial commander of Golden Oaks and the darling of an overwhelmingly female population smitten with any man still breathing.

I spotted him sitting on a sofa and holding court with two ladies on either side and three at a nearby card table, their chairs angled to face him. The flat screen TV mounted on the paneled wall displayed some generic morning talk show. No one was watching. Captain was talking. I slipped up behind him and heard a sentence fragment referencing General Eisenhower.

"Captain Ron Kline," I whispered dramatically. "Please report for duty."

His curved shoulders snapped back and he reached for his walker. One of the elderly women beside him twisted around to see who had interrupted their conversation. The rest of the ladies seemed alarmed at Captain's sudden movement. They hadn't heard me and probably thought Captain was having a stroke.

He got to his feet with surprising agility, whipped the walker around one hundred eighty degrees, and gave me a brisk salute.

I returned it and added a wink. It was our special way of greeting. "Are you up for a walk?"

Captain backed up far enough so he could see all five of his admirers. "I'm sorry, ladies. A mission beckons."

One of the women at the table eyed me suspiciously. She looked familiar but I couldn't recall her name.

"Don't you let anything happen to him," she ordered.

Captain waved his hand. "Don't worry, Joanne. I'll take good care of Sam."

The others giggled like school girls.

Joanne wouldn't be mollified. "I'm serious, Mr. Blackman. Hanging out with you can be dangerous."

I recognized her as part of Captain's CIA. That stood for Corridor Intelligence Agency, a group of residents Captain organized to patrol the halls and keep an eye on the community's well-being. I knew Joanne was referring to the terrible incident when a resident became our client and was murdered after speaking with me.

"I just have to get Captain's advice on something," I said. "I figure he knows more about women than I do."

Even Joanne giggled. "If he doesn't," she said, "you ask any of us. We'll set you straight."

Captain looped around the sofa and stopped beside me. He stood half-a-head shorter, no more than five foot four. Old age probably had knocked a good three inches off his height.

"I fancy a stroll outside," he said. "This store-bought air is like breathing pablum. No zest." He lunged forward with his walker and headed at a brisk clip for a side door.

We exited onto a garden patio. Concrete pathways radiated out in multiple directions. They were painted to look like flagstone but the surface was smooth so as not to trip the unsteady steps of those whose balance had grown a little shaky. Flowerbeds displayed a brilliance of late spring blossoms and their natural perfume permeated the warm air. Zest, indeed.

Captain filled his lungs. "Makes you feel alive. I hope there's a sense of smell in heaven."

"Then you think we'll have to take showers?"

He frowned. "I hadn't thought about that. Could be a problem. Those two women on the sofa keep complaining they've got no one to scrub their backs."

"Sounds like an opportunity in the here and now."

"I'll give them your number. My pension can't support another paternity suit."

We continued down one of the walkways. I was content to let Captain set the pace and decide when to ask what I wanted. The garden wrapped around the building and within a few minutes we were out of sight of the main entry.

Captain pointed to a bench on the far side of a koi pond. "Let's sit a spell. We shouldn't be bothered. Most people stay inside after lunch."

He parked his walker at one end and eased onto the cedar bench. I sat beside him. Two friends separated by half a foot and over half a century.

"I'm glad you came by," he said. "I should have called you first thing this morning."

"Why? What's wrong?"

"The Mayor's in intensive care."

The Mayor was the oldest resident at Golden Oaks. His real name was Harry Young, but, at a hundred and five, everyone affectionately called him by his nickname.

"When did this happen?"

"This morning. Bertha, the head nurse of critical care, told me after breakfast. I didn't want to say anything to the girls until later when the medical team knows more. The Mayor just didn't have the strength to get out of bed."

"Pneumonia?"

"Probably." Captain's eyes glistened. "The old man's friend, we call it. They say it takes you away without pain. There's a breath, and then never another."

I patted his leg. "The Mayor might surprise us."

"Oh, he's done that already. A hundred and five. The things that man's seen."

Captain sounded like he was part of the Facebook generation compared to the Mayor.

"Well, we all go in our time," he said. "But not a day passes I don't think of the young men lost under my command. And wonder why their time was so early."

I didn't say anything. We sat in the sunlight a few moments. The water gurgled through the filter of the pond's pump. The brightly colored koi glided in and out of the shadows cast by the lily pads. It was a good day to be alive.

"What's on your mind?" he said at last.

"Do you know someone named Lucille Montgomery?"

"Sure. Nice lady. Did her daughter get in touch?"

I stared at Captain with surprise. "How'd you know?"

"I'm the one who told her about you. Marsha didn't waste any time."

"When was this?"

"Yesterday afternoon. She came to have lunch with Lucille. We'd all gone to church together. The ecumenical service in the auditorium."

"You'd met her before?"

"Oh, yeah. Lucille's been here about five years. Marsha's good to visit. She works for Lang Paper Manufacturing. I think she's in sales. Lucille says her daughter travels some, but she's usually home on the weekends."

Captain's description of Marsha's job matched the professional appearance of the woman.

"How did my name come up?"

"She caught me at the dessert table. She said she needed some background check run at work but didn't want to use their normal channels. She said it was a sensitive internal investigation. I thought she was probably talking about some sort of suspected embezzlement."

"She didn't say it was personal?"

Captain shook his head. "No. She said her mother told her I'd been involved with some investigators from Asheville. She thought hiring someone from out of town might be better."

"Where's the paper plant?"

"On the outskirts of Brevard."

Brevard was about twenty-five miles from Asheville and paper mills had once been a strong component of its manufacturing base. Many had closed as outsourcing and environmental laws had affected profitability.

"She asked me not to say anything about it because it could reflect badly on the company." He looked at me curiously. "So if it's about her job, why do you want to talk to Lucille?"

"That's a good question. Maybe we should leave it at that."

He grinned. "The private in private eye. Okay. What else do you want to know?"

"How can I meet her?"

"Easy. I'll introduce you." He checked his watch. "She should be in her apartment."

"Thanks." I stood and waited for Captain to man his walker. "You think I could see Harry?"

"While you're with Lucille, I'll speak to Bertha. The Mayor doesn't have any kin so I think they'll be flexible. I'm sure he'd love to see you."

I followed Captain down one of the long corridors to the end. He stopped in front of a door with a brass plaque reading "Montgomery." Beneath it hung cutout wooden block letters of alternating red and white forming the phrase, "Enter with a Happy Heart."

"Lucille's got a trek to the dining hall," I said.

"Yeah, but she's spry. And she saves money."

"How?"

"The farther units aren't as expensive. In this place, a great location means you're close to the food." Captain chuckled. "Amazing how your priorities change as you get older. You just wait." He rapped lightly on the door. "Lucille's hearing is sharp. So's her mind. You won't have any trouble questioning her."

The soft pad of footsteps sounded from within. Then a reedy voice called, "Just a minute."

A few seconds later, the door opened to reveal a petite African-American woman leaning against a lacquered black cane. The wrinkles in her face crinkled deeper as she smiled with delight to see Captain. Then her expression became quizzical as her bright eyes focused on me. Marsha Montgomery said her mother was eighty-five, but Lucille looked ten years younger. Her dark skin held a natural beauty that still shone through.

"Well, what did you bring me, Captain? Can I keep him?"

"This is Sam Blackman, and I'm afraid he's spoken for."

If my name meant anything, she didn't react. Instead she shook her head with exaggerated slowness. "Aren't they all. Except you, of course. The one who always gets away."

"No. They just keep throwing me back."

Lucille's smile broadened. "Your ladies have so many fishing lines dangling in front of you I'm surprised you can walk without tripping over them."

"The secret is to avoid the hooks."

"And you're very adept at that. So, what can I do for you gentlemen?"

Captain looked at me. "Sam wants to talk with you a few minutes, if you have the time."

"Time's all I've got. Come in. Can I get you some coffee or tea?"

"Not for me," Captain said. "I can't stay."

A flicker of uncertainty crossed Lucille's face. "You sure?"

"Yes." Captain dropped his voice. "The Mayor went to critical care this morning. I need to check on him."

Lucille bit her lower lip. "Oh, Lord," she whispered. It wasn't an exclamation but a prayer.

"Yes," Captain said. "I think he's just wearing out." He waved his arm to usher me past him. "You two have a good talk and I'll keep you posted."

I stepped into Lucille Montgomery's apartment and she closed the door behind us.

"What can I get you?" she asked.

"I'm fine. I won't take but a few minutes."

She gestured to a floral upholstered sofa. "Have a seat. I'll stay here with my knitting." She picked up needles and a skein of dark blue yarn.

I looked around the room. The furniture was traditional and simple: the sofa, her rocker, and a velvet armchair. An old picture tube television sat on an oak credenza along the side wall facing her chair. A framed picture of a young Marsha in cap and gown stood to the right of the TV and a black-and-white photograph of a man in a dark suit was in a matching frame on the left. He was a white man and the composition suggested the photographer had been a professional. The soft background appeared to be a studio canvas and the three-quarter profile was one of those contrived, pensive poses where the subject peers off-camera thinking deep thoughts. He must be Marsha's father, the man forbidden by North Carolina law to marry Lucille.

I studied the elderly woman as she sat and placed her knitting in her lap. She wore a light blue dress with white trim collar. Her gray hair was pulled back into a bun. She'd dressed for lunch, although not so formally that my grandmother would have called them "Sunday-go-to-meeting" clothes.

She started slowly rocking. "How can I help you?"

"I'm a private investigator."

She stopped rocking. "Oh?"

"Yes, Ma'am. Your daughter Marsha came to see me this morning."

"Whatever for?"

"She asked me to investigate a theft. She said someone had stolen a picture of you taken by Doris Ulmann."

Lucille Montgomery stared at me like I'd spoken in Japanese. "But that was nearly eighty years ago."

"Not the theft."

"No. That was later. 1967. But I don't know that it was stolen. It could have been lost." Her eyes drifted to the photograph of the man by the television.

"Why would Marsha tell me it was stolen?"

"I don't know. She was only a five-year-old child. She liked it. I might have said something like that at the time."

I looked at the man's picture. "Around the time Marsha's father disappeared?"

I turned back to Lucille in time to see her face harden.

"That's our personal business, Mr. Blackman."

"Yes, μa'am. That's why I'm here. I told your daughter we would consider her case, but I haven't agreed to accept it. You were the property owner and if you're not interested, then there's nothing for us to investigate."

"There's nothing to investigate," she said through clenched teeth.

"And the rifle?"

Again, she looked confused. "What rifle?"

"The one left by Marsha's father. The deer rifle that was taken with the photograph."

"No. She's mistaken. I never touched the thing, but it's somewhere in the house."

I thought for a moment. Marsha had fabricated her own story without taking her mother into her confidence. There was only one reason for that.

"Miss Montgomery, did Marsha mention the discovery made Saturday on the property once belonging to the Kingdom of the Happy Land?"

"No." Her answer was barely a whisper.

"I made it and the story was in all the newspapers yesterday. I found the skeleton of a man hidden in a hollow log."

Lucille took a sharp breath. Her eyes fluttered and then rolled back in her head.

I leaped from the sofa and caught her as she toppled from her chair.

# Chapter Six

"What the hell were you doing in her apartment?" Marsha Montgomery glared at me and made no attempt to hide her anger.

Captain and I sat in a small waiting room outside Golden Oaks' critical care wing. Marsha stood in the door, blocking any exit. Tears lined her cheeks and her hands trembled.

I stood. "We were having an honest conversation. Something you didn't give me in our office."

Marsha looked at Captain. "Would you excuse us a moment?"

Captain gripped the handles of his walker and pulled himself up. "Yes. But I'm the one who introduced Sam to your mother and you're the one who asked me about Sam. The fact that he was with her might have saved her life."

Marsha said nothing. She let Captain pass and then stepped inside, closing the door behind her.

"I never said you could see her."

"You never said I couldn't. And I'm not working for you." I pointed to the chair opposite me. "We can talk or I can tell the doctor the substance of the conversation I had with your mother."

She hesitated, weighing her options. When she sat, I knew she desired to control whatever information I had.

"Why do you think I wasn't honest?" she asked.

"Your mother told me the rifle wasn't stolen."

"My mother is eighty-five and her memory isn't what it once was. I remember that photograph and rifle disappeared at the same time. The missing picture really upset her. She couldn't care less about the gun and she's obviously forgotten about it."

"Uh huh. She was forty and you were only five and she doesn't remember correctly?"

"My father drilled it into me not to touch that gun. What else can I tell you? The rifle was gone."

"Your mother fainted when I told her about the skeleton."

Marsha covered her mouth with her hand. For a second, I was afraid she would pass out.

When she spoke, the words came in a breathy rush. "You just blurted it out?"

I noticed she didn't ask what skeleton. "Why not? What could it possibly mean to her?"

"You know damn well what it means."

"I think I do. Your mother's a smart woman. She remembers quite well the events of 1967 and I think she fears the skeleton is your father. She wasn't shocked because a body was discovered, she was shocked because someone she loved is dead. She held out hope all these years that he went somewhere to make a new life and spare you and her the bigotry of the times."

Marsha Montgomery's lips trembled and she blinked back tears.

"You're a smart woman too," I said. "But you're afraid your mother might be guilty. That's the first thought that crossed your mind when you read the newspaper story. And you over-reacted. Coming to see Nakayla and me must have seemed like a good way to establish the story of the stolen gun in case the log victim had been killed by a rifle bullet. Neither Nakayla nor I swallowed the coincidence of the timing. Not only how you suddenly felt compelled to track down this photograph but also your emphasis on the Kingdom of the Happy Land."

Marsha wiped her eyes with the back of her hand. "Okay. I was stupid. But that doesn't mean what I said isn't true. If that skeleton is my father, then, I tell you, the two are linked. You say you don't like coincidences, Mr. Blackman. Well, neither do I. You find who stole the picture and you'll find who killed my father."

"And the rifle?"

"Let me worry about that." She leaned forward. "Will you help us?"

"No more lies?"

"No more lies."

"I'll still need to talk to your mother."

"When she's feeling better."

"Marsha, as far as I know, there's been no positive identification of those remains. Your father might not be involved in this at all."

"Then I still want to find him. I don't have any children. I don't know how much longer I'll have my mother. I'd like to know what happened to him." Her moist eyes searched my face. There was no trace of duplicity on hers.

I took a deep breath. "Okay. But I'm giving you some advice."

"What?"

"Go to the police. Tell them you read the story in the newspaper. Tell them when your father disappeared."

She shook her head. "I can't do it. They'll want to speak to my mother."

"Of course they will."

"I won't put her through that. It's too painful. My father still has relatives here."

"Then you do have family."

"No. There's been a code of silence. My mother wanted it that way. It was an understanding. We've led separate lives."

"So, you're still trapped in the sixties."

Her eyes flashed. "I don't need to be accepted by some white bigots to have meaning in my life."

I raised my palms in mock surrender. "Fine. But your father wasn't a bigot. Now you're letting someone else's prejudice determine your actions. What would he think?"

"He would think what was best for my mother."

"Then maybe we should let her have her say." I stood. "See how she's doing. I've got a friend to visit in critical care. I'll find you before I leave." I walked out.

Captain sat in a plastic chair in a general waiting area across from the nurses' station. I waved him to keep his seat and slid in one beside him.

"Is Marsha okay?" he asked.

"Yes."

"She's normally very sweet. She must be upset about her mother."

"That's understandable. She's calmed down. Any word on Harry?"

Captain glanced at the nurses' station where a woman sat entering data through a computer keyboard. "Bertha says he's not taking any food. They're running an IV drip, but if they give him too much, then fluid collects in his chest. He's between a rock and a hard place."

"Any pain?"

"He's not complaining. But then the Mayor never does."

"Did you speak with him?"

Captain nodded. "For a few minutes. I didn't want to tire him." He looked back to the nurses' station. "Bertha, okay if Sam checks on the Mayor?"

The middle-age woman turned from her screen. "Just him?"

"Yes."

She studied me a second. "All right. Don't push it if he seems overtaxed. He's in the third room on the left."

Captain grabbed his walker and we stood. "I'm going to give the girls an update on his condition," he said. "Let me know if there's anything I can do for Lucille."

"I will."

"Then let's move out."

We saluted and I paused to watch him waltz his walker down the hall like a dance partner.

"God broke the mold after making Captain," Bertha said.

"And that's too bad. The world could use a few more like him."

"And the Mayor."

"Yes, the Mayor," I agreed.

Harry Young, aka the Mayor, lay on his back in the dimly lit room. The gentle hiss of oxygen and his shallow breaths were the only sounds. His pale skin was nearly translucent and his bony shoulders looked like they might pierce through the thin layer of flesh. His eyes were closed. The hospital bed was slightly raised at the head so that Harry's jaw dropped open. Worn yellow teeth seemed large in the receding gums.

The white sheet had pulled away at the bottom, revealing the scarred stump of the right leg. Over ninety years ago, Harry lost his foot and half his shin to the steel claws of a bear trap.

I became aware of the snug fit of my prosthesis, an engineering marvel compared to the crude wooden one Harry wore as a boy. One hundred and five. The changes he witnessed. Despite his handicap, he lived to the fullest and taught me to do the same.

I stepped closer and smoothed the rumpled sheet over the atrophied limb. He flinched at the brush of the starched fabric and his eyes opened.

For a second, Harry struggled to focus and I thought he might drift back to sleep. But his gaze locked on my face and the slack jaw tightened into the hint of a smile.

"Sam." He exhaled the single syllable.

"Hello, Harry. How you feeling?"

He ran his tongue around the inside of his mouth and across his dry lips. "Plumb tuckered out," he whispered.

"Don't try to talk. I just dropped in to sit a while." I looked at the IV tube hanging from the pole beside the bed. "I should have brought some white lightning for this bag. That would get you up and out of here."

His smile grew a little broader. Then his eyes looked beyond me. "It's okay. I'm ready."

What do you say to a man who's a hundred and five and dying? I pulled a chair from the corner and sat beside him. "I know you're ready." I wrapped my hand around his thin wrist just above where the IV was securely taped in place. "I'm feeling sorry for me. Who am I going to split a pair of shoes with?"

He turned his head and stared at me. There was no mirth in his eyes and I was afraid I'd offended him.

"You gave me a great gift, Sam."

"What's that?"

"My dad." He stifled a sob as his eyes teared.

The lump formed quickly in my throat and I could only nod. In the course of finding the killer of Nakayla's sister, we discovered the fate of Harry's father and ended a mystery that had haunted the old man since 1919.

"There's nothing anyone has done that means more."

I said nothing. Just sat holding onto someone who had been over seventy when I was born, but whose presence would always be with me.

"Thank you," he whispered.

"You're welcome. Tell your dad I look forward to meeting him."

Harry placed his other hand on mine. We stayed like that for a few moments till his breath returned to the shallow rhythm and I knew he was asleep. I slipped free, quietly moved the chair against the wall and left him to travel to a place of no tears, no pain, and no return.

I told the nurse that Harry was sleeping comfortably and asked if she knew where I could find Marsha Montgomery. She directed me to a room at the other end of the hall.

Lucille rested in a reclining chair, still wearing her blue dress. Marsha sat on the edge of the bed next to her. I rapped lightly on the door frame. Both women looked up. Lucille smiled. Marsha frowned.

"Just wanted to make sure you were okay, Miss Montgomery."

Lucille waved me in. "They say it was probably my blood pressure medicine. I took my pills late today and then had a big lunch."

I didn't contradict her as to the timing of her swoon. "I'm glad you're feeling better. Maybe we can continue our conversation some other time."

A look passed between mother and daughter.

Marsha rose from the bed. "Mr. Blackman, I can talk a few minutes now. I suggest we go back to the waiting room. The nurse wants Mother to rest about thirty minutes before checking her blood pressure again."

"All right." I nodded to her mother. "A pleasure to meet you, Miss Montgomery."

Marsha and I walked in silence. The waiting room was empty. I closed the door.

"Can we start over?" she asked.

"Sure." I sat in the nearest chair.

Instead of sitting opposite me, Marsha chose the chair beside me. "I'm sorry if I misrepresented my intentions. You were right. I read the story and I was afraid."

"Afraid of what?"

"I was afraid my mother had killed my father. I wanted to create some other explanation."

"And take the rifle out of the picture."

She nodded.

"What happened to it?"

"I don't know. It hasn't been in the house for years."

I didn't believe her, but I let the statement go unchallenged. I wasn't prosecuting a case and it was none of my business.

"Why would you think your mother was capable of killing your father?" I asked.

"Anger. I thought he refused to marry her."

"But interracial marriage wasn't legal."

"The summer of 1967 was the year of the big change. Loving versus Virginia."

"Sorry. I don't know what you're talking about."

"On June 12th, the U.S. Supreme Court ruled that prohibiting interracial couples from marrying was unconstitutional. The case they reviewed involved an interracial couple named Loving.

Ironic, isn't it? With that decision, the laws imposed by the states of the old Confederacy were swept away along with any legal barrier to my parents living as husband and wife."

"And any excuse for your father not to marry your mother."

"Yes. About a month later, my father disappeared. Mother told me changing the law didn't change people's attitudes."

"She's right about that. Even forty-five years later."

Although Asheville is a liberal town, Nakayla and I sensed the undercurrent of disapproval from some who viewed our relationship as an abomination. How do you argue with people who claim to speak for God? People who feel compelled to force their personal moral code upon others because they're threatened by anything different. We weren't so far removed from 1967. In fact, North Carolina had just gone through a contentious vote on a constitutional amendment banning gay marriage, same-sex unions, and even the legal rights of same-sex couples. The amendment passed with overwhelming support. And the irony was the proponents of this draconian exclusion came as much from the black community as the white.

"Was your mother that angry?"

"No. But I was. Angry and hurt that my father abandoned us. I projected those feelings onto my mother."

"And now you believe her?"

"Yes. I did what I should have done as soon as I read about the skeleton. I asked her. She swears she knows nothing about it and was shocked when you told her."

"And the potential marriage?"

Marsha looked away. "She changed her story. Now she says she was the one who refused to get married. Just because they could didn't mean there wouldn't be reprisals. She was afraid."

"Why did she say otherwise?"

"Because she didn't want me to blame her. Portraying my father as the one who left was easier, and she spun it with the noble motive that he did it for our benefit. The lie created the villains as faceless bigots and my mother and father as victims. It wasn't so far from the truth."

"Will she go to the police?"

"I didn't press the point. She's upset as it is."

"Others must know about your father's disappearance."

"Then they can step forward. Or we'll step forward when we have something to say."

The way she said "we" caught my attention. "What would that be?"

"When you and your partner find the proof of who killed my father. I can't help but believe your discovery of those remains was no accident. You were meant to find them. God and my father have chosen you."

# Chapter Seven

"So, how do we set up a billing account for God?" Nakayla held her fingers suspended over her computer keyboard waiting for me to give her the divine zip code.

I laughed. "More importantly, how do we check his credit?" I'd given her the summary of my encounter with Captain and Lucille Montgomery at Golden Oaks and Marsha's belief that we were destined to find her father's killer.

"Who is her father?" Nakayla asked. "She never said in the office."

I took a small pad out of my pocket and glanced at the notes I'd scribbled in the waiting room. "Jimmy Lang." As I said the name, I remembered hearing it earlier. "Captain told me Marsha works for Lang Paper Manufacturing. I wonder if there's a connection?"

"Should be easy enough to find out. I'll run checks on Jimmy Lang, Jim Lang, and James Lang." She jotted down the names. "Maybe there's something the Internet will flag that people couldn't access in 1967."

"If Jimmy Lang was the victim, I wonder what he was doing on that property in 1967? The Kingdom was long gone."

"We should talk to Mr. Bell. His family owned it then." Nakayla flashed a sly smile. "I assume we're still taking the case?"

Her question sobered me. "We are. And I have Harry Young to thank."

"Harry?"

I told her about my visit with the Mayor in the critical care wing and how our discovery of what happened to his father meant so much to him. "Marsha's plea came right after that. Her need can't be less than Harry's."

Nakayla smiled again, this time with sympathy. "I know. But Harry wasn't facing the possibility that his mother killed his father. Marsha might not like the answer we uncover."

"Lucille Montgomery is a sweet old lady."

"And forty-five years ago she was a single mother trying to raise a daughter in a segregated society—a society forbidding her to marry the father of her child. Who can be sure what happened in the summer of 1967?"

"You're recommending we back away?"

"I'm saying we go into it with eyes open. Harry and Marsha come out of very different circumstances and you're kidding yourself if you envision a resolution that will give Marsha the satisfactory closure we provided Harry."

Nakayla was right. Taking the case meant following the leads and evidence to the conclusion, no matter how painful or ugly it might be.

"Okay. Then here's what I know so far." I looked at my notes, trying to decipher my terrible handwriting. "According to Marsha, Jimmy Lang met her mother in 1956 or 1957. Jimmy ran a trash hauling business. Back then, Hendersonville had a service for the town but the county left it up to the individual residents and businesses outside of town to transport their trash to the county dump."

"He was a garbage man," Nakayla said.

"Yes. Lucille worked as a cook in the cafeteria at Flat Rock High School. Jimmy had the contract for school trash removal for that end of the county. Jimmy and Lucille became friends because she would see that the waste from the cafeteria was divided into food remains and general garbage."

"Why was that important?"

"Jimmy would re-cook the food as slop for his hogs. He had a small farm between Flat Rock and Tuxedo not far from the old Kingdom and not far from Lucille's place that also borders the current Bell property. That first Christmas after they met, Jimmy brought Lucille a home-cured ham for her and her mother."

"Lucille lived with her mother?"

"Yeah. Or her mother lived with her. Lucinda was her name. She died in 1960 before Marsha was born. Breast cancer. Jimmy Lang evidently started checking in on both women, doing handiwork for them, and he and Lucille fell in love."

"Did Marsha say any more about the stolen photograph?" Nakayla asked.

"It was in a black wooden frame and Marsha thinks it was an eight-by-ten but she knows everything looks bigger to a five-year-old. Her great grandmother Loretta, her grandmother Lucinda, and her mother Lucille were in the picture. All Ls. Marsha said her mother decided it was time to move on to M."

"Anybody else in the photo?"

"A few others who came with Julia Peterkin had ties to the Kingdom. That's what Doris Ulmann wanted. A gathering of the king's subjects. They stood in front of an old stone chimney, one of the last remaining vestiges of the cluster of cabins."

"What do you know about Loretta?"

"Her name was Loretta Johnson. She was born in 1875 and grew up in the Kingdom. She died in 1940."

Nakayla thought a moment. "Any men in this picture?"

"Not that she mentioned. Why?"

Nakayla shrugged. "No reason. Just wondering if the photograph could have been stolen because someone knew its value or because someone didn't like the subject matter."

"That's a question for Lucille. Marsha said I can talk to her tomorrow."

Nakayla glanced at the pad in my hand. "Anything else?"

"No. I let Marsha off easy. I didn't go into my hardboiled interrogation mode."

"So, you're saving that bad impression of Sam Spade for an eighty-five-year-old woman who'll probably say anything to make you stop."

"Don't you mean my James Cagney?"

"Please. Show a little mercy."

I tucked the notepad back in my pocket. "How do you want to proceed?"

A knock sounded from the main door to the hall.

"I suggest you see who that is." Nakayla began straightening up her desk.

I crossed the reception area and closed the door on my disaster of an office. It was after four o'clock. Sometimes Hewitt Donaldson dropped in with a bottle of Glenfiddich single malt and rehashed his day in court. But he never knocked.

I opened the door to find an old man leaning on a wooden cane. He wore a blue sport coat over a pale yellow golf shirt that was buttoned to the top. His tan skin was dotted with liver spots. Thin strands of white hair grew in clusters upon his scalp like isolated oases.

"Are you Sam Blackman?" His voice warbled and a loose flap of neck skin jiggled like a rooster's wattle.

"Yes."

"Good. I want you to find who killed my brother."

I hesitated a second while processing his statement. The guy had to be close to ninety. My first prejudicial thought about an octogenarian who showed up without an appointment was that he must have dementia. Someone somewhere wondered where this man was. We would need to notify a family member or retirement center that we had him safely in our office.

"Come in, Mr...." I left the unknown name dangling in the air.

"Lang. John Lang. And I believe you found my missing brother."

I looked at him again and one word flashed in my mind. Recalculating.

John Lang didn't wait for me to regain my bearings. He walked past me, using his cane for support rather than as a jaunty accessory. He stopped in the middle of the room, uncertain what to do next.

Nakayla stepped from her office. "Good afternoon. I'm Nakayla Robertson."

Lang offered his hand and then hesitated. "Robertson?" He repeated the word as if it came from a foreign language.

"As in Blackman and Robertson," I said. "I'm her partner. Why don't you take the seat you find most convenient and tell us more."

The old man shook Nakayla's hand and sat on the edge of the sofa.

"Would you like anything?" Nakayla asked. "Water? Coffee?"

"No, thank you. I prefer to get right down to business."

Nakayla and I each took an armchair. I glanced at her, but she seemed content to let me begin the conversation.

"Mr. Lang, have the police contacted you and confirmed they've identified your brother's remains?"

"They have not."

"Then why are you sure I discovered your brother?"

"Because Lucille Montgomery told me." He looked at Nakayla as if she would more readily understand.

"When did you speak to her?" Nakayla asked.

"A little over an hour ago. While Mr. Blackman was talking to her daughter at Golden Oaks."

"You called Lucille in her hospital room?" I asked.

He smacked the floor with his cane. "No, damn it. She called me. She said you found Jimmy's skeleton and that Marsha was hiring you to investigate."

"Marsha hired us to find a missing photograph," I said. "No one mentioned anything about a murder." So far, I hadn't told anyone about the rifle slug. That information would have to come from the police.

"That damn photograph," he muttered. Lang looked away and his eyes teared.

"You know about the photograph?"

He nodded. "Lucille told me at the time. When it disappeared, she thought it meant Jimmy had caught someone breaking into the house. I told her she was imagining things. But now…" His voice choked and his lower lip trembled.

"Mr. Lang. The police are investigating. They have the resources to identify the remains and follow all the leads. You should go to them instead of us."

"Who? Deputy Overcash? He couldn't find his own ass if you handed it to him on a silver platter."

"The Greenville Sheriff's Department's also involved."

"Bah." He waved his hand like swatting away a horsefly. "They're just as bad and they're from South Carolina."

"Well, we're already working for Marsha Montgomery and trying to learn what happened to the photograph of her mother, grandmother, and great grandmother."

Lang's eyes narrowed in his wrinkled face. "What did she tell you about it?"

"Not much. That she was only five and she associates it with her father's disappearance. She said it was made by Doris Ulmann when writer Julia Peterkin had her meet some descendants of the Kingdom."

"That it?"

"And that Doris Ulmann's work has become valuable."

He nodded. "Yes, but I don't think it was that valuable in 1967. So, you're probably barking up the wrong tree."

"Maybe." I looked at Nakayla. "But it's the case we've accepted."

He pointed his cane at me. "Drop it."

"Why?"

"Because neither Lucille nor Marsha can afford to pay you what it will cost to get to the truth. I can."

"Our financial arrangements with our clients are our business, Mr. Lang." I made no effort to mask the annoyance in my voice.

"And if I get them to withdraw?"

"I'd like to ask a question," Nakayla said.

Lang leaned back against the corner of the sofa. "All right, dearie. Ask away."

Nakayla's jaw tensed. "Dearie" wasn't the way you addressed a professional investigator. She took a deep breath before speaking. "Where did you think your brother was all these years and why didn't you report his disappearance to the police?"

"That's two questions, but I take your point. My brother and I weren't seeing eye-to-eye. He'd brought me into his business, but then wouldn't let me expand it into new markets. He got tied up with Lucille, fathered a mulatto child, and kept an ongoing relationship that went against the law. Then when that law changed, the woman he could now marry rejected him. He told me I could do whatever the hell I wanted with the company. He was starting over. He took ten grand out of his checking account and was never seen again."

"And you never got worried that something had happened to him?" Nakayla asked.

"Of course I did. But I had my pride, and Jimmy knew where I was if he wanted to find me. Look. It was a tough time. My wife had just died of cancer, my only son William was in Vietnam, and my brother was acting like a damn fool."

"And you blame Lucille Montgomery," Nakayla said. "That's why you want her out of this."

His face flushed. "Hell no. Lucille's the one who called me. Lucille's the one who thought something had happened to Jimmy. I was just too damn stubborn to listen to her."

Lang worked himself up into such a frenzy that spittle foamed in one corner of his mouth. I became concerned he'd have a stroke if he didn't calm down.

"Okay," I said. "I think we understand. And you've kept up with Lucille all these years?"

"Yeah. And I've tried to help out. She never had any money to speak of. I gave her a job that paid higher than her cafeteria work. I helped her with daycare expenses. Then I hired Marsha when she graduated from high school. I guess you could say Jimmy's absence bound us together."

"And your relationship is public knowledge?" Nakayla asked.

Lang glared at her. "We did what was best for both of us."

I thought of Marsha Montgomery's phrase, "There was a code of silence. My mother wanted it that way." It appeared Lucille shared that desire not to cross the color line.

"All right. Here's what I propose," Nakayla said. "We'll talk to Lucille and Marsha. If they want you involved in the investigation, then we'll consider it. If they don't, well, there are other private investigators."

"Lucille said Blackman and Robertson were the best."

"We are," Nakayla said. "And whoever hires us deserves our full attention."

Lang looked to me, but I said nothing.

He shrugged, put his weight on his cane, and rose from the sofa. "Then I'll wait to hear from you." He fumbled in the side pocket of his sport coat and pulled out a business card. He handed it to Nakayla.

"Don't wait," she said. "Go to the police and tell them what you told us. Better you find them than they come looking for you."

When we heard the elevator in the hall descending to the ground floor with Lang, I said, "Tomorrow let's both talk with Lucille and Marsha Montgomery. This is too strange for me to follow up on my own."

"Agreed." Nakayla went into her office and returned with her purse. "But let's leave it till tomorrow. Tonight, you can take me to dinner."

"All right, dearie. Right after I forward the phones."

We walked to Bouchon, a favorite French restaurant a few blocks from the office. The mountain air was invigorating and the setting sun cast that magical golden aura on everything it touched. We were early enough to beat the crowd, but not so early that we couldn't start dinner with a bottle of wine. And it was all-you-can-eat mussels night. Life couldn't get any better.

Actually it did. We split a bottle of Pinot Grigio, if my three glasses to Nakayla's one qualifies as a split. Then Nakayla insisted she drive me home. To her home.

Somewhere in the fuzzy realm of wine, mussels, love, and sleep, I heard ringing. Nakayla threw a bare hip into me in case I had any doubt as to whose cellphone was the culprit. I rolled over and grabbed the offending instrument from her nightstand.

"Yes," I croaked.

"Mr. Blackman?" The woman's voice sounded breathy and frightened.

"Yes."

"This is Marsha Montgomery. I'm at the Henderson County jail. They've just booked my mother on suspicion of murder and charged me as an accessory. Please help us!"

# Chapter Eight

As I gathered my wits during Marsha's call, I realized it was only ten-thirty. Immediately upon hanging up, I phoned Hewitt Donaldson and told him the story. When he heard an eighty-five-year-old woman was sitting in a county jail, the pit bull side of his personality launched into high gear. What I intended to get on his agenda for the morning became an instant crusade. He asked where I was and said he'd pick me up in thirty minutes. I had no chance for rebuttal. You don't argue with Perry Mason on steroids.

Nakayla, Hewitt, and I arrived at the Henderson County Detention Center shortly after midnight. A deputy behind the reception window asked for identification. Nakayla and I flashed our P.I. licenses. They struck the deputy with all the force of an airborne dandelion seed.

The deputy eyed Hewitt. In his wrinkled orange and yellow Hawaiian shirt, Hewitt looked like someone we were bringing into custody.

"And who are you?"

Hewitt leaned in till he was less than six inches from the protective window of thick glass. "Hewitt Donaldson, attorney-at-law, and I'm here to see that elderly woman and her daughter you have egregiously incarcerated."

The deputy wet his lips. He had heard of Hewitt Donaldson. "Visiting hours are in the morning."

Hewitt leaned even closer and tilted his head to read the deputy's name badge. "Officer Stinson. I am not a visitor. I am their attorney. I am not waiting until morning for them to exercise their constitutional rights. Now, you can let me talk to them under the protection of attorney-client privilege or I will make one phone call to the editor of the *Hendersonville Times-News* and tell him how the Sheriff's Department dragged an eighty-five-year-old lady out of the critical care wing of her retirement center and dumped her in a jail cell."

Deputy Stinson's face turned scarlet. "That's not true. We went after hours when we wouldn't be disruptive to the whole complex, and Miss Montgomery was in her own room. She came willingly."

"Fine. Those will be nice quotes, but they don't refute the fact that less than twelve hours ago the woman was in a critical care facility. Need I remind you that your boss is an elected official and that the actual voters in this county who elect him are disproportionately retirees? Who do you think they're going to identify with in our drama tonight?"

Deputy Stinson didn't say anything. Hewitt just waited, letting the silence build.

Finally, the deputy looked at Nakayla and me. "Tell your friend here that they're sleeping. If Miss Montgomery didn't feel well earlier, then she needs her rest tonight."

"I can hear you," Hewitt said. "I have two good ears. I also have two good eyes." He looked around the room. "No offense, but this isn't the Ritz-Carlton. If you think she's sleeping, then she's probably in a coma."

The deputy glared at Hewitt for a few seconds. Then the anger in his face dissolved into the tired recognition that Hewitt wouldn't yield to any argument or threat.

"All right. I'll buzz you through." He pointed a finger at Nakayla and me. "But you two stay here. This isn't going to turn into a circus."

Hewitt gave me a nod. He would cover us later.

Nakayla and I sat in two chairs across the small lobby from the duty officer. A second deputy appeared from the back rooms and waved Hewitt inside. He acknowledged Nakayla and me with a "Good evening, Sir. Ma'am." I was tempted to correct him that it was after midnight but decided I was skilled enough at making enemies without putting in extra effort.

Twenty minutes later, the interior door opened again and Deputy Overcash stepped into the room. He wiggled his index finger for us to follow him. Without saying a word, Nakayla and I walked behind him until he led us into an empty interview room and closed the door.

I noticed that his shirt was mis-buttoned and part of the tail wasn't smoothly tucked into his trousers. He'd been roused from his bed and probably dressed in the dark.

"Have a seat." He gestured to two chairs on the far side of a wooden table.

"What are we doing here?" I asked.

"That's what I'd like to know. Hey, no skin off my nose if you prefer to leave, but I thought a little talk might be helpful to all of us."

Since Overcash knew more about what was going on than we did, I saw no point in being antagonistic.

When we were seated, Overcash clasped his hands in front of him. "No notes. No recordings. Just a simple chat. Okay?"

"Sure," I said. "I'll even answer that first question. We're here because Marsha Montgomery hired us to find a missing photograph. Through us, she met Hewitt Donaldson who is now engaged as her attorney." Technically Hewitt and Marsha had met only for a brief moment in our office, but I was confident that by now Hewitt was part of the Montgomery family. "Hewitt brought us in case this mix-up has anything to do with our investigation."

Overcash looked incredulous. "A photograph? You expect me to believe this is about a photograph?"

"Believe whatever the hell you want. That's not going to change the facts of what happened. All I see from your side is an overzealous rush to book a suspect."

Overcash studied my face for a few seconds, probably deciding how much to reveal in our simple chat. We were about the same age, but I seriously doubted he possessed either the investigative experience or the discipline my years in the military had provided me. I counted on his vanity to prompt him to show me his hand. He might not like me, but he didn't want to appear foolish.

"An overzealous rush to book a suspect." He mimicked my words. "Tell me, Mr. Blackman, what would you do if you found a rifle freshly buried in a woman's backyard that had her fingerprints all over it. A rifle that hadn't been fired or cleaned for some time because of the extensive corrosion in the barrel, yet not in such poor condition that rifling marks couldn't provide a clear ballistics match to the slug we found in our friend in the log."

"So, Marsha Montgomery disposed of her own property. The skeleton has to be so old that she was only a child when the shooting occurred."

"Maybe. But I can guaran-damn-tee you her mother wasn't a child. There's no statute of limitations on murder, no matter how long ago, how old the perp, or how many years later someone conspired to cover it up."

"You've identified the remains as someone Marsha or her mother had a motive to kill?"

His eyes flicked down to the table just for an instant, but long enough for me to tell I'd hit the weak spot in his case.

"We have a strong lead on a person missing during the timeframe consistent with the skeletal remains, and there is a clear link between that person and Lucille Montgomery."

"Oh, so an official missing person's report led you to dig up Marsha Montgomery's backyard?"

Again, the flick of the eyes. "We have our methods."

"I'm sure you do. Discovering Jimmy Lang's name when no missing person's report exists is outstanding detective work. Of course, you could have called Nakayla or me and we would have told you Jimmy Lang disappeared in the summer of 1967. We're detectives too you know."

His face flushed. "Who told you that?"

"We have our methods. I figure you got a tip on the rifle before Lang gave you the name. You had to have found it yesterday in order to turn around even a fast-tracked ballistics report."

"Someone said they saw Marsha Montgomery burying a rifle on Sunday morning."

The morning the story of the log skeleton first appeared in the newspapers, I thought. "Anonymous, or are you withholding the name?"

"Anonymous. The caller told our dispatcher he didn't want to cause any trouble in case there was an innocent explanation. He claimed he was out walking his dog when he saw Marsha bury the gun in her garden. Then William Lang contacted me Sunday afternoon and told me about his uncle's disappearance."

I kept my eyes on Overcash, forcing myself not to look surprised. He hadn't learned about Jimmy Lang from John Lang but from John's son, and an entire day earlier. Furthermore, if John was to be believed, William hadn't told his father. John got that information from Lucille.

Overcash leaned across the table. "We got a search warrant for Marsha Montgomery's exterior property. She wasn't home and since we weren't going inside the premises, we simply proceeded with our search. We saw the freshly turned earth, found the rifle, and got it to the ballistics lab."

"And you didn't talk to Marsha or her mother in the meantime?"

He shrugged. "Nothing to talk about. Not till we got the report."

"And then you made a grandstand arrest of an eighty-five-year-old woman and her daughter, both of whom have lived in this county all their lives."

Overcash remained calm. "Nothing grandstand about it. We had probable cause, obtained an arrest warrant, and went to Golden Oaks after things had quieted down for the evening. Marsha was visiting her mother and both came peacefully. After booking the women and matching Marsha's prints to the rifle, each was given her right to a phone call and here we are."

I wondered if Lucille made a call and to whom.

Overcash shifted his gaze between us. "To be perfectly straight with you, I feel they're better off in our custody than the Greenville Sheriff's Department. If the victim was Jimmy Lang, then he was a Henderson County resident, most likely shot in Henderson County, and he happened to die only a few feet across the state line. This is clearly our case."

"If Jimmy Lang is your victim," I said.

Overcash couldn't keep a smirk off his face. "Oh, we'll know that through any dental records or if not then DNA testing."

Nakayla touched my wrist, a subtle signal that I should be careful what I said.

"Is it a crime to be related to someone?" she asked.

"What do you mean?" Overcash asked.

"I assume you've taken a saliva swab from both Marsha and Lucille."

"Yes. That's all perfectly legal."

"And if you find their DNA matches DNA evidence collected at a crime scene, then you have something to pursue. But using that for victim identification might be another matter. I'm not a lawyer. I'm just saying I'd hate to see your case collapse on a technicality."

Overcash looked confused. I understood how he felt. I didn't know where Nakayla was heading with a legal argument more suited for Hewitt's maneuvering. North Carolina law had recently required the collection of a DNA sample from anyone charged with a felony, but I didn't know if there were restrictions on its application. Then I realized Nakayla was expanding my own argument. Proving the victim was Jimmy Lang and irrefutably establishing Marsha's kinship to him made the link between Lang and Lucille only stronger. That might not play well with a jury if the case ever came to trial.

Overcash's face brightened. "Well, don't worry your pretty little head about that. We've got a better way of identifying the skeleton. You might say the perfect way. John Lang is Jimmy Lang's twin brother. It'll be like looking in a DNA mirror."

He was correct, as if DNA markers weren't accurate enough already. "Anything else?" I asked.

"Nope. I just wanted to establish a cooperative relationship with you both. You know, before the D.A. gets involved."

"All right. You can check that off your to-do list. Now, do you want a description of the stolen photograph?"

Overcash laughed. "No. I'll leave that matter to you big city detectives." He stood. "We'll piddle along with our little murder and let you solve the high-profile cases."

We followed him back to the main entrance. Seated in the chair I'd occupied was John Lang. He looked madder than a wet hen, and I immediately knew whose number Lucille Montgomery dialed for her one phone call.

"What the hell's going on?" He pounded his cane on the floor and then leveraged himself to his feet.

"We have a suspect in your brother's murder." Deputy Overcash couldn't keep a note of pride out of his voice.

"Are you talking about Lucille?" Lang hurried forward as fast as he could. "Overcash, you jackass. What proof do you have it's Jimmy?"

"Your son said your brother went missing during that time."

"My brother left town and my son was in Vietnam. So, again, what evidence do you have that it's Jimmy?"

"There's the timeframe."

"And how wide is that?"

The Adam's apple on Overcash's thin neck bobbled as he swallowed nervously. He didn't like the way the old man was grilling him, especially in front of us. "That's for the Medical Examiner to determine. But Lucille's gun definitely shot the man."

"That old Remington fourteen and a half? Lucille's gun might have shot the man, but Lucille couldn't hit the broadside of a barn if she were standing inside it."

"She was a lot younger then."

Lang waved his cane at Overcash. "Of course, she was younger then. We all were. Jimmy tried to teach her to shoot, but he told me she was hopeless."

I looked at Nakayla. She smiled. Hewitt Donaldson would love this old codger as a defense witness.

Overcash didn't have the good sense to let Lang's rant go unchallenged. He put his hands on his hips and squared off facing him. "Even a blind man can hit something if he stands close enough."

"Right." Lang pressed the end of his cane against the deputy's chest and pulled an imaginary trigger. "And at that distance, what bone in your body do you think will stop a thirty-eight rifle slug from passing clean through?"

Overcash's mouth dropped open. Nakayla arched her eyebrows and looked at me. That was a damn good question and we all knew it. An old cartridge that wasn't sealed properly might acquire some moisture that dampened the powder and an uncleaned gun could have barrel corrosion, both of which might reduce muzzle velocity. I wasn't familiar with the Remington model Lang mentioned, but a bullet fired from a thirty-eight caliber rifle at point-blank range should penetrate and exit. The fact that it didn't suggested the shot had been taken from a distance, where the broadside of a barn would look like a postage stamp.

Lang didn't wait for Overcash to fabricate an answer. He dropped his cane, reached in his back pocket and pulled out a checkbook. "I'm bailing her out. How much is it?"

"Bail? You can't bail her out."

"Why the hell not?"

"Only a judge sets bail on a murder charge. That won't happen until the bond hearing."

Lang pointed to the phone on the desk behind Overcash. "Then get a judge on the phone."

"I'm not authorized to do that."

"Then get the High Sheriff or someone else who can."

"It's already done." Hewitt Donaldson stood in the doorway to the rear of the jail. He looked from Lang to Overcash. "I called Judge Mercer at home. Lucille and Marsha are on his docket for nine o'clock. He's calling the D.A now. You'll probably hear from a prosecutor in about fifteen minutes."

"Who the hell are you?" Lang asked.

"I'm their attorney. Hewitt Donaldson."

"You any good?"

"I got the judge, didn't I?"

Lang stepped past Overcash like he no longer existed. "Then I'm hiring you."

"For what?"

"Lucille's defense."

"I'm already her lawyer."

"Well, I'm paying you."

Hewitt shook his head and his long gray hair flowed out like the whirling swings at a carnival ride. "Sir, here's my legal advice. For free. Go home. Get a good night's rest, or whatever's left of it. The bond hearing is open to the public. Come to the Henderson County Courthouse a little before nine, and we'll see how this plays out. If bail is set and you want to pay it, that's your business. Mine is giving Lucille and Marsha Montgomery the best defense I can."

"Okay," Lang whispered. He turned back to Overcash. "Finally, someone who knows what he's doing."

Overcash reddened. "Mr. Lang, we know what we're doing. And if you'd help us, we can find out if that dead man was your brother."

"How's that? You think I can recognize a skeleton?"

"No, sir. But you can tell me who was his dentist."

"Ben Isaacs. But he retired in 1965 after his office burned to the ground. Jimmy only went to him once. For a tooth ache. So good luck with those x-rays."

"Then DNA. You two were twins. I'll just get a simple swab of your saliva and we'll learn if we've got a match."

Lang studied the deputy for a few seconds. "Son, nobody's sticking anything in my mouth unless I'm eating or drinking it."

"But we'll know for sure," Overcash protested.

"I got nothing else to say. At least not till I talk to my attorney in the morning." He looked over his shoulder at Hewitt.

Hewitt nodded. He'd just picked up his third client in less than an hour.

# Chapter Nine

"Who's hungry?" Hewitt Donaldson whipped his Jaguar into the Waffle House parking lot before either Nakayla or I could answer. "A little sparring makes me ravenous."

I wanted to point out that it was nearly two in the morning. I wasn't ravenous, I was sleepy. But Hewitt was in control.

We sat in a booth in a back corner, Nakayla and I on one side, Hewitt on the other. A gray-haired waitress set a pot of coffee and three mugs in front of us. I held up my hand to stop her from filling mine.

"Just a half cup, please," Nakayla said.

"Darling, I'll fill it and you drink what you want. Half cup, three-quarters, makes no never mind to me."

Hewitt pushed his cup forward. "You can leave the pot. And I'll take two eggs over easy with hash browns." He looked at us. "Order up. My treat."

"Whole wheat toast," Nakayla said.

"You got any apple pie?" I decided I wasn't going to sit there with a glass of water and packets of Sweet'N Low.

"Sure do. You want that a la mode or with ice cream?"

"What's the difference?"

"Ain't no difference with the pie. If you say a la mode, you ain't from around here."

"Since my grandfather's paying, make it a la mode and with ice cream."

"You got it, honey. Two scoops' worth." She left to turn in our orders.

Hewitt looked around, checking who might be sitting near us. The only other customers were two state troopers at the far end of the restaurant.

Hewitt leaned forward and put his fingertips together like a church steeple. "Interesting case. Overcash has crawled out on a limb, but I think that has more to do with usurping Greenville, South Carolina, than any desire to make an example of Lucille Montgomery."

Nakayla frowned. "What do you mean 'make an example'?"

Hewitt turned his hands palm up. "Nothing really. Just that a murder's a murder no matter how old. He wants to look tough on crime and not be accused of going soft on Lucille because of her age. That's part of his motivation."

"He wants to look better than his Greenville counterparts," I said.

"Yeah," Hewitt agreed, "and he might be motivated by something else. Another shoe may fall in addition to the rifle."

"Any ideas?"

"No. But Overcash isn't stupid and neither is Noel Chesterson."

"Who's he?" Nakayla asked.

"The D.A." Hewitt smiled. "And just like Overcash doesn't want to play second fiddle to the Greenville Sheriff's Department, Chesterson won't want to look intimidated by yours truly. Overcash had to have probable cause to get the warrant. Chesterson will press on if the case has the least hint of being successfully prosecuted."

"Which hinges on that skeleton being Jimmy Lang," I said.

Hewitt took a deep sip of his coffee and smacked his lips. "Correct. Which means it's in Lucille's best interest not to have the remains identified. Old man Lang latched onto that fact and Deputy Overcash has no way to coerce a DNA sample from him."

"What about Marsha?" Nakayla asked. "She's Jimmy Lang's daughter and they have a sample of her DNA."

"If I can get the charges dismissed or reduced from a felony to a misdemeanor, then her DNA is inadmissible and must be destroyed. At that point she has the same rights to privacy as John Lang."

Nakayla shook her head. "I don't understand why John Lang is so adamant about protecting Lucille. Seems like he'd be anxious to cooperate with the prosecution."

"Sounds like once Lucille refused to marry his brother his animosity toward her disappeared," I said. "He told us he's tried to do right by Lucille and Marsha."

"I'll explore that with him tomorrow," Hewitt said. "We also need to determine who else could provide a DNA sample."

"We know Lang's son William is a prospect," Nakayla said. "And he might have children."

"Hope for the best, plan for the worst," Hewitt said. "I've got to build the defense upon the assumption that the remains will be identified as belonging to Jimmy Lang. We need to show that even though Lucille had the rifle she couldn't have fired the fatal shot. Someone else had access to the gun."

"Which brings us back to the missing photograph," I said. "The theft Marsha brought to us in an attempt to establish the lie that the rifle had been taken at the same time."

"A lie we have to reshape into not only a possible theft but also a return," Hewitt said.

Nakayla sighed. "It's going to be a challenge convincing a jury."

Hewitt grinned. "That's my job." He looked up as our waitress arrived with our food. She set a generous slice of hot apple pie in front of me. Two large scoops of melting vanilla ice cream cascaded over the brown crust.

Without asking, Hewitt reached across the booth with his spoon and scooped a healthy sample. "And that's why I'm treating you to this feast. From now on you're working for me. I know it's hard to believe, but I'm going to have to stand in front of that jury with more than my good looks."

◇◇◇

Hewitt Donaldson rose from his chair and faced Judge Mercer. His gray hair, so scattered the previous night, was pulled back in a neat ponytail that fell a few inches below the collar of his blue pinstripe suit. He'd sat quietly while District Attorney Noel Chesterson reiterated the seriousness of the charges of capital murder and conspiring to conceal evidence of a crime. Chesterson hadn't opposed bond, but requested the bail be commensurate to the crimes and demonstrate that murder isn't discounted by the passage of time.

That final phrase annoyed Mercer, as if the comment had been designed to lecture the veteran jurist. It was clear to me the judge had presided over enough bond hearings that neither histrionics nor exaggerations would sway his rulings. He'd dismissed the D.A. with a wave of his hand, the cue that brought Hewitt to his feet.

"Your Honor. I'm pleased the district attorney acknowledges my client Lucille Montgomery deserves bail consideration while reminding us that murder doesn't erode to petty larceny over time. But time has also transformed Lucille Montgomery into an eighty-five-year-old woman in a retirement and critical care facility. She was born and reared in Henderson County, has no criminal record, and lives on a fixed income. She's not a flight risk, she's not a threat to anyone, and anything above the most minimal of bail levels will be a financial hardship, even if a bondsman posts her bail."

"Fine." Mercer cut him off. "Bail is set at one thousand dollars."

The D.A. appeared startled by the low amount but he didn't protest. He knew Lucille wasn't going anywhere.

"And regarding Marsha Montgomery?" the judge asked Hewitt.

Hewitt shrugged. "I believe the circumstances leading to the charges speak for themselves. That's why I would ask your Honor to consider her bail in light of our request for a probable cause hearing to be held as soon as possible."

"What?" Chesterson blurted. "We have probable cause. That's how the deputy acquired a warrant. Your Honor, that would be a waste of the court's time. I can't remember the last time we had a probable cause hearing."

Hewitt turned to the D.A. "Then perhaps you can't remember Articles 29 and 30 of the North Carolina Criminal Procedure Act." He looked back at Mercer.

The judge frowned. He was obviously unhappy with where Hewitt was going. "Mr. Chesterson, does Mr. Donaldson need to read you Articles 29 and 30, or perhaps impress both of us by reciting them from memory?"

"No, your Honor." The D.A. glared at Hewitt.

Hewitt smiled. "And, your Honor, I agree with Mr. Chesterson's concern for the court's time. That's why bringing charges against Marsha Montgomery, who was five at the time of the alleged murder, warrants our request for the probable cause hearing provided for under North Carolina law."

"The charge is for conspiracy after the fact, Mr. Donaldson." The D.A.'s voice quivered with barely suppressed rage. "We're talking about last weekend."

"Okay. Then I'll be interested to see how you demonstrate a conspiracy when neither Marsha Montgomery nor her mother saw or spoke with each other between the time of the skeleton's discovery and when your anonymous witness said he saw Marsha bury the gun. You have checked the phone and visitation records at Golden Oaks, haven't you?"

Chesterson said nothing.

Hewitt shifted his argument back to the judge. "Your Honor might be interested to know the weapon in question is an old Remington fourteen and a half, and yet Marsha Montgomery is supposed to have dug a hole for its full length."

"What's that have to do with anything?" Chesterson asked.

Hewitt looked at the judge.

"That model is a short range deer rifle," Mercer said. "The barrel and stock separate into two pieces with a simple thumbscrew. Much easier to bury in two short segments."

Hewitt nodded at the judge's answer. "I mention that only to show that, like the esteemed district attorney here, Marsha Montgomery was neither familiar with the gun's workings nor had any conversation with her mother during the time specified. I'm interested in how Mr. Chesterson defines conspiracy if there's no evidence of communication."

Mercer stared at Chesterson. The D.A. said nothing.

"You raise an interesting question, Mr. Donaldson. Now this isn't a probable cause hearing, but I would appreciate some enlightenment from the prosecution since a probable cause hearing will likely wind up in my court."

Chesterson held up his hands in mock surrender. "I'm certainly not one to contribute to the overload of the judicial docket. For now we'll wave the conspiracy charges against Marsha Montgomery, but I'll take what I consider sufficient evidence to the grand jury and seek an indictment. Is Mr. Donaldson also seeking a probable cause hearing for Lucille Montgomery?"

"No," Hewitt said. "Her bail has been set and we're anxious to go to trial. We have no interest in seeing Mr. Chesterson subject Lucille Montgomery to the trauma of re-arrest should he receive his grand jury indictment."

"Then we are set," Mercer quickly interjected. "Bail for Lucille Montgomery is set at one thousand dollars and her daughter is free to go. Anything else, gentlemen?"

Chesterson shook his head and gathered his papers from the table in front of him.

Hewitt made no move to leave. "There is one thing, your Honor."

"Yes."

"Since Mr. Chesterson has dropped the charges against Marsha Montgomery, the law stipulates that any DNA samples collected during the booking process are to be destroyed. I would appreciate if the bench would reinforce that by direct order."

Suddenly, Hewitt's ploy became crystal clear. All of his maneuverings with probable cause hearings had one goal: eliminate Marsha Montgomery's DNA from the investigation.

Chesterson looked at Hewitt with dawning apprehension that he had been outfoxed. He just didn't know why.

"Write up a brief order," Judge Mercer told Hewitt. "I'll sign off on it." He brought the gavel down in one quick stroke. "This hearing is adjourned."

# Chapter Ten

The sign on the door read "Hewitt Donaldson and Associates." The plural noun barely qualified since Hewitt had only two associates and neither was an attorney. Hewitt claimed he dealt with so many lawyers in the courtroom that he couldn't stand to be around them in his office. Truth be told Hewitt was a lone gun, beholden to no one but his clients and he was very picky regarding who joined that elite club.

Nakayla and I entered his hallowed chambers at ten thirty after successfully overseeing Marsha and Lucille's release from the Henderson County Detention Center and the posting of Lucille's bail by John Lang. Nakayla and I were to gather at eleven for a strategy session with Hewitt and the two women, but I wanted an advance conversation where we could talk freely without concern for the clients' sensitivities.

"Will his Highness receive two humble servants?" I asked the question of the dark-haired woman scowling over the morning mail at her desk.

Without looking up, she snapped, "The only throne his Highness sits on is porcelain and I advise you not to be received there."

"Good morning, Shirley," Nakayla said cheerfully.

The woman dropped the mail and flashed a welcoming smile. "Hi, girlfriend." She glanced at me. "Why's Sam Spade with you? Didn't you get that restraining order?"

"It was invalid," I said. "Like most of the legal work done in this office."

"What are you talking about? Every legal service performed comes with Hewitt Donaldson's personal guarantee."

"Which is?"

"That no matter what happens, he'll still be your Facebook friend."

"Does he even know what Facebook is?"

"I told him it was the book of mug shots at the police station. Hell, most of them are his friends."

Hewitt might have been the best defense attorney in western North Carolina, but if he ever had to go against Shirley in a courtroom, she'd turn him into steak tartare. I didn't know if she had a college degree. She wasn't an attorney or paralegal. All I knew was that she ran Hewitt's law practice like a well-oiled machine. She was one of those people born with so much common sense and intuitive insight that she would have been a quick study in any business.

She was also weird. Her hair was so black that it looked like a hole in the fabric of space/time. She wore white makeup and deep purple eyeliner. If I met her on the street, I'd guess her occupation as Queen of the Zombies.

But, if you needed something done and done right, Shirley was unbeatable. I couldn't imagine Hewitt surviving without her. She kept him focused and her quick wit kept him honed for verbal jousting in the legal arena. In short, Shirley was Shirley and anyone trying to categorize her or change her would have better luck teaching a cow to speak French.

"Is he in?" Nakayla asked.

"If you mean that corpulent mass he calls his body, then yes. If you mean the neurological mess he calls his brain, then your guess is as good as mine. He came in all fired up from the bond hearing. So, he might be back there writing his lawyer-of-the-year acceptance speech."

"Do you want to tell him we're here?" I asked.

"Only if you'll take him away. I was hoping to get some work done this morning."

"Sorry. The clients are coming at eleven."

"Well, then I'd appreciate you keeping him tied up till they show." She hit a button on her phone console. "Hey, Horace Rumpole, wake up. Nakayla and the bionic man are here to see you."

Hewitt's voice came through the tinny speaker. "I'll meet them in the conference room."

"Words cannot describe how thrilled they are." She released the intercom button and swept her thin, pale hand toward the rear of the office. "You know your way to the inner sanctum."

Nakayla and I took chairs one seat apart at Hewitt's round conference table. He hadn't yet appeared.

The room bore the trappings of Hewitt's personality. The circular table meant no one would be seated at the head. The walls were devoid of the leather-bound legal volumes and framed diplomas that seemed to be the mandatory decor of law firms wanting you to believe they had the Supreme Court Justices on speed dial. Instead, Hewitt had framed classic album covers from the 1960s and 70s that ranged from *The Freewheelin' Bob Dylan* to the Stones' *Sticky Fingers*. I considered the display to be Hewitt's chronicle of his own transformational decade, the turbulent time that shaped him into the firebrand who stood with his clients against all odds. The fact that Lucille Montgomery's case went back to 1967 would be an irresistible force pulling Hewitt into the genesis of his own identity.

He came through the door, shed of his tie and suit coat and with sleeves rolled up near his elbows. He carried a mug of steaming coffee in one hand and a legal pad in the other. "You guys want some java? You got less sleep than I did."

"I'm coffeed out," Nakayla said.

"Me too," I added. "We thought we'd better go over a few things before Marsha and her mother arrive."

"All right." Hewitt took the seat with his back to the door.

I noticed he'd filled the top sheet of his pad with scribbling, and I assumed he was mapping out a strategy for building the defense. "Nakayla and I think we should agree on our priorities so that we're not sending them mixed messages."

"My priority is having the charges dismissed. If that fails, then the only remaining priority is for their acquittal. Do you have another priority?"

"No. Of course not. But this whole business with the missing picture seems like a wild goose chase. It was fine to pursue it when Marsha thought it would divert suspicion from her mother, but now that Lucille's been charged and the murder weapon was in her possession, a more realistic approach seems warranted."

Hewitt rested the palm of his right hand against his chin and rubbed his broad fingers across his lips while he thought. Then he pushed his legal pad aside and leaned over the table. "Look, we've been through some challenging cases together but never in the courtroom. So, it's good we're talking because there's a difference in our perspective." He looked at Nakayla. "Before you hooked up with this bozo, you worked for insurance agencies exposing fraudulent claims. That's basically a prosecutorial perspective." He looked back at me. "And as a Chief Warrant Officer, you worked for the military investigating crimes to reveal a suspect, someone who would be charged and prosecuted."

"We're all after the truth," I said.

"No. You might be after the truth, but I'm after the story. And the members of the jury might think they're after the truth, but it's the story that seals the verdict one way or the other."

"How does that change our investigation?" I asked.

"It means everything is fair game and nothing is too insignificant. I won't lie for my clients and I won't condone their perjuring themselves. But, I will choose what to emphasize and what to marginalize." Hewitt glanced at the legal pad. "I've already started outlining a possible narrative. As facts are determined and we get discovery from the prosecution, I'll shape that story into the most favorable light for Lucille and Marsha."

"You think Chesterson will go to the grand jury for an indictment against Marsha?"

Hewitt shrugged. "If I had to bet, I'd say no."

"You certainly caught him off guard with how the rifle breaks apart."

"I made a quick Internet search for specs on the Remington fourteen and a half and I knew Judge Mercer collects guns. If he didn't see the possibility for digging a smaller hole, I would have raised it. But Mercer made the point for me, and Chesterson was odd man out. The judge and I knew more about his evidence than he did."

"Can't Chesterson wait and charge Marsha after Lucille's trial?" Nakayla asked.

"That's the smarter play," Hewitt said. "Then, if he has a conviction on Lucille, his conspiracy charge is tied to a proven murder."

"How'd you discover the lack of contact between Lucille and Marsha so quickly?" I asked. "That's what backed Chesterson down."

Hewitt smiled. "I didn't. I took a chance and believed my clients. I also believed Deputy Overcash moved so quickly for the arrest that he hadn't checked. I bluffed and Chesterson folded. He had no evidence to the contrary."

"And you kept Marsha's DNA out of the identification pool."

Hewitt sat back and rested his hands on his stomach. "And that's the first part of our story that I want to protect. If the remains stay unidentified, then the lack of a provable relationship between Lucille and the deceased eliminates motive."

"But the DNA could definitively prove it wasn't Jimmy Lang," Nakayla said.

"Yeah, but let's face it. Odds are Jimmy Lang was shot by Lucille Montgomery's gun, crawled into that hollow log either in an attempt to hide or get shelter, and bled to death." Hewitt's face tightened as he made the grim assessment. "We need to plan that the first part of our story will have to be rewritten. When, not if, Chesterson determines the skeleton is Jimmy Lang, I need to make sure the jury has plenty of other options for the story's ending. Who else stood to gain by Jimmy's death? Who bore him grudges? And, yes, who could have stolen a photograph and a rifle, a rifle that was returned for the purpose of incriminating Lucille in the event Jimmy's body was ever discovered."

"Okay," I said. "So our priority is everything you just listed."

"Yes. As well as what we don't know that we don't know. That's the most crucial because that's the biggest surprise." Hewitt's eyes narrowed. "And I don't like surprises."

"All right," I said. "We'll work all the angles. Are you billing them for our time?"

"What were you planning to charge them?"

I glanced at Nakayla, signaling her to answer.

"We really hadn't gotten to those details. Actually, the odds were we'd be taking it pro bono." She smiled at me. "It let Sam worm his way into the investigation of the remains."

"Worm," Hewitt said. "Bad word choice. But accurate."

The phone on a side credenza buzzed. "Lucille and Marsha Montgomery are here," Shirley said through the intercom.

"Thank you. I'll be out in a minute."

"You still want us to stay?" Nakayla asked.

"Yes. If I sense we're moving into sensitive issues better left just between the clients and me, then I'll suggest you start following leads while we finish. I'll handle informing them that we're unifying your investigation with my legal defense."

"What's the status with John Lang?" I asked.

"I'm seeing him at noon. I'll advise him he's under no obligation to give the authorities DNA material and that goes for anyone else in his family." He stood. "Wait here and I'll get the ladies."

As soon as he left the room, I asked Nakayla, "What do you think? Are we getting in over our heads?"

"Probably. And you're loving it. You who didn't want to go mushroom hunting. How dull your life would be without me."

When Marsha and her mother came into the conference room, I stood and helped Lucille into the chair beside me. She looked frailer than yesterday. Worry and exhaustion plagued her lined face. Nakayla slid over and Marsha sat on the other side of her mother.

Hewitt took a seat diametrically across the round table. "I've asked Nakayla and Sam to sit in so they can investigate any leads that might grow out of our conversation."

Lucille gave me a faint smile. "That's fine. Will they find out if that poor man in the log was Jimmy?"

"No, ma'am. The police will determine his identity."

"But how will they do that unless they use a DNA sample? Marsha told me how that works."

Hewitt paused a moment. I figured he was assessing how to best sell the first part of his defense strategy.

"Miss Montgomery, I have one duty and one duty only. That's to provide you with the best defense possible."

"I didn't kill anybody."

"I know. But our justice system isn't perfect. I wish I could say otherwise. Unfortunately, there are troublesome elements like the rifle and what John Lang says was your rebuff of Jimmy's affections."

"I never rebuffed his affections." She looked at her daughter, undeniably Exhibit A in that regards. "Jimmy and I loved each other."

"I understand," Hewitt said. "And before June of 1967 you couldn't get married. But when the Supreme Court changed that, the question arises why didn't you? Mr. Chesterson will say Jimmy refused to marry you. That when he finally could, he wouldn't."

"That's a lie." Her voice rose with indignation. "I'm the one who didn't want to get married."

"And the D.A.'s going to ask why. Why wouldn't a black woman in 1967 leap at the chance for the security for her and her child by marrying a white man?"

I heard both Nakayla and Marsha draw a sharp breath. Hewitt's question sounded too accusatory, too judgmental.

Lucille Montgomery laughed. "Oh, Mr. Donaldson, you know better than that."

"I do." He smiled, pleased with her reaction. "But there are people that don't and twelve of them might be on the jury."

"Then they need to understand something. Men can change the law, but a new law doesn't change the human heart. A judge's gavel isn't a magic wand. People who opposed our right to marry didn't change just because the law did."

"You were afraid for your safety?"

"No. They wouldn't do anything to us. To the contrary, they'd have nothing to do with us. Jimmy and John were trying to make a go of their company. Can you imagine what would have happened to their business if Jimmy had married a black woman?"

"Seems like that would have been Jimmy's decision," Hewitt said.

"Really? A woman's got no say in a marriage proposal?"

I witnessed one of those rare events—like an eclipse or double rainbow. Hewitt Donaldson blushed.

"Of course she does," he said.

"And to go into a marriage with no income and a five-year-old child to feed was not my idea of a marriage that could endure. Folks would look the other way if a white man was dallying with a black woman on the side. That's been going on since before Mr. Jefferson and Sally Hemings. But to desecrate their holy ideal of the racial purity of marriage? Well, that wasn't crossing the color line, Mr. Donaldson, that was blowing it up."

Lucille's words rang true but I wasn't sure how they fit with what John Lang said about his brother. Maybe that's why Jimmy pulled ten-thousand dollars out of the bank and left his job. To show Lucille he couldn't lose what he no longer had. If that were the case, how angry would she have been? Her explanation was far from exonerating.

Hewitt saw the same problem with her story. "Miss Montgomery, I have no doubt as to the truth of what you're telling me, but you know people, how they like to gossip and think the worst."

"Yes, sir, I do."

"Then did Jimmy Lang tell you he was leaving town? That he was taking his money and going away?"

"No, sir."

"You loved each other, but he didn't even say goodbye?"

Tears spilled down the old woman's cheeks. "He didn't. It pains me to this day. Maybe it pained him too. That's why he couldn't bear to tell me."

"Who did tell you?"

"His brother John."

"And if that skeleton belongs to Jimmy?"

"Then he didn't leave me. That's why I want to know."

Hewitt shook his head. "Not now. I can't advise you to do anything that would jeopardize your defense. After we get through the trial and you're acquitted, then we'll do everything we can to help identify those remains." He stated those final words to Marsha and kept staring at her until she nodded her agreement.

Lucille had brought a small black clutch purse with her. She unsnapped it and pulled out a folded piece of paper. The white color had yellowed with age. She passed it over to Hewitt.

"The day Jimmy disappeared, he was supposed to pick me up when I got off work at the cafeteria."

"Was that his normal routine?" Hewitt asked.

"No. I usually rode with a co-worker and paid her something each week for the gasoline. Both of us had a child in a church daycare which made it convenient. But this day Jimmy said he would be by because he had some place special to take me."

"Did he say where?"

"No. Just that it was time for a new beginning."

"A new beginning," Hewitt repeated. "Was he going to tell you he was leaving?"

"I didn't think so at the time, but then he never showed. At the end of the day, I had to get a ride home."

"And what's this?" Hewitt unfolded the paper.

"A letter to my grandmother from Miss Julia Peterkin. It came with a copy of the photograph Miss Ulmann took on the site of the Kingdom of the Happy Land. Miss Peterkin and my grandmother were friends. They'd made arrangements for us to have our picture made."

"The one that was stolen?"

"Yes."

Hewitt read the letter silently and then aloud. "Lang Syne Plantation, Fort Motte, South Carolina, November 3, 1932. Dear Loretta, I hope this finds you, your daughter, and your granddaughter well. Enclosed is a framed print of the photograph of descendants of the Kingdom. Doris Ulmann was determined to see that you received a copy. She is quite pleased with it and with the stories you shared. She is a dear friend but I am very worried about her. She continues to suffer from the stomach ailments that plagued her last summer. And she is still under the spell of that insufferable gigolo John Jacob Niles. I tell you that man is aiming to take her for every penny. He knows the value of her work and I'm convinced he'd sell every last photograph if it meant liquor money. Doris will hear nothing against him. I only tell you because you met him that day. I'm sure you quickly sized him up for the no good leech he is. It pains me that he has separated her from me for I am concerned not only for her health but for her safety. The man will be her ruin, if not her death. Sorry to trouble you with my concerns. If I ever decide to pick up the pen again, I'd like to set a story in the Kingdom. I hope you will grant me the opportunity to be inspired through your memory of those days. With gratitude, Julia Peterkin."

Hewitt scanned the letter one more time and then handed it back to Lucille. "You brought this to show me that the Ulmann photograph existed?"

"Yes, sir. And prove it has value. And that this John Jacob Niles knew it."

"Okay," Hewitt said. "But I don't see the relevance."

"Miss Ulmann died in the summer of 1934 after she took sick in Asheville. Miss Julia said John Jacob Niles tried to steal her estate. Miss Julia said he could have even caused her death."

"How does that relate to 1967?"

"Not just 1967, Mr. Donaldson, but Friday, July 14, 1967. That's the day Jimmy disappeared. And when I finally got home that evening, Miss Ulmann's photograph was gone. John Jacob Niles was the only one still alive outside the family who knew about it. If he killed Miss Ulmann, he wouldn't think twice about killing my Jimmy."

Hewitt nodded. "Then Sam and Nakayla will look into it."

"We certainly will," I said. I looked to Nakayla for confirmation but she turned sideways in her chair and scrutinized Lucille like she thought the woman might be carrying explosives.

"July 14th," Nakayla said skeptically. "Jimmy was picking you up at the school cafeteria?"

Lucille smiled. "I see nothing gets past you. Not the school cafeteria. The camp cafeteria. During the summer break, I worked at Camp Quail Cove. They served the boys three meals a day and I worked the breakfast through lunch shift."

"Where is it?" Nakayla asked.

"Between Flat Rock and Tuxedo, but it stopped operating in the eighties. I think it's now a gated community."

"Quail Cove Estates," Marsha added. "It borders the Kingdom of the Happy Land."

"That's right," Lucille said. "The Bell family let the camp use their trails for hiking and horseback riding."

"How about hunting?" I asked.

"Oh, no," Lucille replied. "The only weapons allowed in the camp were bows and arrows and they were only used under strict supervision."

"What time were the meals served?" Nakayla asked.

"Breakfast was from eight to nine, lunch noon to one, and dinner from five to six."

Nakayla looked back to Hewitt, satisfied with Lucille's explanation.

The lawyer gave Nakayla an appreciative nod. Her catch of the summer date was something both he and I should have noticed.

"You mentioned John and Jimmy were expanding their business," Hewitt said. "Was there anyone who stood to lose if they were successful?"

Lucille grimaced as if she'd just bitten into a rotten apple. "Mr. Earl Lee Emory. He was also bidding for the contract."

"What contract?"

"The county school board was going to consolidate garbage collection for all the schools. Jimmy and John would have doubled their business."

"They had the east side of the county?"

"Yes, sir. And Earl Lee Emory had the west."

"So, it wasn't simply a matter of expanding. One company was going to lose business." Hewitt pulled his legal pad closer and jotted down Emory's name. "Did Jimmy and Emory have any dealings with each other?"

"No. Jimmy couldn't stand the man. He was bad to drink and everybody knew he beat his wife. Jimmy and John had a much better reputation for never missing a pick up."

"Did the dislike go both ways?"

"What do you mean?"

"Did Emory ever express animosity for either Jimmy or his brother?"

Lucille sat quietly, not answering for a moment.

"Miss Montgomery, it could be important if we can show there was bad blood over business."

"They had words after they made their proposals to the school board."

"Was this in public?"

"Yes, sir. Mr. Emory presented first while Jimmy and John waited in the lobby of the education building. Then, when they came out after their turn, Mr. Emory was waiting for them. He asked Jimmy if he told the school board he was sleeping with a…" She halted, unable to complete the sentence.

"He used the N word," Hewitt said.

Lucille blinked back tears. She took a deep breath. "Mr. Emory said a man like Jimmy wasn't fit to set foot on school property let alone pick up children's garbage."

"Jimmy told you this?"

"John did. He had to hold Jimmy back from punching Mr. Emory. Jimmy didn't deny it."

Nakayla and I looked at each other.

Hewitt then stated what had become clear to all three of us. "So, you refused to marry Jimmy because you knew there was no way that school board would give him the contract if he married a black woman."

"Yes, sir."

"When did this confrontation with Emory occur?"

"Two weeks before Jimmy disappeared."

"And had the school board made a decision before he disappeared?"

"No. That would be announced at their August meeting. By then, everyone knew Jimmy had left."

"John got the contract?"

"Yes, sir. And the company's grown ever since."

Hewitt caught my eye and we read each other's thoughts. Earl Lee Emory might be a suspect with a grudge, but Jimmy's disappearance erased the main obstacle standing in the way of his brother John's path to becoming a very wealthy man.

Pursuing that line of inquiry would need to be done with extreme subtlety. And by me.

# Chapter Eleven

At three in the afternoon, I pulled into the meadow where Nakayla and I had met the mushroom club on the previous Saturday. Now she was in the Pack Library in Asheville researching photographer Doris Ulmann, her companion John Jacob Niles, and Pulitzer-Prize-winning author Julia Peterkin.

In the passenger seat beside me rode my fellow veteran and amputee Jason Fretwell. He wore the only clean non-hospital garb he had, fatigues that fit his lean frame too loosely. With his good left hand, he clutched the printout of my Internet research on the specifications and characteristics of the Remington fourteen and a half. The young sniper was the closest thing to an expert I knew, and I figured the afternoon release from the V.A. hospital would be welcome physical and psychological therapy.

We saw the slim form of Ed Bell leaning against the hood of his muddy Jeep. He gave a wave and I parked the CR-V alongside him.

My vehicle had barely stopped before Jason hopped out, tucked the papers under his right arm and extended his left hand. "Hi, Mr. Bell. I'm Jason Fretwell. A pleasure to meet you."

Without so much as a glance at Jason's prothesis, Bell grasped the young man's hand. "Welcome to the Kingdom of the Happy Land."

The introductions were done and I had yet to unfasten my seatbelt. I sat a moment, marveling at the transformation of the soldier I'd seen sulking in the cafeteria the day before. Then I took a point-and-shoot digital camera from the glovebox and got out to begin the hunt for indisputable evidence that Lucille Montgomery couldn't have shot our log-entombed victim.

"What would you like to see first?" Bell asked.

I looked to Jason but he only shrugged.

"Let's start at the log and work back toward spots where he might have left a vehicle," I said.

"No abandoned vehicle ever turned up," Bell said.

"I know. But there were no keys found with the skeleton, so he might have hiked in, or ridden with the person who killed him, or simply left his keys in the ignition. Would that have been common back in the sixties?"

Bell smiled. "Considering we never locked our houses? Definitely."

His answer raised another question. "How much of this area has changed since then?"

"What do you mean?"

I swept my arm across the field. "Was this meadow here? Were there more of them? Are there roads that no longer exist or new ones that weren't here then?"

Ed Bell surveyed the landscape as if trying to see more than forty-five years back in time. "This is pretty much it. The land was logged in the thirties, but the basic footprint of the acreage is the same."

Jason took a few steps forward. He turned, shielded his eyes with his left hand, and looked at the afternoon sun behind me. "Did you bring a compass?"

"No. I should have thought of that."

Bell pointed over my left shoulder. "That's due west." He swung his arm almost a hundred and eighty degrees. "The spot where the skeleton was found is east-southeast of here."

"Are we considering a certain season of the year?" Jason asked.

"Yes. Summer. Friday, July 14, 1967 to be exact."

"They worked that out just from the bones?" Bell asked.

"No. That's the day Jimmy Lang disappeared."

"The trash guy?"

"Yes." I realized Bell hadn't heard the news of Lucille Montgomery's arrest. I gave him a brief update. "Did you know Jimmy and Lucille?"

"I knew Lucille in passing. Her family went back to the Kingdom days. I didn't know the Lang brothers. I think they came here from South Carolina." He paused, trying to be more specific. "I believe during the late forties."

"Do you know any reason why Jimmy Lang would have been on the property?"

Bell shook his head. "No. Unless he was just hiking. We took care of getting our own trash to the dump."

Jason Fretwell rotated slowly in the meadow, examining the tree line and particularly the ridge to the north. "Do you happen to have a time of day?"

I thought about Lucille Montgomery being stranded at Camp Quail Cove, waiting for Jimmy to pick her up. "Probably before two in the afternoon. Maybe between noon and one or even eight to nine in the morning."

"Why those times?" Bell asked.

"Camp Quail Cove meal times. I'm not saying it had to be during those periods, but if someone wanted to be on the property unseen, there was less likelihood of being spotted."

"You are a detective," Bell said.

I didn't tell him Nakayla had been the one to make the connection.

"So, the remains were found in that direction." Jason pointed toward the spot Bell had indicated. "The bullet didn't penetrate the body which means there had to be some distance between the shooter and the target. From the information you gave me on the muzzle velocity of the Remington Fourteen and a Half, I'd estimate at least over a hundred yards." Jason looked at the sky. "The date was about three weeks after the summer solstice so the sun would have risen early, but between eight and nine the angle could still have impaired an eastwardly shot." He looked back at the western edge of the meadow. "I'd want the higher ground with cover. If the victim were shot from across the meadow, then I'd say you're looking at the noon to one time slot. It would make sense that a wounded man would run in the opposite direction. He would figure that out from the impact of the bullet."

"If he were shot in this meadow," I said.

"Yes. So, let's see how far he would have had to run and if there are any other areas with a clear enough sight line to give us the necessary distance." Jason walked back to the CR-V. "I'll leave these papers in the car."

We followed Bell into the woods. He kept to an old logging road, a route that was faster than my meandering mushroom search. Jason would stop now and then to estimate line of sight, but the road twisted too frequently to give him the distance he wanted.

We walked about three hundred yards before Bell veered to the right and headed across a fern-covered rise. "This is the little knoll where the king's cabin stood. Up ahead is the South Carolina line."

I saw the swarth cut through the trees and the red paint on the trunks.

"The queen's cabin was just across the state line," Bell said.

"Coincidence?" I asked.

Bell laughed. "No. They knew exactly what they were doing. Supposedly, one of their enterprises was distilling corn liquor. If they got wind of a raid coming from one state, they'd quickly move everything across the line. The states never made a coordinated attack. Of course, if the Kingdom had lasted into Prohibition, that little scheme wouldn't have survived the federal revenuers and their government axes."

Bell turned right on the boundary and we headed down the hill. Approaching the hollow log from the upper slope, we first saw strands of yellow crime scene tape twisting in the breeze. The perimeter was still marked and within the enclosed area leaves had been carefully raked clear of the soil. Scratch marks approximately six inches apart scarred the bare dirt where some implement had dug several inches into the ground looking for any object that might have been deposited. The log had been dissected so that the bottom half of the shell was completely exposed. If anything in addition to the skeleton and mangled bullet had been uncovered, the police report hadn't mentioned it.

Jason stared at the site. "He was in that log all these years?"

"Yeah," I said. "We figure he crawled in there to hide. If he'd been running after taking the bullet, his heart rate would have accelerated the bleeding. Probably passed out and then bled out."

Jason shook his head. "Man, what a way to die."

"Not much different than being enclosed in a wooden coffin," Bell said. "It's the anonymity that's most disturbing. To think you can disappear and it makes no difference."

Jimmy Lang's disappearance did make a difference to Lucille, I thought. And Marsha.

"So, what do you think, Jason? Any possibilities other than the meadow?"

"Not so far." He looked at Bell. "Is there any other stretch of open road or a clearing?"

"Only the first hundred yards coming off the highway."

"He would have had to run uphill all the way," I said. "That's at least half a mile from here."

"You mentioned those cabins," Jason said to Bell. "Were any of them still standing in 1967?"

"No. All the cabins had been gone for years. There's a storage shed and a picnic shelter, but those were built after the Kingdom. The only remnants that survived into the mid-twentieth century were the cabins' stone chimneys, and by 1967 all but one had been destroyed."

"To reuse the rocks?" I asked.

"To look for treasure."

"Treasure?" Jason's face lit up, showing a kid's excitement over a possible adventure worthy of the Hardy Boys. "What kind of treasure?"

"The kind that exists only in the imagination. Or in the hopes of desperate people."

I looked at the disassembled log. "We're talking about desperate people. Desperate people who murder."

"I guess we are." Bell stuck his hands in the front pockets of his jeans and leaned against an oak. "Well, any time you have a king and a queen you have rumors of treasure. A story circulated in the forties that the founding king had brought his plantation valuables from Mississippi. Not just household silver but the hard currency his wealthy white father had amassed. The rumor was fueled by the tale of a workman on this property."

"Someone you knew?" I asked.

"No. I was just a kid. As the story goes, my family had given permission for one of the stone chimneys to be demolished for a friend to rebuild for a cabin a few miles away. The worker and his assistant dynamited the chimney because the masonry was too tight to disassemble by hand. When the younger assistant showed up on the construction site of the new cabin the next day with the load of rocks, he asked the owner if his boss told him what happened the day before. The owner hadn't seen the assistant's boss. The apprentice said after the small charge of dynamite exploded, gold coins poured out of the chimney."

"Like a slot machine?" Jason asked.

"Maybe. If you blew up a slot machine. Anyway, the boss never returned to the project and word was he left suddenly for a northern city, maybe New York, maybe Chicago. For the next few years we had trouble with vandals destroying the chimneys. Usually teenagers, but on occasion a couple of adults would get liquored up and come seeking their fortune. No one ever found so much as a penny. Today only one chimney remains and that's because it wasn't part of the cluster around the king and queen."

"Where is it?" I asked.

"To the right of the road you drove in on. About two hundred yards above the meadow."

"Do you believe there were gold coins, Mr. Bell?" Jason's eyes had grown wider during the course of the man's story.

Bell laughed. "Sure. Somewhere. Sometime. But no one in my family has any such knowledge. I've heard the same tale about a cabin in Georgia. It makes the rounds, being customized for each location. The man who allegedly made off with the loot returned a few years later. Turns out he came back after the husband of the wife he'd been caught cheating with died. If he found any gold, he'd spent every last cent."

I nodded to the log. "That wouldn't have been the aggrieved husband?"

"No. I'm told he had a fatal heart attack. In the throes of ecstasy with another man's wife." Bell looked to Jason. "Probably saw nothing hypocritical about threatening one man's life for doing what he was doing himself."

"Mountain justice," I said. "To spite his own wife."

"Yes, there's that," Bell agreed. "Mountain folk have their own way of settling scores."

We were silent a moment, staring at the site where a score had been so violently settled.

I turned to Bell. "I'd like to see that last remaining chimney. Is it a tough hike?"

"No. Just off a trail where you can't see it. That's why it's survived so long."

We walked in single file, skirting the meadow and veering up the northern slope. Then Bell led us into the underbrush. The dry leaves crackled underfoot and we spaced ourselves to avoid the backlash of branches. After about fifty yards, we emerged into a small clearing of ferns ringed by white pines. In the middle stood a partially toppled stone chimney, a silent sentinel watching over the ghosts of a bygone era.

"There it is," Bell said. "The last vestige of the Kingdom of the Happy Land."

"Not a gold coin to be seen," Jason said.

"No," Bell agreed. "If there was any treasure in the Kingdom, it was the communal spirit that bound them together after the hardships of slavery and the war."

I looked above the chimney to the afternoon sun. Marsha Montgomery's voice broke into my thoughts. "The light streamed through the pine boughs like beams from the Kingdom above." Her words to describe the Doris Ulmann photograph of her mother, grandmother, and great grandmother.

"Do you keep this little clearing cut?" I asked.

"No. There's only a thin layer of soil covering the granite under this knoll. No tree of any size can put down roots."

"So, it's always been this way?"

"Depends upon what you mean by always. Not in geological time, but certainly since the cabin was erected. The bedrock made a great foundation."

I stepped back a few yards. The afternoon sun streamed through the pine needles in visible rays, peppering the chimney with hot spots and shadows. I felt certain that over eighty years ago, a world-renowned photographer would have found that scene worth shooting. But where was her photograph? And, more importantly, was the missing picture worth another kind of shooting?

When we returned to the meadow, I thanked Bell and drove Jason back to the V.A. hospital. I stopped short of the front door to avoid any questions of where we had been.

"Thanks, Sam. I really appreciate you springing me from this place for a few hours."

"Thank you. I appreciate the help. You make a good case for the shot coming from across the meadow."

"That's what I would've done. Good sun position, no twigs or branches to deflect the bullet. Distance far enough to keep the shooter out of sight and allow for the slug staying in the body." He paused. "I guess we don't know the angle of penetration."

"Why's that important?"

"It could give us a more precise elevation difference between shooter and target. Maybe support the theory that the shooter was on the higher ground. And we might know if the victim was coming or going from his car."

"Wouldn't that depend upon whether he parked facing in or out of the meadow?"

"Yeah. You're right. But it would be nice to know."

"Why?"

Jason looked at me like I was overlooking an elephant sitting on the hood. "Wouldn't that help you know if the killer had been in place ahead of time, either luring the victim to the site or anticipating his arrival? Otherwise, he probably followed him there and found a shooting spot where he had a clear but distant view, particularly if he wasn't sure from what direction his target would be returning."

I just stared at him.

"What?"

"Jason, I'm the professional investigator."

His face fell. "Sorry. Guess you knew all that."

"Here's what I know. That was very good thinking. But I outrank you. Didn't you learn in the army not to make a superior officer look stupid?"

He grinned. "Yes, sir."

"Good. Because I'm perfectly capable of looking stupid all by myself."

# Chapter Twelve

Wall Street. The name has become synonymous with greed, corruption, and cronyism. An environment that fostered the fleecing of America and made the robber barons of the nineteenth and twentieth centuries look like altar boys.

But not Wall Street in Asheville, North Carolina. Only a few blocks from the Pack Library, the short street of shops and restaurants begins at Asheville's triangular Flat Iron Building and runs along the edge of a city hill. Buildings on the lower side have their first story on Patton Avenue while their Wall Street entrances actually open to the second floor.

At five-thirty on Tuesday afternoon, Nakayla and I strolled hand in hand past the ever-present street musicians to one of our favorite Wall Street dining spots, Cucina24.

Nakayla had spent the afternoon in the library and an early supper sounded like the perfect way to swap information about the day's discoveries. The restaurant was not yet crowded and the maitre d' led us to a table by the rear window overlooking Patton Avenue thirty feet beneath us. He handed Nakayla a menu but she waved it off.

"I want a glass of Chianti and the wild mushroom pizza."

"Mushrooms?" I rolled my eyes. "Really?"

She nodded toward the wood-fired oven visible behind the bar. "Sorry. The sight of those flames gets me every time."

The maitre d' extended the menu to me. "We have dishes without mushrooms."

I lifted my hands. "I surrender. When I see her pizza, I'll regret any other selection. Bring two. But change her Chianti into a draft Porter for me."

"Very good, sir. I'll tell your server. Miracles are her specialty."

The drinks arrived in less than a minute. I clinked my beer against Nakayla's stemmed glass of red wine. "To our case."

"Whatever it might be. How was your field trip?"

I gave her a recap of the scout of the Kingdom of the Happy Land, Ed Bell's history of the place, and Jason Fretwell's opinion of where the shooter could have been positioned.

"What do you think about Jason's theory for the time of the shooting?" Nakayla asked.

"Makes sense. If the victim was Jimmy Lang, then he could have been on the property around noon and had plenty of time to pick Lucille up from the nearby camp at two. But why was he there?"

Nakayla ran her finger around the lip of the glass. "That's the question. One of several that we need to ask Lucille."

"But let's hold off until we've talked to more people."

"Who do you have in mind?"

"I made a mental checklist of the names I heard over the past two days. John Lang, his son William, this Earl Lee Emory who was the business competitor." I paused, wondering whom I'd left out.

"Quite the list. Three names. The computing power of your brain is astonishing."

"I know. Especially since I had to squeeze those names in among all the women madly in love with me."

Nakayla lifted her glass of Chianti. "Wow. That makes a total of four names. And I can give you a fifth."

"I'll take it. Who?"

"David Brose. He's the folklorist and curator for the John C. Campbell Folk School."

"Where's that?"

"Brasstown, North Carolina. Near Murphy. About as far west as you can go and still be in the state."

"How's Mr. Brose fit in?" I grabbed my beer and leaned back, ready for Nakayla's story.

"I hope he might provide some insight into the missing Doris Ulmann photograph. I spent the afternoon researching her and Julia Peterkin. Everything matched what Lucille and Marsha told us. Julia Peterkin was the mistress of Lang Syne Plantation and she wrote novels in the Twenties. She drew upon her experience with former slaves and the first-generation born into freedom. Her characters, particularly black women, were strong and lusty."

"I like a lusty black woman." I tried to wriggle my eyebrows like Groucho Marx but only managed to wiggle my ears. Not exactly a seductive come-on.

"Cute trick. Better if you were wearing a hat."

"A hat and nothing else."

"Please. I'm getting ready to eat." She took a healthy sip of wine. "Anyway, for a while Julia Peterkin was the literary darling of New York and Chicago. Carl Sandburg introduced her to his circle of friends in the Windy City."

"Heady stuff for a talented woman stuck on a plantation in South Carolina."

"Yes. She spent a lot of time in New York, had a long running affair with a writer named Irving Fineman, and became good friends with Doris Ulmann. They even shared another lover."

"This John Jacob Niles?"

"No. Someone else."

"Speaking of lusty women." I took a swallow of beer and wiped my lips with the back of my hand. "How ya gonna keep 'em down on the farm after they've seen Pareé?"

"Funny thing is Julia Peterkin eventually returned to her plantation role. This was shortly after Doris Ulmann died."

"Would she have had a motive to steal Lucille's photograph in 1967?"

"She might have had a motive, but the means and opportunity would have been a problem. Julia Peterkin died in 1961."

"Oh. So much for her role in the case."

Nakayla cocked her head and eyed me like a teacher disappointed in a prized student. "Don't be so quick to dismiss her. We do have the letter she wrote Lucille's grandmother. It's proof the photograph existed and no one can contradict Lucille and Marsha's claim that it disappeared the same time as Jimmy Lang."

"But what good is that if it doesn't provide another suspect?"

"We have Julia Peterkin's disparaging remarks about John Jacob Niles." She slid her wine aside and leaned across the table. "And in 1967, he was very much alive."

I mulled that possibility for a moment, struggling to see how Hewitt Donaldson could concoct a believable story about a man returning to steal a photograph thirty-five years after it was taken. "Where is John Jacob Niles today?"

"Very much dead. But in 1967 he was seventy-five and still composing and performing concerts."

"Did he have a criminal record?"

Nakayla shook her head. "No, but Julia Peterkin's misgivings seem to have played out during his relationship with Ulmann and afterwards. He was with her during her final illness. She was severely stricken in Asheville. They made it back to a hotel in Scranton, Pennsylvania, where her personal physician was vacationing. Other than the doctor, Niles kept everyone away from her, including her longtime chauffeur. Then he had a total stranger witness a will she allegedly wrote in the hotel leaving him ten thousand dollars and all her photographic images."

"Nice work if you can get it."

"Yeah. But Ulmann made it back to New York and had her attorney draw up a proper and more complete will that still included Niles. She died a week later. Then a big struggle ensued as Ulmann's sister and brother-in-law contested the will. They tried to get Julia Peterkin to testify against Niles."

"Did she?"

"No. As much as she disliked Niles, she wanted no part of dragging Doris Ulmann's name through the mud." Nakayla fumbled through her handbag in the chair beside her and retrieved a notepad. "I had to jot down one Julia Peterkin quote that she wrote to a friend explaining her decision. I found it in a book called *The Life and Photography of Doris Ulmann.* 'I could not help resenting the man who seized upon her like some horrible leech, never to let go until he had gotten what he aimed from the start to get, her property. I plead with her once, only once, to save herself from his clutches. Poor child, she had not the strength, maybe not even the will to do so. Of course, it seems a pity that a scoundrel should have all her work in his filthy hands, but even that seems better to me than to have her name and reputation smirched more than it already is.'"

Julia Peterkin's visceral loathing of John Jacob Niles flowed through the words. I could hear Hewitt latching onto "leech," "scoundrel," "clutches," and "filthy." Still, the letter offered no proof of villainy, just the opinion of a Pulitzer-Prize-winning novelist. Making it relevant to the legal case would be Hewitt's job.

"Did Niles wind up with everything?" I asked.

"No. In the end, he received a trust fund. Other money from the estate went to care for Ulmann's photographs and to two institutions, Berea College in Kentucky and the John C. Campbell Folk School in Brasstown."

"Where your Mr. Brose works."

"Yes. I stepped out of the library and called the school. They said Brose was the expert I should speak with." She paused as another thought crossed her mind. "I didn't try to reach him because I had an incoming call from Donnie Nettles."

"The mushroom guy?"

"Yes. He'd heard Lucille had been arrested for murder and wondered if the victim was Jimmy Lang."

That got my attention. "How did he link the two together?"

"He knows John Lang's son William. William was a year ahead of him in school, but they played sports together. He said William told him his uncle disappeared while William was in Vietnam."

"So, Nettles grew up here?"

"After he was twelve. His folks came from Kentucky. Then he moved to Asheville when he got out of the army."

"He told us he was also in Vietnam."

"That's right. But he and William didn't serve together. William enlisted the year before."

"Was Nettles in town when Jimmy vanished?"

"No. Especially when I told him the date was July 14th. He said he was at Fort Bragg, only days away from deployment to Vietnam."

"Did he know about the relationship between Jimmy and Lucille?"

"He said there were rumors, but he never talked about it with William. It wasn't the kind of thing you discussed back then. Do you want to interview him?"

"No. Sounds like we're dealing with nothing more than Nettles' curiosity."

"Excuse me, these are hot." The waitress and an assistant set the two pizzas in the center of the table.

My mouth watered at the sight and all unpleasant memories of mushrooms vanished.

"Will there be anything else?"

I pointed to Nakayla's glass. "A Chianti for the lady and I'll have another Porter."

"Very good, sir," she said, as if a customer could ever make a bad selection.

Nakayla wriggled her beautiful eyebrows while her elegant ears remained motionless. "Are you playing the role of John Jacob Niles and trying to get me to change my will?"

"Trying to get you feeling lusty."

"No problem. Nothing like three hours in the library to jump-start a woman's libido."

I kept quiet, counting on my physical charm to seal the deal.

We chewed our pizza and enjoyed our drinks in silence. Sometimes companionship is felt strongest when no words are spoken.

When my plate was empty, Nakayla said, "You can have my last slice. I'm full."

Without hesitation, I grabbed it before she could change her mind.

"You know how much money John Jacob Niles was given a year in the settlement of the estate?" she asked.

My mouth was already full of pizza. I shook my head.

"Thirty-five hundred dollars."

I grunted an "mmm."

"In 1935, that would have been a comfortable sum, but in 1967?"

I swallowed. "A lot less."

"I ran an inflation calculation. The dollar was worth less than half. About forty cents."

I understood where Nakayla was headed. "So, depending upon other income sources, Niles could have been facing a money squeeze. It would explain why, as the photographs grew in value, his need for money could have also grown."

"It's a possibility," Nakayla said. "And maybe this photograph was one no one else knew about. Unfortunately, a lot of Ulmann's negative plates were lost in 1954 when Columbia University ran out of storage space and gave the Ulmann Foundation an ultimatum to have them removed. They only found housing for part of the collection. Thousands of plates had to be destroyed. Lucille might have had the only copy of any photographs from the Kingdom of the Happy Land, and Niles might have been the only person alive outside the family who knew about it."

"What's your next step?"

"I'd like to get a better description of the photograph from Lucille. Then I thought I'd call Berea College, the Getty Museum, Oregon University, the major centers of Ulmann collections. Multiple prints were probably made and one of those institutions should either have it or know of its existence."

"What about the folk school in Brasstown?"

"I think the school and Mr. Brose warrant a personal visit. Would you like to join me in a excursion to the most western frontier of North Carolina?"

"Yes, but not before we make an excursion to your place in West Asheville. I'm worried about your libido."

Nakayla laughed. "So, that's your next step? What about the case?"

"See if you can schedule an appointment with David Brose toward the end of the week. I'd like some time to run down our local interviews before then. You can contact the colleges and museums."

"I'll need to talk to Lucille first."

"I know. We'll move her up and see her first thing in the morning."

Nakayla pursed her lips as if my agreeing made her reconsider the idea.

"What?"

"Shouldn't we clear any conversation with Lucille through Hewitt?"

Her question raised an interesting point. Immersing myself in the investigation, I forgot we were no longer working for Lucille and Marsha Montgomery. Our client was Hewitt Donaldson, and if anyone was going to question Lucille, he might want to clearly establish that her answers fell under attorney-client privilege.

"You're right. I'll call him right away."

Nakayla stuck out her lower lip in a mock pout.

"What now?"

"What do you think? My libido just came in second to Hewitt Donaldson. You really know how to woo a girl, Sam."

I heard the clock in the hallway strike three. The muted chime of Nakayla's family heirloom was just loud enough to wake me. She lay snuggled into my back, her left arm draped across my chest. As my mind surfaced from sleep, I gently grasped her hand like a child waking to clutch a comforting stuffed toy.

She stirred. "What's wrong?" she murmured.

"Nothing."

"Sam, you're not a light sleeper. Something's bothering you."

I felt the bed shift as she broke free of my grip and propped herself up on her right elbow.

The room was dark except for a patch of moonlight sneaking through a crack in the curtains and reflecting off the metal of my prosthesis I'd left on the floor. The thought that disturbed my sleep returned.

"Just thinking."

"About the case?"

"About Jason Fretwell."

Silence. I started to remind her who the young amputee was, but waited. Nakayla wouldn't have forgotten his name.

After a moment, she asked, "You think his analysis was wrong?"

"No. I think his analysis of the terrain and weapon was spot on. He was very helpful and he knew it."

"Hmmmm. Why do I get the feeling I'm sleeping with Sam the Do-Gooder?"

"You didn't see his face. The kid loved the whole afternoon, getting out of the hospital, using his training again."

"We're too young and he's too old for us to adopt him."

"No, but we can give him a start."

Nakayla sat up. I rolled over and tried to read the expression on her face. In the darkness, all I could see were the narrow slits of her eyes. She was trying to read me as well.

"Are you thinking of hiring him?"

I laughed. "Are you kidding me? You and I aren't busy enough. I was thinking of trying to get him a job with Nathan Armitage. Like Tikima tried to help me."

Bringing Nakayla's sister Tikima into the conversation might have been unfair, but relevant. When Tikima had visited me in the veterans hospital, she'd offered to set up an interview with her employer Armitage Security Services. Her murder had been the horrific event that brought Nakayla and me together.

"But you were a Chief Warrant Officer," Nakayla argued. "You knew security and you knew your way around a crime scene. I don't think Nathan's changing his company name to Armitage Security and Sniper Services."

"No. But a sniper has patience and discipline. Those are solid attributes."

"Okay," Nakayla conceded. "Then is he cute?"

"What's that have to do with anything?"

"Well, I assume he'll need a place to stay. That's what you're hinting at, isn't it? So, if Jason Fretwell and I are going to live together, I want to prepare myself against the temptation of a good-looking, younger man."

Now I sat up. "Hey, I'm all the man you'll ever need. I was thinking of offering him my apartment till he gets settled. That is if he even wants a job in the area."

"And where would you sleep? On your sofa?"

I patted the mattress. "This is a big bed. And I wouldn't be moving in. Just looking for shelter."

"Like a stray cat."

"I prefer virile yet affectionate tomcat. Missing a leg. Who could turn such a charmer away?"

"Who indeed?" Nakayla lay back, pulling me with her. "My Sam Do-Gooder. Let's see how good you really are."

# Chapter Thirteen

At the office the next morning, I telephoned the veterans hospital and asked for the Rehab department. I knew most of the nurses and physical therapists so when an authoritative voice said, "Reilly," I visualized Sheila Reilly, a large woman carved from the side of a mountain who had pushed my butt through every tortuous exercise conceivable till I could walk again.

"My favorite dominatrix. Surprised you set down your whip to answer the phone."

"Is this my favorite one-legged candy ass?"

"I hope so."

She laughed. "Sam, how are you? Did Tikima's sister come to her senses and dump you?"

"No. She's still blinded by my wit and good looks." I heard Nakayla groan from her office.

"I'm translating that as she still feels sorry for you," Sheila said. "Are you calling because you miss the sound of my commands?"

"That and to see if I can weasel some information out of you."

"About what?"

"Actually about whom. Jason Fretwell. Have you been working with him?"

"Yeah." A note of skepticism crept into her voice.

"Is he scheduled for discharge soon?"

"Probably Friday. We've done about everything we can for him."

"How do you think he'll fare?"

Sheila Reilly was quiet a moment. I could hear the garbled sound of the hospital P.A. in the background.

She cleared her throat and then spoke softly. "You know I can't talk about a patient's private medical information."

"Then don't," I said. "You're his physical therapist. I'm interested in your opinion of his psychological progress and you're not a damn shrink. Whatever you say is speculation just between us."

She sighed. "Well, two days ago I'd have said he was facing a tough row to hoe. You know how that is."

I did. Losing a limb is small potatoes in comparison to losing your self-worth. When you can only see yourself as a cripple, you believe that view is shared by the world. It's a dark spiral downward and some can never break free of its grasp.

"Something changed?" I asked.

"At our Monday afternoon session, Jason was as chipper as a teenager who just scored a date with the most popular girl in high school."

After our little cafeteria encounter, I thought.

"Same for yesterday morning. Things started clicking for him with the arm, but that was only part of it. Then he didn't show for his afternoon session, and I thought he'd returned to the dark side. But, I ran into him this morning and he was all smiles. Wouldn't say where he'd been. Just that he had an appointment with his mentor." She paused. "You wouldn't know anything about that, would you?"

"Who me? I'd never come between him and your physical abuse sessions."

"Right. Whatever you're doing, Sam, keep it up. He's a good kid."

We hung up and I placed a call to Nathan Armitage to make my pitch for Jason joining his company. I caught Nathan on his way to a client meeting, but he told me he'd set up an interview as soon as Jason was released. Now I had to talk with Jason. That conversation was too important to conduct over the phone.

"Sounds like you made progress on your project." Nakayla stood in my office doorway, her smile a beacon of approval.

"Yeah. But Jason might have his own plan in mind. All I can do is offer him an option."

"Well, it will have to wait till later today. Hewitt wants to see Lucille with us. We need to leave now."

"Let's take separate cars and you ride back with him. I want to get to John Lang and his son right after Lucille."

"No problem. Hewitt was in Henderson County for Lucille's arraignment. They'll meet us at Lucille's apartment. And I suggest you talk to John Lang and his son separately."

"Why?"

"Because Hewitt said the early discovery from D.A. Chesterson lists William Lang as a prosecution witness."

That information stopped me. "But his father put up Lucille's bail."

Nakayla shooed me out of my chair. "Yes. Curious, isn't it?"

Lucille, Marsha, Hewitt, Nakayla, and I entered Lucille's small living room. Lucille lifted her knitting from her rocking chair and set the needles and yarn on the coffee table. She collapsed onto the cushion with a sigh. Even though the arraignment had been a brief formality, the trauma to an eighty-five-year-old woman compelled to stand in public and proclaim not guilty to a murder charge had to be exhausting.

Hewitt took the seat on the sofa closest to her and Marsha sat next to him, poised on the edge where she could spring between the lawyer and her mother if she felt her mother needed protection. I motioned for Nakayla to take the armchair beside the rocker and I pulled a hardback chair from the dinette set in the kitchen. When we were settled, everyone looked at Hewitt Donaldson to begin.

"Miss Montgomery, you did very well in front of the judge. I know that wasn't easy."

She shook her head in disbelief. "A bad dream. That's what I told myself. It's a bad dream."

"A good way to look at it," Hewitt agreed. "But you're not in it alone. We're here with you and we'll get through it together."

"I just want it to be over, and I want justice for my Jimmy."

Hewitt glanced at me. I knew he wanted to keep Jimmy buried and unidentified. The D.A.'s case was very weak without a provable connection between the murder victim and Lucille.

"Of course," Hewitt said. "But justice means first clearing you. Then the police will move on to discover the real killer. That's why I'm pushing for a speedy trial. Understand?"

"Yes, sir."

"Good." Hewitt shifted on the sofa. "Now it's come to light that the prosecution is calling John Lang's son William as a witness. Any idea why?"

Lucille leaned forward as if she didn't hear him clearly. "Willie? He's talking against me?"

"We don't know what he's saying. We'll schedule a deposition, but I wondered if you had any idea why he'd be testifying."

Lucille folded her hands in her lap. "No. Not for the life of me. When Jimmy left, Willie wasn't even here."

"Where was he?"

"Vietnam."

"When would Jimmy have last seen Willie?"

"The week before. Something like that. Willie was home for his mother's funeral."

"Right before he began his tour of duty?"

"No, sir. He was already over there. He got bereavement leave. Had to return the day after the funeral."

Hewitt thought a moment. "So, John Lang's wife died about a week before Jimmy left?"

"Yes, sir. Breast cancer. Just like my mother. I took turns tending to her and preparing meals for the family. We tried to make Gladys comfortable."

My first thought linked the death of John Lang's wife to the disappearance of Jimmy Lang. Had there been a rift between the brothers? Was John's wife simply someone who kept the family together, or was there more going on? I wasn't sure of a delicate way to frame the question. Fortunately, that was Hewitt's job.

"Miss Montgomery, did Gladys Lang's illness and death put a strain on Jimmy, as far as his relationship with the rest of the family?"

Lucille looked at Hewitt with incredulity. "A strain? We were all under a strain."

"Yes, ma'am. I know." Hewitt, the skilled courtroom interrogator, seemed at a loss for words. "But was there anything that could have caused Jimmy to leave when his sister-in-law died? Anything that would have been too great a conflict for the brothers to resolve?"

"Not over Gladys. Their only quarrel was over me. Jimmy marrying me and what that would have done to the business."

"You mean the county-wide school garbage contract?"

"Yes."

"Okay." Hewitt leaned on the armrest, moving nearer the elderly woman. "Then back to William Lang. Was he close to Jimmy?"

Lucille spoke without hesitation. "Yes. They were tight. In some ways, Jimmy was more his father than an uncle. He'd take Willie hunting and fishing. John was always too busy. John loved his son but just wasn't as natural in showing it. Some men are like that."

"When did William return from Vietnam?"

Lucille thought a moment. "Must have been late 1968. He was there eighteen months. There was some talk of him re-enlisting, but John advised against it. Said the war was getting too crazy and he needed him here. The business was expanding. By then I'd gone to work for John myself."

"Could William have blamed you for Jimmy's disappearance?"

"Me?" The question seemed to throw her.

"My mother loved Jimmy," Marsha interjected. "And she loved Willie too. She's the one wrote him letters when Gladys was too sick to do it herself."

Hewitt ignored Marsha and kept his eyes focused on Lucille. "But if you wouldn't marry Jimmy and that could have been a reason for his leaving, don't you see how William could have blamed you?"

Lucille slowly nodded. "Yes, sir. But he would have also blamed his father. John made no secret he disapproved of Jimmy and me marrying."

"And that would have come to a head about the time John's wife was in the final stages of her cancer?"

"What do you mean?" Lucille asked.

"The Supreme Court ruling. Loving versus Virginia. It came down only a few weeks before. Suddenly your marriage became a legal possibility. And that prospect happens at the same time as the garbage contract, Gladys Lang's dying, and William heading back to Vietnam. Seems like a lot of stress on one family."

"Yes, sir. It was a tough time for sure."

Hewitt nodded. "And William never talked about his uncle after that?"

"No. Not with me. I suspect he and his father hashed that out when Willie returned. But we never spoke of it. Willie's always been respectful and polite. To me and Marsha. I don't know why he'd be talking for the other side."

Hewitt rested his palms on his thighs. "Well, Miss Montgomery, neither do I. But we'll learn soon enough." He looked at Nakayla and me. "I believe my associates have a few questions, if you're not too tired."

"My mother is exhausted." Marsha stood, signaling the conversation was over.

Lucille raised her right hand and waved her daughter to sit. "You sought them out, Marsha. We should listen to what they have to say."

Marsha gave Nakayla and me a hard stare. "All right. But my mother's had a very trying morning."

As Nakayla and I had discussed during the drive from the office, she took the lead, not only because she could build the stronger bridge, but also because she would be pursuing the Ulmann photograph.

"Miss Montgomery, Sam and I are investigating any possible connection between Jimmy's disappearance and the theft of the picture of you, your mother, and grandmother."

"I told you Jimmy wouldn't have stolen it."

"Yes, but somebody else might have. We can't ignore that it went missing the same day Jimmy failed to pick you up after work."

Lucille looked at Hewitt. "They're saying whoever took that picture killed Jimmy?"

"We don't know that the victim in the log is Jimmy. Yet we can't just say the timing of the two events is a coincidence." Hewitt turned on the sofa to Marsha. "You were wrong to bury the rifle, but your instincts were correct about the stolen photograph. If anyone had access to your mother's home, they could have also taken and returned the rifle. We need to find the picture and link it to someone who had means and opportunity. Motive will follow."

"And what if it was destroyed?" Lucille asked.

"I thought it was valuable," Hewitt said. "What would be the motive in that?"

"No motive at all," Lucille said sharply. "But if you can understand all the reasons for human behavior, Mr. Donaldson, then you are a very smart man indeed."

Hewitt smiled. "Miss Montgomery, I get the feeling that even if I were as smart as I think I am, I'd still have only half the insight you do." He gestured toward Nakayla. "That's why we need your help if we're going to end this bad dream."

Lucille turned to Nakayla. "All right, dear. What would you like to know?"

"How big was the photograph?"

Lucille pointed across the room to the pictures on the table with the television. "Smaller than those. I guess six by eight. Something like that."

On Monday, I'd noticed the graduation portrait of Marsha on one side of the TV and the second photograph of an unknown man on the other. I examined the man's face more carefully. "Is that Jimmy?"

"Yes," Lucille said. "It was a thirty-fifth birthday present for me. He had it taken at Barber's Studio in Hendersonville."

I studied the black and white, three-quarter profile of the handsome man. He looked like a younger John Lang, his twin. I tried to peer beneath the tan skin and dark hair to the skull I might have seen up close and personal.

"Who was in the missing photograph?" Nakayla asked.

"My grandmother Loretta, my mother Lucinda, and me."

"No one else?"

Lucille shook her head.

"The boys," Marsha added.

"They're interested in our family," Lucille said. "Not people we don't know."

Nakayla leaned forward in her chair. "We're interested in everything. What boys?"

Lucille looked at her daughter. "Just some children who came up with Miss Julia for the day. A chance to see the mountains."

"Do you know who they were?"

"No. I was only five. If they told me their names, I've long forgotten. I think there were five or six boys and girls from Miss Julia's plantation."

I looked at Marsha to see if she would offer more details, but she said nothing.

"How many people total were in the picture?" Nakayla asked.

Lucille looked up to a corner of the smooth, white ceiling as if the number might be written there. "Seven, I think. That sounds right, doesn't it, Marsha?"

Her daughter nodded, but she didn't look certain.

Nakayla shifted her gaze between the two women. "So, you were posed in front of one of the remaining chimneys of the Kingdom. Do you know which one?"

"No," Lucille said. "I can tell you it wasn't from the king's or the queen's cabin. I remember we walked a piece till the photographer found the light she wanted. I didn't know what she meant. It was the afternoon. There was light all around us."

I wondered if it was the stone chimney Ed Bell showed me yesterday. In 1932 there were others, and the photograph had been taken before the treasure-hunting vandals struck. "Would you recognize the spot?" I asked.

"Maybe. But woods can change in eighty years. And as a five-year-old girl, I was struck by the people, not the setting."

"What about the people?" Nakayla asked.

"There were four adults. I remember the photographer wore a long dress and a hat. Like someone out of a magazine. I marveled that she could walk through the woods without tripping. Miss Julia had what you'd call everyday clothes. Nice, but more suitable." Lucille stopped and collected her thoughts. "I'm wrong. There must have been five adults. Someone drove the second car."

"Weren't there two men and two women?"

"Yes, but four adults rode in one car. I'd never seen a car so big. A chauffeur, Miss Julia, the photographer, and a man who never left the photographer's side."

"John Jacob Niles?" Nakayla asked.

"I guess, but only because I have the letter Miss Julia wrote my grandmother. She sure didn't care for Mr. Niles."

"What do you remember about him?"

Lucille shrugged. "Not much. He was big and carried the camera. He sang a song for us. "Froggy Went a Courtin'" in a high warbly voice. We laughed more at him than the words of the song."

"And there was a fifth adult?"

"Yes. He drove the smaller car. The one with the children."

"Can you describe him?"

"A black man. He wore overalls and his hair'd gone completely gray. He stayed with the cars while they took the picture up at the chimney."

Nakayla glanced at me, her invitation to ask a question. I shook my head. Lucille had given me all I needed confirmed. By the year 1967, John Jacob Niles had to be the only adult of the five who was still alive.

# Chapter Fourteen

While Nakayla rode back to Asheville with Hewitt Donaldson, I set out for my encounter with John Lang's son, William. Hewitt instructed me not to ask William about his possible testimony against Lucille, but instead to concentrate on questions regarding the investigation of the missing photograph and anything William could tell me about his Uncle Jimmy. Furthermore, I didn't call ahead for an appointment. I didn't want to give William Lang the opportunity to contact D.A. Chesterson, who might take a dim view of my parallel investigation. From Chesterson's perspective, I could be harassing his star witness.

As a Lang employee, Marsha confirmed that William was scheduled to be at the paper plant all week and that his calendar wasn't busy. In the event William refused to see me, I would use his father's name as the interested party spurring my inquiries. For once, I'd be gaining access by telling the truth.

I took old Highway 64 from Hendersonville to Brevard. The two-lane blacktop wound through a picturesque mountain valley and the clear blue sky and midday sunshine enriched the hills and spring wildflowers with a colorful brilliance that hurt my eyes. Besides, that route ran between two of my favorite spots: the cemetery housing Thomas Wolfe's monument from *Look Homeward, Angel* and Hawg Wild, a barbecue restaurant on the outskirts of Brevard. Lucille Montgomery might be facing a murder charge, but that didn't mean I couldn't take time for a pork sandwich before facing William Lang.

At two o'clock, I pulled into a blue-stone gravel parking lot adjacent to several large metal buildings that bore more resemblance to airplane hangars than factories. A large white sign with black block letters read "Recyclable Deliveries Proceed to Gate House." An arrow pointed to the right and I saw a tractor-trailer idling by a guardhouse about fifty yards away.

To the left of the operational complex stood a single-story brick office. An apron of grass provided enough space to anchor a polished black granite stone that looked more like a cemetery memorial than corporate signage. Carved into its smooth surface were the words "Lang Paper Manufacturing" with a smaller font beneath proclaiming "Green and Clean."

John Lang had definitely come a long way from hauling school garbage to the dump.

There was no designated parking for visitors, just two handicapped spaces on either side of a concrete walk leading to a white front door. LPM had been stenciled across its mantel in textured hues replicating brown paper. I figured this logo was the newer image, reduced to initials to show the company was in the big leagues with the likes of IBM and UPS. Easier to paint over a door than re-chisel a tombstone.

A bell chimed as I stepped into a small lobby. A counter split the room in half with a few mismatched chairs on my side and a middle-aged woman at a desk on the other. She was on the phone and held up her index finger signaling she'd be with me in a moment.

The walls were made of the cheap paneling lining the family room of every home built in the seventies. Plaques and framed certificates populated its surface, chronicling everything from environmental awards to company bowling championships. The community impact of small business USA. I was sure more than one little league baseball or football team sported the Lang logo on their uniforms.

I sat in a green vinyl-covered chair and examined the magazines spread on the coffee table in front of me. All were esoteric trade publications. *Pulp & Paper International, Paper360, PaperAge,* and *Corrugated Today*. The last one caught my eye because its cover featured John Lang and another man flanking the granite sign out front. I picked it up and read the caption. "John and William Lang: Two Generations of Paper Manufacturers Setting the Standard for Generations to Come." The resemblance between father and son was obvious. William was taller, although John might have shrunk a few inches as he journeyed through his eighties. William's hair was still salt and pepper and he wasn't as tanned as the old man. Probably didn't get in as much golf.

The magazine was six months old, hot off the presses for a waiting room. I flipped through the pages till I found the article. There were photographs of stacks of cardboard waste, steaming hot water transforming the crushed boxes into a brown sludge, and ribbons of new paper flowing between pressure rollers onto giant spools. Next to the sludge picture was a photograph of a clear mountain stream right beside the plant. The caption lauded Lang's use of a closed loop water treatment system that insured no stream pollution.

The layout highlighted a quote from William Lang: "Thank God for pizza." Puzzled, I searched for the explanation until I found the paragraph in which William explained the surge in pizza delivery generated tons of recyclable takeout boxes.

"May I help you?"

I looked up. The woman stood behind the counter. Her smile was uncertain, like maybe I was a salesman she'd have to keep at bay.

I stood and walked to her, resting my empty hands on the counter surface to show I carried no brochures or product samples. "I'm here to see William Lang."

"Do you have an appointment?"

"It's a personal matter." I leaned closer. "John asked me to see him. He told me Willie was free this afternoon."

I used Lucille's name for William, hoping Willie was what family and close friends called him.

Her smile broadened. She offered her hand. "I'm Edna Collier. I don't believe we've met."

"Sam Blackman. But you can call me Sammy." I spoke the word without grimacing. I hated being called Sammy, but, hey, her boss was Willie.

She returned to her desk. "I'll let him know you're here."

"Thanks." I headed toward the interior door at the end of the counter, demonstrating my confidence Willie would welcome me with open arms.

"Hold a second, please." She picked up the receiver with one hand and punched an intercom button with the other. Then she pivoted away from me. Her voice dropped to a whisper except when she emphasized one sentence: "Yes, your father, but he's still at lunch."

When she turned back to me, the smile was gone. "I'll escort you to Mr. Lang's office."

I got the feeling Edna would want to frisk me before I left the building.

I followed her down a hallway lined with more certificates and commendations. I wondered if these environmental organizations ever tallied how many trees died to create their awards.

She stopped outside a door to a proverbial corner office. I figured old man Lang occupied another corner of the building. I was lucky he was at lunch so that William couldn't buzz him in an effort to learn why I was here.

Edna knocked.

"Come in." The reply was quick and curt.

Edna nodded toward the door and swiftly retreated like we'd disturbed a dragon in his lair.

I smiled. "Thank you, Edna. See you on the way out."

I stepped into the office. Beneath my feet, the carpet turned from heavy-duty industrial to soft, plush pile. The cheap paneling became genuine oak and the plaques and certificates transformed into fox hunt prints and mountain landscapes. A small conference table was on my right and two red-leather upholstered chairs occupied the space between the table and a massive mahogany desk. Behind it sat the man I'd seen on the magazine cover, only now he sported a neatly trimmed, graying beard.

The desk surface was clear except for a blotter and brass name plate used as a paperweight. "William P. Lang" was etched in 3-D letters. Handy in case your guest forgets your name. A closed laptop sat on the credenza behind him and on the wall above hung the mounted head of an eight-point buck.

William P. Lang's eyebrows gathered in an unmistakable scowl.

I'd gotten what I wanted, a chance to question him. There was no need to start with a hostile tone.

"Thank you for seeing me, Mr. Lang. Things are moving quickly and I appreciate your time."

He didn't stand or offer his hand. He simply nodded to the chairs on the other side of his desk.

I closed the door behind me. "I assume your father told you I might be dropping by." I sat and crossed my good leg over my damaged one.

Lang's eyebrows arched. "No, he didn't. I don't know why you're here."

I paused, as if this was a monumental development. I decided not to say John Lang had come to our office or tried to hire us. Perhaps the son knew nothing about those events. But posting bail was a public action.

"I guess your father's been preoccupied, what with Lucille Montgomery's arrest. I saw him at the courthouse yesterday morning. We talked after he put up her bail."

"He did what?" William interjected.

"He posted her bond. I understand your family has a long connection with her."

"Lucille worked for us. Her daughter Marsha heads our customer service department." He leaned forward and laced his fingers together. "What's your interest in this?"

"I've been hired by her defense attorney. There's a valuable photograph that was stolen from Lucille's home about the time your uncle left the area. If the remains that were found turn out to be his, then the theft might have a bearing on Lucille's defense."

"You mean whoever stole the photograph could have stolen the rifle?"

I nodded. "I see you're familiar with the case. That information hasn't been made public."

William Lang reddened. He realized he'd made a mistake. "I don't know about any photograph."

"It was taken by a world-renowned photographer named Doris Ulmann in 1932. Lucille, her mother, and her grandmother posed for the picture on the site of one of the old cabins left from the Kingdom of the Happy Land. You've heard of it?"

"Yes. I hiked the property when I was a kid."

"How old were you in 1967?"

"Twenty."

"And you don't remember the photograph? Six by eight. Lucille kept it in her home."

"I was never in her house."

"But your uncle was, wasn't he? He's Marsha's father."

"That was then, and that was my uncle's business. When he left, I was humping it in the Mekong Delta."

I pretended that was news. "A vet? Thank you for your service."

He smiled for the first time. "No. You deserve the thanks. You're the Sam Blackman who solved that death at the Sandburg farm, aren't you?"

"Guilty as charged."

"I read you lost your leg in Iraq. My service pales by comparison."

"No, it doesn't. My injury could have happened to anyone. The fact that you were there, in harm's way, is what matters."

William Lang's eyes moistened. He seemed to reconsider our conversation. "You're wondering how I knew about the rifle."

"It crossed my mind."

"When I read about the discovery of the skeleton, I thought about Uncle Jimmy. Particularly the last conversation we had."

"I'm listening."

"I was on compassionate leave. We'd just buried my mother and Jimmy told me the legal obstacles to marrying Lucille had been struck down by the Supreme Court. But he wasn't sure he was going to marry her after all. He was afraid she'd take the news badly. They can have quite a temper."

"They?"

"Black women."

My first thought was if Nakayla were here she might have proved him correct by punching him out. Lang must have read the disapproval on my face.

"I'm not prejudiced or anything," he quickly added. "Look, I'm Irish. I admit they're bad to drink and fight too."

"You're saying Lucille's a drunk?"

"No," he snapped. "Forget it. I'm upset that's all. I guess when I read the story in the paper the conversation with my uncle came back to me. I shouldn't make generalizations or draw conclusions."

"You contacted the Henderson County Sheriff's Department, didn't you? They didn't come to you."

Lang shrugged. "Like I said, the article upset me. I felt a duty to step forward."

"In person?"

"I spoke over the phone with a Deputy Overcash. He told me about the rifle and I confirmed my uncle kept it at Lucille Montgomery's house."

The phone call fit with what Overcash said and must have been the testimony that rushed him to make an arrest.

"So, you haven't met with D.A. Chesterson yet?"

"Tomorrow morning."

"And a DNA sample?"

The door to Lang's office swung open and John Lang entered. "What's going on?" He stared at me. "Edna said you were here."

"Nothing's going on." I answered before William could speak. "I was asking your son about the missing photograph."

"William knows nothing about that."

"So he told me. We were just chatting about the DNA sample he's giving tomorrow." I rose from the chair. "Well, I guess I'll see you at your deposition." I turned around. "And nice to see you, Mr. Lang."

I walked to the door, stopped and faced them. "Oh, does the name Earl Lee Emory mean anything to you?"

John Lang's jaw tightened.

William stood. "What's he got to do with anything?"

"I don't know. But I heard there was bad blood between him and Jimmy. Is that true, Mr. Lang?"

John Lang's eyes narrowed. "Earl Lee Emory was a son of a bitch to the core. And his spawn is worse."

Earl Lee's spawn sounded like a bad horror movie. "Are you talking about his children?"

John Lang sneered. "I'm talking about Mick Emory. The son of the son of a bitch."

"Earl Lee and Mick tried to put my father and uncle out of business," William Lang explained.

"But they didn't," I said.

"No. Between them they didn't have the brains."

"What are they doing now?"

William smiled. "I guess you could say Mick's in the recycling business too. Last I heard he runs a pawnshop in West Asheville. Double G Pawn."

"Double G?"

"Yeah. Guitars and Guns. Your one-stop redneck Christmas store."

"And Earl Lee?"

William Lang looked to his father to answer.

"Earl Lee's on the wrong side of the grass. Way I heard it he took one of the pawned guns and blew his brains out. Gotta respect a man who tests the product he sells."

"When did this happen?"

"Oh, twenty years ago I reckon. He'd folded up his trash business. I guess desperation can cause a man to do extreme things. Like killing himself."

"I hear he was pretty desperate to get that county contract forty-five years ago."

Nobody said anything. I suspected we were all thinking the same thing. A man who proved desperate enough to kill himself could also have been desperate enough to kill someone else.

The intercom on William's phone buzzed.

"Yes," he snapped.

"Mr. Lang," a woman said. "Joe Caspar from the American Legion is on line two."

"I'll have to call him back."

"Yes sir. He just wanted you to know someone shot and killed Donnie Nettles."

William collapsed back in his chair. "Jesus." He glared at me. "I think we're done here."

I walked out of the office without saying another word. I was too shocked myself.

I'd gone no more than ten feet when I heard old man Lang's angry voice.

"Just what the hell's going on, Willie?"

# Chapter Fifteen

As soon as I left the Lang parking lot, I called Detective Curt Newland of Asheville homicide. I had no idea where the shooting of Donnie Nettles had occurred, but "Newly," as he was nicknamed, would be my fastest source of information. He and I had a strong friendship, cemented when Nakayla and I uncovered the murderer of his partner.

"What's up?" he asked.

"Know anything about a shooting involving a Donnie Nettles? I think he's an Asheville resident."

"Yeah, but it's out of our jurisdiction. Evidently Nettles was killed in his home last night, a gated community called The Cliffs at Walnut Cove in southwest Buncombe County. What's your interest?"

"Nettles was the guy who organized the mushroom hunt where I found a skeleton."

"Yeah, I read about that. You working it?"

"Hewitt Donaldson's the defense attorney for a woman charged with the crime. He's hired us to investigate."

"Could his client have popped Nettles?"

"No way. She's eighty-five years old and I believe she's innocent."

Newland laughed. "There's a first. Donaldson defending someone who's innocent. So what's your tie-in to Nettles?"

"None that I know of. He called yesterday curious about the case, but he didn't have any connection to it that we know of."

Newland sighed. "Sometimes coincidences are just that. But if you like, I'll contact a friend in their investigative unit and see what I can learn."

"Thanks, Newly."

Next I phoned Hewitt Donaldson. I summarized my conversation with Newland, and then moved to the real purpose of my call. "I think I kicked a hornets' nest with the Langs."

"How so?" he asked.

I gave him the rundown on my encounter with William Lang. How he'd volunteered the details of his last conversation with his uncle and that I figured he was giving a DNA sample the next day.

"William's the other shoe," Hewitt said. "Overcash got the rifle match and then William's testimony directly contradicted Lucille's story. Overcash thought he had motive, means, and opportunity. And he wanted jurisdiction even before the remains were identified. We're fortunate he rushed the arrest."

"Why's that?"

"Your hornets' nest. The arrest brought John Lang into the picture and now you've gotten him and his son on opposing sides. Interesting to see how that plays out." He paused a second. "What's your next move?"

I checked the time. After two thirty and I was forty minutes from Asheville. "I've got a meeting unrelated to the case and then I'll head to the office. Tomorrow morning I'll talk to Mick Emory at the pawnshop. It's clear there was no love lost between his father and the Langs."

"Could be tough tying Earl Lee Emory to Lucille's rifle."

I laughed. "Not my problem. You're the storyteller. I'm confident you'll create a more than plausible explanation for the jury."

"True. But I'd welcome a supporting fact or two. Like maybe Earl Lee taught Annie Oakley how to shoot."

Hewitt and I set a tentative appointment for lunch the next day after my conversation with Mick Emory. Meanwhile Hewitt planned to schedule the deposition of William Lang.

I'd driven about ten miles farther when the call came from Newland.

"That was quick," I said.

"Caught my man on the scene. And he's their top guy with gunshot wounds. Matches the autopsy about eighty percent of the time."

That was impressive. On-site examinations can be tricky, particularly if there are multiple entry and exit points that aren't always clear as to which is which.

"What's he say?"

"Contact wound. Back of the head. All six tells."

That was shorthand for a definitive evaluation based upon six markers. There would have been an abrasion of the skin as the projectile created the entry wound, unburned gunpowder tattooing the scalp, soot from burned gunpowder, seared skin from the muzzle flame, triangular tears from the hot gases injected into the wound, and finally, a muzzle contusion from the gases pushing the skin back against the barrel. I thought of the horrific damage such a contact shot would inflict, and then saw Donnie Nettles' smiling face as he handed me my whistle and welcomed me into the club. I felt sick to my stomach. Nettles was a guy I'd like to have known better.

"Any brass?"

"No. The shooter picked up the spent cartridge."

"How do you know it wasn't a revolver?"

"Muzzle contusion has the u-shape."

That told me that the muzzle had the slide mechanism of a semiautomatic pistol.

"Is your guy good enough to speculate on the model?"

"He's smart enough not to. But if he were pressed, he'd go with a nine millimeter Beretta, mainly off the muzzle contusion."

"And the slug?"

Newland grunted. "That's the odd part. From the angle of the entry, exit, and the point where it then struck an interior wall, Nettles had to be standing at the time, facing away from the shooter. When my friend's team went to remove the slug, they discovered it had already been dug out."

That was odd. That also signaled there would be no prints. Someone had done a careful cleanup.

"They got a motive?"

"Nettles was in his pajamas. Looks like forced entry in the middle of the night. His wife was in Washington D.C. visiting their new grandson. His car was in the shop overnight. The theory is the perp thought no one was home."

"You said it was a gated community."

"Wouldn't stop someone coming in on foot," Newland said. "The house had been tossed, jewelry boxes empty, no wallet for the deceased, but big items like the TV and computer system weren't taken."

"Nettles put up a fight?"

"Not that they can determine. Again, they're still on the scene."

"Who found him?"

"Landscape crew noticed the back door was open and the area around the latch splintered. That was at eleven this morning."

"I don't like it, Newly."

"Yeah, me neither. Too professional for a run-of-the-mill break-in. Most of these guys are methed up and make a run at a house with an old cargo van." He paused. "Of course, the guardhouse eliminated that possibility. Maybe they came for jewelry and cash, something more likely to be found in these multimillion-dollar homes."

"You know what Nettles did for a living?"

"No. Not my case. I just got the report from the scene."

"Thanks. I owe you."

"No problem. What are you going to do?"

"Nothing. It's not my case either. It's a matter for the Buncombe County Sheriff's Department. But I'd appreciate a heads-up if you hear anything that sounds like it's more than a burglary gone bad."

"Like what?" Newland asked.

"Like the name Jimmy Lang surfaces for some reason."

"He's your bones in the log?"

As much as I trusted Newland, I wasn't about to make any comment that undercut Hewitt Donaldson's carefully orchestrated efforts to keep the skeleton unidentified. "I don't know, Newly. He's still a John Doe. It's just that I don't like surprises. I met Nettles at the scene of a crime, and less than a week later, he's murdered."

"All right. I'll keep my ear to the ground." He laughed. "And my mouth shut."

I hung up and tried to shake off the feeling of despair a senseless killing always gave me. I shifted focus to the immediate task ahead. Sam Blackman, Ace Investigator was about to become Sam Blackman, Do-Gooder.

I parked in a visitor's space near the rehab section of the V.A. hospital. Jason Fretwell might not be in a physical therapy session, but it was a good place to begin looking for him.

I stopped outside the open door to the therapy room. The men and women inside were stark reminders of our soldiers' sacrifices that too many people in this country choose to ignore. I watched a young man struggle to walk on two artificial legs and a woman brush her hair using a prosthetic hand. An elderly man with an oxygen tank rolled a plastic bowling ball at a few pins, a recovering stroke victim I assumed. I thought of Mr. Carlisle, my roommate during my stay here. The World War Two veteran passed away shortly after my discharge. Mr. Carlisle particularly liked bowling with the plastic set, calling his fellow veterans contestants rather than patients. That's what it took, a competitive spirit and the determination not to give into bitterness and frustration.

"Couldn't stay away from me, could you?"

I turned to see Sheila Reilly smiling down at me. The woman must have been six three or six four, at least half a foot taller and fifty pounds heavier than me. When she told you to do something, you did it. No drill sergeant commanded more obedience.

"Yeah. Most of the bruises you gave me have healed so I came back for more."

She glanced at my left leg. "I saw you walk from your car. Impressive."

"Are you in the market for a poster boy? I'll have my agent call you."

Sheila's smile faded. She looked beyond me to the veterans struggling to regain their health and, for some, their very identity. I turned and scanned the room. The ages ranged from two octogenarians who could have served in Korea or even the Second World War to three young men who couldn't have been out of their teens or a few weeks out of Afghanistan.

War rolls like a wave across the generations, leaving shattered lives in its trough while lifting up others as examples of heroism and devotion. I was no such hero and I regretted my remark.

"No, not a poster boy," Sheila said, as if reading my mind. "But a man who didn't quit. And that's all we can ask of these men and women. Don't quit. Don't give up on life."

"I know. Giving up on life dishonors those who served beside you and died. It took me a while to realize that."

We stood quietly for a few moments, watching the patients go through their therapy.

Then she said, "If you're looking for Jason Fretwell, I just finished with him about fifteen minutes ago."

"Is he back in his room?"

"No, he was headed outside. He likes the fresh air."

"Thanks. I think I know the spot."

"Don't be a stranger, Sam."

I looked up at this woman's strong face, a face that had pushed me beyond my endurance more than once. "I won't." I stepped forward and wrapped my arms around her. It was a bear hug except the bear was the huggee.

She gave a responding squeeze that collapsed my lungs like a cheap accordion. "Take care."

She released me and I staggered backwards. "Take care? Another hug like that and you'll be taking care of me on one of the wards."

I found Jason on the grounds where I thought he'd be. He sat alone on a bench by a bed of blue and pink pansies that would soon fade as spring crossed into summer. He was staring at his prosthesis, slowly opening and closing the fingers. It was a marvel with microprocessors and miniature motors that responded to the muscle actions of his lower arm. I could tell from his expression that Jason would push the device to the limit. The world that had seemed so closed to him was opening again.

"Hey, hotshot. Learning to count on your new fingers?"

He grinned and raised the back of his prosthetic hand toward me. "No, I'm trying to get the middle one to stand by itself. Just for you." He scooted down the bench, inviting me to join him.

I sat and stretched my legs. Easing the weight off my stump always felt good. "You're getting pretty proficient with that thing. You'll be dealing cards before long."

"Not unless I'm capable of pulling aces out of my sleeve."

"So, when are they cutting you loose?"

"Doc Anderson says Friday. I've been here longer than the government would like, but he was insistent I stay an inpatient until I mastered the basics."

"He was like that with me too. One of the good guys."

Jason nodded. "Doc Anderson's why I came back."

I knew Jason was a farm boy from Indiana. I hadn't thought about why he was in Asheville for his care. The government isn't the most logical when it comes to assigning the wounded to bed space.

"Was he your doc the first time?"

"Yeah. When I'd healed enough, they discharged me and I went back to my folks near Fort Wayne. Then when it came time to be fitted for a prosthesis, I pushed to return to Asheville. Anderson pulled some strings and said I was a candidate for the microprocessor hand. And here I am."

"Where will you be after Friday?"

"Back in Indiana." He shook his head. "Moving in with my parents, I guess. Starting over."

I turned on the bench and looked directly at him. "What would you think about staying in Asheville?"

"And do what? Make a cardboard sign and stand on the corner of Broadway and Patton Avenue?"

"No. I mean get a job. A friend of mine owns a private security company. He'd like to talk to you."

"So, I'd be a damn mall cop?"

"I don't know what the hell you'd be. Maybe you'd clean out his toilets."

Jason flinched. My anger at the emergence of his dark mood surprised both of us.

"Okay," he said softly. "I deserved that."

"Look, I'm not trying to push anything on you."

"I know. Sure, I'll talk to him."

"I'll set it up for tomorrow. His name's Nathan Armitage. He was a big help to me when I was in your position, and he helped Nakayla and me start our detective agency."

Jason's face brightened. "Hey, what about you guys?" He lifted his prosthesis. "Need an extra hand?" He looked at the gap between my khakis and left shoe where the metal of my prosthesis gleamed in the sunlight. "Or extra legwork?"

"I'm afraid Nakayla and I don't have enough work to keep us busy. But we're not in competition with Nathan, so if the need arises, you could probably freelance for us."

He beamed. "That'd be great."

"Well, we've got to get you a full-time job first. Nathan might not work out. But if you're serious about staying in Asheville, we'll find something. You're welcome to stay at my apartment till you get on your feet."

His brown eyes filled with tears. He looked like he wanted to say something but couldn't trust himself to speak.

"Don't get misty on me. You have to take out the trash."

"And clean the toilet," he managed to say.

I slapped him on the thigh. "You got it."

◇◇◇

Nakayla was on the phone when I returned to the office. From her side of the conversation, I deduced she was talking to someone about the Ulmann photograph. I closed my door and went to work lining up the next day's agenda.

An Internet check revealed Double G Pawn opened at ten. A call to Nathan Armitage led to a breakfast meeting with Jason Fretwell. We planned to meet at the Sunny Point Café in West Asheville, a favorite morning haunt for Nathan, so that the two men could have an informal conversation before taking the next step of an official job interview with Nathan's Director of Human Resources.

I told Nathan that Jason would be staying at my apartment for the immediate future and looking for other opportunities in case nothing worked out with Armitage Security Services. I didn't want Nathan to feel pressure to give the young vet a job.

A quick call to Sheila Reilly elicited her promise to make sure Jason knew I would pick him up at eight. Nakayla must have seen the light go out on my line because as soon as I hung up, she opened my door.

"Got a few minutes to bring me up to speed?"

We sat in the middle room, Nakayla on the leather sofa with her bare feet tucked under her and me in the armchair across from her. Holmes and Watson. I was pretty sure I was Watson.

She smiled. "So, how'd you do?"

"I'm afraid I've got some bad news."

Her smile vanished. "What?"

"Someone shot and killed Donnie Nettles last night."

Nakayla's right hand flew to her mouth. "Oh, my God. Not Donnie?"

"Yes." I shared the information Newland had given me.

"Do they have any leads?" she asked.

"I don't think so. I wonder if it was someone who knew he'd be alone. Maybe someone at the garage where he left his car."

"Maybe. Or someone who thought he'd gone to D.C. with his wife." She shook her head. "Such a nice man. It had to be someone who didn't know him. Everybody liked Donnie."

"Newland's going to keep me posted."

"I wish there was something we could do. Donnie really went out of his way to make me feel part of the club. And when Tikima died, he was the first person who called."

"I understand how you feel," I said. "But we're already locking horns with the Henderson County Sheriff's Department. At this point, we need to let the Buncombe County investigation proceed on its own. We can't be everywhere."

She nodded. There was nothing more to say.

I moved on to my meeting with William Lang, remembering how stunned he'd been by Nettles' death. Nakayla listened without interrupting.

When I finished, she asked, "I wonder who owns controlling interest in Lang Paper?"

"Why?"

"It will determine how much clout John has over his son." She thought a moment. "The interesting thing about this case is all the testimony revolves around dead people. Julia Peterkin calls John Jacob Niles a leech, Lucille says she refused to marry Jimmy Lang while William claims just the opposite, and John Lang characterizes Earl Lee Emory as desperate enough to inflame racial prejudice against Jimmy for his relationship with Lucille. Each conflict involves a person no longer among the living and thereby beyond interrogation."

"What are you suggesting? We buy a Ouija board?"

"No. But when we started this agency you said there were three key aspects of detective work."

"Right. Physical evidence, testimony uncovered through Q and A, and deductive reasoning."

Nakayla raised her index finger. "Number one—physical evidence. We have an unidentified skeleton, a rifle slug, and a matching rifle tied to Lucille Montgomery. We have a letter from Julia Peterkin to Lucille's grandmother Loretta referencing a photograph and her distain for John Jacob Niles. And that's it as I see it."

She raised a second finger. "Number two—testimony. We have Lucille and Marsha saying the photograph in question disappeared the same day as Jimmy Lang. No one refutes that, but the theft wasn't reported for forty-five years. We have John Lang and Lucille claiming Lucille wouldn't marry Jimmy. We have William Lang saying the opposite, that Jimmy told him he wouldn't marry Lucille. We do have consensus that business competitor Earl Lee Emory was a son of a bitch. Finally, everyone agrees that John and William Lang bore no hard feelings against Lucille and Marsha."

"Earl Lee and Mick had nothing to gain by killing Jimmy," I interjected. "Keeping him alive kept his relationship with Lucille a sore point in the contract bid."

"Right," Nakayla said. "But who can count on a hothead to think rationally. As for opportunity, everyone except John Jacob Niles and William Lang was in the area. Niles could have been, but that's a real stretch, and William was in Vietnam."

"As you pointed out, with so many dead people in the mix, what are we likely to learn that's new?"

Nakayla smiled and held up a third finger. "Which brings me to deductive reasoning. What conclusions can be drawn from this mishmash?"

"That a confused jury is more likely to either be hung or find for acquittal?"

Nakayla pursed her lips. "A possible consequence, true. But not a deduction we can use. Not a conclusion that you and I can build from." She swung her feet to the floor and leaned forward. "The corroborating testimony is this: Lucille, John, and William Lang agree on the character of Earl Lee Emory. Lucille strikes me as someone who doesn't speak ill of others without strong motivation."

"I agree."

"So, I think your investigation into the confrontation that ensued over the garbage contract is a top priority."

"I'm seeing Mick Emory tomorrow as soon as the pawnshop opens."

"Good. I'll do a background check on both men." Nakayla stood, slowly paced back and forth along the length of the sofa, and then stopped in front of me. "Now the other deduction we can make is that the Doris Ulmann photograph existed."

"You found it?"

"No. I'm basing that on the testimony of Lucille and Marsha and my belief that the handwriting in the letter from Julia Peterkin matches the images of her signature I found on the Internet. And there's the indisputable fact that Ulmann loved photographing the people of the region. The Kingdom of the Happy Land would be a story that appealed to her, especially if its former residents and descendants assembled one final time."

Nakayla stopped and searched my face for a reaction. "You're frowning."

I waved her to sit down. "What you've said is true, but it doesn't provide any proof that the photograph was stolen the day Jimmy Lang disappeared. The prosecution will claim the timing was fabricated to suggest the rifle was also stolen."

"Because Marsha told that story after you found the remains."

"Exactly."

Nakayla smiled. "I called several museums that have Ulmann photographs in their collection. The Getty in California was particularly helpful."

"You said you didn't find it."

"I didn't. And they weren't aware of its existence. That is until about a month ago when they received an inquiry from an art gallery seeking the same photograph. The woman I spoke with had taken the other call. No mistake. She told me the photo was described as a group shot of descendants of the Kingdom of the Happy Land. The woman told the caller she'd never heard of such an Ulmann photograph or the Kingdom."

"Did she remember the name of the gallery?"

"She did. Dimensionless Horizons. Not only have I heard of it, I've been there. It's down Lexington five blocks from here."

I stood. "Then let's go."

"Not so fast. The gallery's closed Wednesday afternoons. They open at ten tomorrow." Her smile broadened. "I believe you're supposed to be pawning a guitar or a gun."

"I'll postpone that. You know what this means?"

"I do. Someone was looking for the photograph before the skeleton was discovered. It wasn't just a sham Marsha created to explain away the rifle."

"So why delay?"

"Because I know who owns the gallery and I want us to go together. Stick with your original schedule. She won't be going anywhere."

"She?"

Nakayla made an invisible checkmark in the air.

"Score one for me. The co-owner of Dimensionless Horizons is Jennifer Lang. William Lang's daughter and John Lang's grand-daughter. Asheville's a small city but it's not that small for it to be a coincidence."

"And William Lang denied knowing anything about the photograph."

"I thought you'd find that interesting." She blew me a kiss. "I believe my hard work deserves dinner tonight."

"Whatever you want, Sherlock."

# Chapter Sixteen

The most difficult part of eating at the Sunny Point Café was getting parked. The restaurant encouraged patrons to either walk or ride bicycles because their small lot and the limited street spaces quickly overflowed.

Jason and I scored a spot a block away, not bad at eight-twenty in the morning, but as we neared Sunny Point, we saw Nathan Armitage pull his black Lexus into an open space not more than thirty feet from the front entrance. He stepped out wearing his usual dark blue suit, white shirt, and muted burgundy tie. His well-coiffed steel gray hair gave him the aura of sophistication and business acumen, two traits that were more than image. Nathan was a self-made man in his late forties who had managed to become successful without becoming arrogant, an accomplishment as admirable as the company he built.

I waved. "Do you pay someone to hold that spot?"

Nathan threw up his hands. "What can I say? Some people are lucky in love, others in finance. I'm lucky in parking." He walked around the rear of his car. "I'm Nathan Armitage, Jason. A pleasure to meet you." He dispelled any awkwardness of the moment by immediately offering his left hand.

"Thanks for seeing me," Jason said. "Sam's told me a lot about you."

"Not everything I hope." Nathan winked at me.

Jason thought Nathan was kidding, simply making the remark nine out of ten people would say. What he didn't know was Nathan and I had our secrets, secrets forged in a deadly showdown with some very bad people that nearly cost Nathan his life.

"I'll put our name in for a table." I left the two men at the edge of the parking lot talking in the morning sunshine. A young woman took my name, handed me one of those buzzers that looks like a miniature UFO, and told me it would be about a fifteen-minute wait.

When I returned to Nathan and Jason, they were well into a conversation that meandered from their common roots in the rural Midwest to Jason's special training in sniper school. We were summoned to our table as Jason talked about his time at Fort Benning, Georgia, and some of the more demanding sniper exercises.

When the waitress came, Nathan and I ordered our favorite, the MGB. The initials stand for Mighty Good Breakfast and the MGB consists of two free-range eggs and local sausage. Nathan always goes for the cheese grits for his side and I take the herb-seasoned spuds. Jason selected an egg and cheddar biscuit that was easier to eat with one hand.

As we ate, Jason described having to get close enough to a target in the woods to make a kill shot while his commanding officer scanned the terrain for any sign of his approach. Success meant patience, ingenuity, and determination. Those qualities weren't lost on Nathan.

"We're making you do too much of the talking," Nathan said. "Eat up."

Jason didn't hide his prosthesis. With his mechanical fingers, he gripped the plate to steady it while he used a fork to cut his side order of sausage.

Nathan told Jason about the scope of services offered by his company. He took the conversation in an unpredictable direction when he asked if the young vet might be interested in sales and customer service.

"You mean like calling on people? In person?"

Nathan laughed. "Yeah. I've found that works better than randomly tweeting them. No substitute for a flesh and blood encounter."

Jason reddened and glanced at his hand.

"And that's not what I mean," Nathan said. "I'm talking about people looking you in the eye and seeing you stand behind what you're saying. You can have no hands or no legs and still make a personal connection. Did Sam tell you how we met?"

"No. Just that you helped him start his detective agency."

Nathan looked at me. "Sam's giving me too much credit in that regard. We met through the sister of his partner Nakayla." He shook his head and dropped his voice to barely above a whisper. "Tikima was a great woman, a Marine like me, only with real courage. She lost an arm in the early days of Iraq when insurgents first started car bombing during the post-Saddam power struggle." He studied Jason's prosthesis for a second. "Tikima didn't have something as advanced as that. Maybe too much of her arm had been blown away. Instead, she had a mechanical pincher that closed when she shrugged her shoulders. She could make it click like a damn castanet." Nathan halted as his voice choked.

Jason stared at his plate in silence. Then he looked Nathan square in the eye. "I heard she was murdered. You and Sam found who killed her, didn't you?"

"Yes," Nathan said. "But my point to you is this. No one was better in sales than Tikima. No one else was even close. The sheer force of her personality and exuberance for life obliterated any perception that she was handicapped in any way. I think you have the same qualities, Jason. Sales and customer service might not be your thing, but I encourage you to think about it."

"Don't get me wrong," Jason said. "I'm grateful you'd consider me for any job, but snipers are loners."

Nathan pointed at Jason's chest. "So are salesman. It's you and your quarry. We just try to keep you supplied with good ammo to help you bag him."

"What kind of ammo?"

"Top on-site security personnel who know their jobs, strong customer support, professional sales literature, and, most importantly, a training program so that you'll have confidence in your skills. Think of it as Fort Benning except you've got a security contract in your sights instead of a human being."

"And I won't have to stand out in the rain or be eaten alive by bugs?"

"Nope. Not unless you lock your keys in your car." Nathan scooted closer to the table. "We'll have HR give you an aptitude test. We do that for every potential hire. And maybe your talents are in a different area. But, I'm a pretty good judge of character, and I think you've got potential. Just like Tikima Robertson."

Jason looked to me for reassurance. I kept a smile on my face. Tikima had been in a league of her own, a person who made a lasting impression on me even though I was with her for only ten minutes. Jason was a good kid but I'd seen the dark brooding side of him that Nathan hadn't. I recognized how it could cloud your judgment because it had clouded mine. Jason had a tough road ahead, but I smiled and nodded, determined not to undermine Nathan's gift, the gift of hope.

We left Sunny Point Café a little after nine thirty. Nathan apologized that he had an appointment in Sylva about forty minutes away or else he would have taken Jason back to his office. I promised to get Jason to HR as soon as I could, and Nathan assured us he would see that Jason returned to the hospital that afternoon.

As we walked the block to my CR-V, I said, "Are you okay hanging with me a little while?"

"Sure, whatever you need. Are you still working on that shooting in the woods?"

"Yeah. But this is just a conversation with a guy who might have known someone who disappeared from that area." I thought a second. "He runs a pawnshop heavy on guitars and guns. Why don't you come in with me? We'll talk about guns a few minutes before I find a way to steer the conversation where I want it to go."

His eyes widened with excitement. "You mean like undercover?"

"No. Like a veteran who knows guns and is just looking over the inventory."

"Okay. I can do that. We'll say I'm looking for a rifle most adaptable for my hand. How's that sound?"

I slapped him on the back. "The CIA couldn't have come up with anything better."

Double G Pawnshop was in one of those small strip malls that blighted the American landscape in the sixties and seventies. The store was at the far end next to a dry cleaners. Other establishments included a nail salon, a tanning booth, and a tattoo parlor that at one time must have been a barbershop because a faded red and white pole sat dormant by its door. The strip mall was an oasis of image improvement: beautify your nails, tan your skin, ink your body, press your wardrobe, and then buy a pawned, knockoff Rolex.

I parked right in front of the Double G. At five after ten, customers weren't breaking down the door. Not that they could have. Iron bars shielded its plate glass and the display windows flanking it. Over the door glowed a red neon sign shaped like a classic Fender guitar with a rifle in place of the fretted neck. Two large capital Gs bordered the guitar like bookends.

An electronic chirp sounded as I pulled open the door. I waved Jason to enter ahead of me. The room was deeper than it was wide. Cheaper items were displayed on tables and wall shelves. A lot of the merchandise appeared to be army surplus: canteens, ponchos, USMC KA-BAR knives, and mess kits. There were clocks and camera bodies, estate jewelry and old coins, used band instruments and archery equipment. In short, a military, musical, sportsman's flea market.

A gruff voice called out, "I'm in the back if you need some help."

We followed the sound to the rear counter. The wall behind was covered in gun racks hosting a variety of rifles and shotguns. A locked glass case displayed handguns ranging from single-shot derringers to forty-five caliber semi-automatics. I surveyed a row of Berettas ranging from pocket to full-size models. They lay on a blue velvet display cloth with a gap in the line-up where a pistol had been removed.

Flanking the guns on either side were racks of guitars: electric solid and hollow bodies, twelve-string acoustic, bass, classical, dobro, and even a rare seven-string model.

No one was behind the counter. I saw saloon-style swinging doors that must have led to a storage room. Above them a sign read "Employees Only."

"Hello?" I called to the empty doorway.

"Be right there," came the reply.

Jason leaned over the glass counter of handguns to get a closer look at the rifles. "I wonder if a bolt action or lever action would be better for me."

The saloon doors swung open. "Depends on how you use it." A thin man with a scruffy gray beard and stringy gray hair eyed us like we might have hidden merchandise in our pockets. He walked closer to Jason. "Don't push up against the counter, son. Your belt buckle will scratch the glass."

Jason stepped back and we both stared at the countertop. The crisscross of prior etchings looked like a flock of chickens had stampeded over it.

"Sorry," Jason said.

"So, what are you boys looking for?"

He used the word "boys" in that down-home way that could be directed at anyone from age seven to seventy-five. He wore baggy camo pants and a black t-shirt that hung loosely around his scrawny chest. A faded eagle held up a middle claw over a red, white, and blue banner proclaiming "Don't F K With The USA!" Classy guy.

"Something to do a little deer hunting," Jason said. "Maybe a thirty-thirty."

The man scratched his chin. "How good a shot are you?"

"At one time, I used to be real good."

"My friend was a military sniper," I said. "He never missed."

"Well, put her there." He stuck out his bony hand. "I'm Mick Emory and I'm always glad to give a discount to a man who served his country."

Jason held his gaze as he reached out and grabbed the offered hand with his prosthesis. A low whir sounded as the mechanical fingers wrapped around the other man's palm.

Mick Emory jerked his hand free as if he'd touched a red-hot stove.

"This is why I used to be real good," Jason said flatly.

Emory's sallow complexion reddened. "Jesus, man. You startled me. I didn't mean nothin' by jumpin' like that."

"Forget it. I startle myself every time I look down." Jason pointed to the racks of rifles. "I'm thinking the lever actions would be faster and load more cartridges but this damn hand could get hung up. A bolt action might be easier for me to grip and to get a finger inside the trigger guard."

"You'll just have to try some." Emory's desire to make up for his embarrassing handshake was obvious. He walked to the wall and surveyed his inventory. "I've got a nice thirty-thirty Henry that would be my choice of lever action. And then I've got a real clean Winchester Classic 70 from 2005. They don't make 'em like that anymore."

Jason scanned the guns. "What about a Remington fourteen and a half?"

Emory turned to him. "That's a collector's rifle. I ain't seen one of those come through here in years."

"It's light and the pump action with my left hand might be something I could handle. I hear they're pretty accurate. You ever shoot one?"

I stepped closer to Jason, afraid he was pushing Emory a little too hard in an area tied to the murder.

"Yeah," Emory said. "But it's been years ago. Maybe you ought to consider the Remington 7600. Nice pump action. I ain't got one in stock, but I can probably find one for you. I know every pawn dealer in western North Carolina." He turned to me, making sure I was impressed with his standing in the hock-your-valuables community.

"Sounds good," I said. "But as long as we're here, Jason, you ought to handle both the Henry and the Winchester."

Emory pulled down the two rifles and laid them on the counter. So much for protecting the glass top. Jason lifted the bolt action first, getting a feel for its balance.

"That's a nice collection of Berettas," I said. "I might be in the market for one if I ever stop living paycheck to paycheck."

"I hear you." Emory looked down at the display. "Sweet piece of action."

"From the empty spot looks like you sold one recently."

Emory grinned. "A Compact PX4. They move real good. Nothing gums up a Beretta. Dirt, mud, sand." He looked at Jason who had switched to the Henry. "Soldiers knew they could count on them to fire."

"You shoot a lot?" I asked Emory.

"Not as much as I used to. But I'm a pretty good shot."

"Were you in the service?"

"No. Bad feet. I tried to enlist. Maybe I could have gone with the Navy but who wants to sit in the middle of the god-damned ocean? You know what I mean? If I was goin' in, I was goin' in all the way. This was back during 'Nam and I was primed to hunt me some gooks."

Behind Emory, I saw Jason roll his eyes. He shared my reaction. Those who didn't serve were typically the biggest blowhards when it came to pontificating about what they would have done or what our military should have done. We let Emory's self-aggrandizing statement pass unchallenged.

"So, you've always lived around here?" I asked.

"Depends upon what you mean by here. I'm originally from Henderson County."

"That's funny."

Emory scowled. "What's funny?"

"Henderson County's where I first shot a Remington Fourteen and a Half. Sweet gun." As innocently as I could, I added, "It belonged to the Lang family. You know them?"

The scowl lines on his face deepened into canyons. "They friends of yours?"

"No. I was introduced to William Lang by someone who belonged to his hunt club." I didn't know if Lang belonged to such a club but I remembered the buck on the wall behind his desk. I also figured it was a safe bet Lang and Emory didn't run in the same social circles. "I was a guest and we were sighting in rifles. He had the Remington and let me fire a couple rounds. Frankly, he was a little aloof for my taste."

"Aloof? I reckon that's one word. Asshole's another."

"I take it he's got a lot of money. Owns some paper plant?"

"That's his daddy's business." Emory swung his arm in a wide arc. "Because of them Langs, I'm stuck in this place. They stole a contract that drove me and my daddy out of business. So, when you look at Willie P. Lang, you're seein' everything that shoulda been mine."

I nodded sympathetically while I thought there was no way this bitter man would have been able to parlay a school trash collection business into an industry-leading paper mill.

"Willie P. Lang?" Jason laid the Henry back on the counter.

As Emory turned to him, I shook my head. Jason and I hadn't discussed any names and I didn't want him inadvertently jumping to the skeleton before I was ready.

"You know him?" Mick Emory asked.

Jason caught my warning. "No. I'm from Indiana. Just sounds funny that a guy who heads a big company would be called Willie. It's more like something you'd hear in the army."

"And maybe that's why we lost 'Nam because Willie P. was over there instead of me."

"Then he and his dad destroyed your business after he came home?" I asked.

"No. I think Willie was still in the army. But I'm sure he was part of the scheme. He made no secret he had big plans. He and his uncle Jimmy."

"Jimmy Lang?"

"That's right." Emory cocked his head and studied me a second. "But how would you know him? He ain't been seen round these parts for over forty years."

"Maybe he has. Rumor is the skeleton they found over near Tuxedo might be his remains."

Emory stared at me, the shock clearly evident on his face. "They found Jimmy Lang's body?"

I shrugged. "Nobody's saying anything official. I know some people in the Sheriff's Department."

Wariness replaced shock. "Who are you, mister?"

"Sam Blackman. And this is Jason Fretwell."

"And you know people in the Sheriff's Department and just happened to come in here and get me talking about the Langs."

"We came shopping for a rifle."

He gritted his yellow teeth and looked back and forth between us. "Sounds to me like a setup."

"Yeah," Jason snapped, "I cut off my arm so we could pretend to find me a gun." He reached out with his prosthesis. "You want to touch it again? Make sure it's real?"

Emory took a step back. "Look, I'm sorry. Forget I said anything." He picked up the two rifles. "I'll hold these for you, if you like, and I'll try to find a pump 7600 for you."

"Okay," Jason said.

"How can I get in touch?"

Jason looked to me. We had to go through with the charade. I pulled out my wallet and handed Emory a card.

As he studied it, the wariness returned to his eyes. "Sam Blackman. You're a damned detective?"

"Yeah. I investigate secrets and my speciality is detecting the bullshit used to hide them. I'll be expecting a call about that rifle. Now that we know where to find each other."

Jason pointed his prosthetic hand at Emory again but this time he shaped the fingers like a pistol, pulled an imaginary trigger, and dropped his thumb mimicking a hammer. "Catch you later, Mick."

# Chapter Seventeen

"Awesome." Jason shouted the word as soon as he closed the passenger door. "You manhandled him. He never saw it coming."

I started the engine. "But he's on full alert now, and he didn't say anything incriminating."

"He admitted shooting a Remington fourteen and a half," Jason argued.

As I pulled away from the Double G Pawnshop, I saw Mick Emory watching us through the front door. "The man has hundreds of guns coming through his store. There probably aren't many models he hasn't shot. The woman charged with the crime has had only one gun, the murder weapon."

"Oh." Jason's euphoria fizzled. "So we didn't accomplish anything? I didn't help?"

"You were great. We caught him off guard by the way you played it. We just have to proceed carefully. Don't push too hard or fast if you don't need to. As it is, we got confirmation that there was bad blood between the Lang and Emory families. I knew that was the truth going in so I used his responses as an indicator of how truthful he might be in his related statements."

"I see. Know more than he thinks you know."

I took my eyes off the road long enough to flash him a grin. "Exactly. And my job is to uncover possibilities for Hewitt Donaldson to pursue."

"Who's that?"

"The attorney we're working for. He's the person to best catch Mick Emory in a lie. Preferably in front of a jury."

Jason thought about that a moment. "Is that the rule about never asking a question you don't know the answer to?"

"A large part of it. You want the surprise to be on the suspect or witness, not the other way around. That's why when you started to ask about Willie P. Lang, I signaled you to drop it. We don't want Mick Emory thinking we're involved with the Langs. He'll shape his story to either match or contradict what he thinks the Langs will say, depending upon what's in his best interest."

"But I meant—"

"You meant no harm," I interrupted. "And I hadn't given you the full background on what we already know. I have to respect the attorney-client privilege Hewitt Donaldson is working under. Let's just leave it with what you said earlier. Know more than your adversary thinks you know. Get as many facts as you can before any confrontation. And when you're working for an attorney, always run the information by him or her first because in the end the defense attorney is going to have to present it to the jury."

"I got it. Know when to pull the trigger."

I laughed. "That pretty much sums it up." I looked at my watch. Ten thirty. "If you don't mind, I'll let you hole up in our office a while. My partner and I have an eleven o'clock appointment I need to prep for and I won't get to Armitage Security Services and back in time."

"No problem. Do what you need to."

We drove in silence the rest of the way into downtown Asheville. I was thinking ahead to the interview with William Lang's daughter that could change the course of our investigation. Jason's thoughts must have been about the upcoming HR interview that could change the course of his life.

When we entered the office, Nakayla was sitting in a leather armchair studying a few sheets of paper. I made the introductions and explained that Jason would wait here while we walked to the art gallery.

"Can I answer the phones or something?" Jason asked.

"Thanks," Nakayla said, "but that's not necessary. Sam will forward them, won't you, Sam?"

"Always do."

"Right." Nakayla grabbed her purse, folded the papers she'd been reading, and stuffed them inside along with a small notepad. "Make yourself at home, Jason. There's a coffee maker in my office and the computer's on if you want to check email or the Internet. All other files are password protected so you can't get in trouble."

"Thanks. I'm good. Don't rush back for me."

I switched the incoming lines to our cellphones and we left Jason to manage the empty office.

We stepped out into the diverse humanity that made Asheville Asheville. Tourists snapped photos as they rode by in open-air buses with guides spewing historical facts and anecdotes. On the sidewalk, white-haired retirees mingled with the pink-haired and the pierced. A field trip of middle schoolers stood in Pack Square beneath the monolithic monument to Civil War Governor Zebulon Vance while a teacher tried in vain to hold their attention. There were young couples pushing strollers, people of all ages walking dogs of all sizes, and the competing sounds from street musicians playing everything from tenor sax to fretless banjo.

As we turned the corner on Walnut Street headed toward Lexington, Nakayla said, "Jason seems like a good kid. I understand why you want to help him."

"And he really wants to help us." I gave her a summary of our visit to Mick Emory.

"Well, there might be occasions when we could use him." Nakayla slid her arm through mine. "Hewitt will be glad to get the info about Emory."

"Damn it. I forgot I'm briefing him at noon. Maybe we should get Jason a cab to Armitage Security."

"I'll run him out there. I don't need to be in the meeting, do I?"

"No. And I am kinda tired from forwarding the phones."

She squeezed my arm tighter. "Poor baby. Then lean on me while I give you the background on Jennifer Lang."

"Were those the papers you stuck in your purse?"

"Yes. Printouts I made off the Internet. Jennifer Lang is thirty-two. She majored in Business at UNC-Chapel Hill and she started Dimensionless Horizons four years ago with a mMaster's degree in Art History. I assume Jennifer runs the business side while Judith makes the artistic decisions."

"Do we know which of them placed the call to the Getty?"

"No. And I didn't push it with the museum."

"Just as well," I agreed. "Did Jennifer Lang have other jobs between college and the gallery?"

Nakayla waited to reply until we navigated around an old man in bib overalls who was playing a musical saw on the corner of Walnut and Lexington. I think the tune was "Barbara Allen," although the sliding notes made it difficult to tell.

"Yes," Nakayla said. "Jennifer worked for five years in the billing office of Lang Paper Manufacturing. In fact, she was the youngest member on the board of directors. Then she abruptly left to start the gallery."

"Does she have siblings?"

"No. Her mother and father divorced when she was fourteen. Neither remarried. The mother moved back to her home town of Raleigh taking Jennifer with her. Jennifer spent summers with her father and interned at the plant."

"Looks like she was being primed to run it someday."

"Maybe," Nakayla said. "Maybe she saw enough to decide paper manufacturing wasn't for her."

"She would have crossed paths with Marsha Montgomery," I said.

"Yes, and surely she knew Marsha was her illegitimate cousin."

I mulled that over. "Maybe not. Marsha and her mother both said the kinship wasn't publicly acknowledged. I'd say we let it alone unless she mentions it."

"Okay. So, we'll play it straight. I'll tell her we're working for a client trying to recover a stolen photograph and we learned her gallery was searching for the same one. We'll see where that leads."

I opened the door to Dimensionless Horizons. "And it will be you doing the leading. I'm just here to watch a professional at work."

"Right. It has nothing to do with the fact that you wouldn't know a Van Gogh from a Van Winkle."

"I know Van Winkle fell asleep for twenty years and then woke up to find his ear ripped off. What kind of rube do you take me for?"

"My mistake. You're in a class by yourself."

"Thank you." I pulled the door closed behind me.

Dimensionless Horizons had worn hardwood floors that had a protective coating of polyurethane to preserve the authentic patina without further deterioration. The plaster walls were painted off-white. Exposed, rough-hewn beams overhead provided the anchor for numerous sets of track lighting directed to illuminate particular works. Pieces included framed photographic and painted compositions on the walls—some impressionist, some detailed landscapes, some black and white documentary-style images of mountain people, and some streaks and swirls of multiple hues with meaning inaccessible to my unappreciative eye.

There were also handblown glassworks that refracted the spotlight beams into pools of vibrant colors. A few metal sculptures suggesting human forms in limber, elongated poses stood on pedestals of varying height. The gallery housed an eclectic array, but all shared a common trait—a powerful sense of human creativity breaking through dimensions beyond craftsmanship and into a realm of unique artistic expression. Dimensionless Horizons was an apt name indeed.

"May I help you?" A woman in black slacks and a white blouse approached. Her shoulder-length brown hair showed strands of gray and she looked like she could have been the branch manager of a bank. I wasn't that familiar with the art world, but the few galleries Nakayla had dragged me to were usually run by people dressed to draw more attention to themselves than the works they sold.

"We're here to see Jennifer Lang," Nakayla said.

The woman gave each of us an appraising glance. "Do you have an appointment?"

"No." Anticipating the next question, Nakayla added, "We're not selling anything. It's a personal matter."

"Personal." She repeated the word as if we'd announced we were here for an IRS audit. "And you are?"

Nakayla handed the woman her card.

The front door opened behind us and an older couple came into the gallery.

"This might be just the place to find something for over the mantel, Herb. It won't hurt to look." Herb's shopping companion smiled at us and headed for the larger glassworks. Herb followed a few steps behind wearing an expression most commonly worn entering a dentist's office.

Jennifer's gatekeeper hesitated, caught between a potential sale and a potential scene with two people she now knew were private detectives.

"We need to speak to her." Nakayla's voice carried both urgency and authority.

"Wait here." She whirled around and disappeared through a door to a back room.

In less than two minutes, she returned with a younger, auburn-haired woman by her side.

"I'm Jennifer. How can I help you?"

"We'd like to talk to you about a photograph," Nakayla said. "Preferably somewhere private."

The older woman took a step closer to Jennifer like a big sister protecting her younger sibling. "I'm Judith Crenshaw and I'm in charge of our acquisitions."

"I'm pleased to meet you," Nakayla replied. "But this is a legal matter involving Ms. Lang."

Jennifer Lang clasped the other woman's hand. "It's all right, Judith. I'll speak with them in the office." She nodded to Herb's wife who was fawning over a glass bowl. "You'd better engage them before hubby drags his wife out on the sidewalk."

Before Judith could reply, Jennifer said, "Follow me. And don't mind the mess."

She led us into the back where two desks sat among storage shelves and shipping supplies. Other than the chairs behind each desk, there was no other place to sit.

"Sorry. We rarely get office visitors. You can wheel Judith's chair into the open. One of you is welcome to sit at my desk."

I gestured to her chair. "Please take it. I'm fine to stand."

Nakayla rolled the second chair directly across from Jennifer. She sat and took out her notepad. When Jennifer was seated, Nakayla asked, "We've been hired to find a stolen photograph."

"The Kingdom of the Happy Land," Jennifer said.

I relaxed. Her ready identification meant we weren't starting on a confrontational note.

"That's correct," Nakayla said. "And we know you've been looking for it as well."

"As a favor. Nothing more. May I ask why you're interested?"

"We were approached by the daughter of the original owner. She's recently become aware of the photograph's value."

"Marsha Montgomery. Did she tell you she asked me to find it?"

"No."

Jennifer frowned. "She didn't tell me there was any secret about it. If what you're saying is true, I don't know why she wouldn't have mentioned it."

"Maybe she didn't want to get you involved. Maybe since you failed, she didn't want us eliminating any of the possibilities you pursued. I spoke with the Getty. Did you contact anyone else?"

"I didn't contact anyone. Judith made the calls. She's more tied into the network of galleries and museums than I am." Jennifer shifted her gaze from Nakayla to me and back to Nakayla. "What do you mean by not getting me involved? Involved in what?"

Nakayla looked at me. I picked up the cue that we were going to play good detective, bad detective.

I cleared my throat. "This is a very serious matter, Ms. Lang. We were originally asked by Marsha Montgomery to search for the photograph, then by your grandfather—"

"My grandfather?" Her face flushed as she interrupted me. "What's he have to do with it?"

"Nothing right now. We're working for a defense attorney. As you may know, Lucille Montgomery has been arrested for murder."

The blood that rushed to Jennifer Lang's face only a second earlier drained just as suddenly. "Murder?"

"Yes. And the theft of that photograph might be a crucial part of the defense's case."

"The woman's in her eighties. Who's she supposed to have killed?"

"The remains haven't been identified, but the prosecutor is working under the assumption the victim is your great uncle Jimmy."

Her mouth dropped open. "He left before I was born. This is the first I've heard of it. Marsha didn't tell me."

I realized Jennifer Lang was completely in the dark. And that wasn't only Marsha's doing. "Your father or grandfather hasn't said anything to you?"

"No. We're not exactly on speaking terms. My grandfather left me a couple messages this week but I haven't called him back. He just said we needed to talk."

I cut my eyes to Nakayla. She would be better at shifting the interview into the personal area we needed to explore.

"Why are your family relations strained?" Nakayla asked.

Jennifer shrugged. "It's no secret. They don't approve of my life style. And they don't approve of Judith."

Life style. My mind replayed Judith Crenshaw's protective attitude in the gallery and the clasp of hands when Jennifer said she'd speak with us alone. Jennifer and Judith were a couple.

"Is that why you left the company?" Nakayla asked.

"Yes. I was given a choice between Judith and my job. As far as I know, my father disinherited me."

Nakayla sighed. "And that's his loss. I think bigotry is more destructive on the bigot than the target of his fear."

Jennifer's eyes moistened. "But it still hurts."

The room was silent a moment. I looked around and for the first time noticed the pictures on the two desks. Framed photos of Jennifer and Judith hiking, smiling next to the base of the Eiffel Tower, working side by side at a soup kitchen. In short, making a life together. And the irony was that Jennifer was experiencing the bigotry that Jimmy Lang and Lucille Montgomery faced a generation earlier. A generation within her own family that still didn't understand how love doesn't recognize restrictions or limitations.

Nakayla's jaw tensed. She was wrestling with how to proceed. "Jennifer, has anyone ever told you about the special relationship between Jimmy and Lucille Montgomery?"

"No. I've heard from my grandfather how Lucille helped care for my grandmother when she was dying of cancer. But, again, that was before I was born."

"Jimmy and Lucille were lovers. They wanted to get married but North Carolina law prohibited it."

"What?" Jennifer turned her stunned face to me for confirmation.

"It's true," I said. "And when the law forbidding interracial marriage was finally overruled by the Supreme Court in 1967, Lucille decided not to marry Jimmy. Both she and your grandfather agreed the climate was still highly charged and the company would have suffered."

"Business over love," Jennifer said with undisguised sarcasm.

"That may be too harsh," Nakayla said. "Lucille was doing what she thought was best at the time for the man she loved. I know the prejudice my own family experienced."

"Is that why Jimmy left?" Jennifer asked. "My father said there was rift between my grandfather and his brother."

"That's what everyone thought," Nakayla said. "But now, well, the remains that have been discovered on the Kingdom of the

Happy Land have focused attention on Jimmy's disappearance and what might have been behind it."

"And that's why Marsha wants to find the photograph?"

"Yes," Nakayla said. "What reason did she give you?"

"That she'd checked out a book for her mother called *Roll, Jordan, Roll* and it contained photographs by Doris Ulmann. Lucille told her Ulmann had taken her photograph years ago."

"Marsha told us she was already familiar with the photograph," Nakayla said.

"And that's what she told me. But as a kid she never thought about who took the picture. When she learned of Ulmann's stature in the art world, she realized the photograph could be valuable and asked me to check into it. She didn't seem particularly urgent about it."

"When did she ask you?" Nakayla said.

"I guess more than a month ago. Judith got right on it but found nothing."

Jennifer's answer matched what we'd learned from the Getty Museum. Evidence was stacking up that Marsha's interest in the photograph was generated completely unrelated to the discovery of the skeleton. She only shifted emphasis to the theft when she sought to explain the missing rifle, the one she tried to bury.

"Could I have a list of galleries and museums Judith queried?" Nakayla asked.

"Yes." Jennifer ran her tongue over her lips nervously. "Did Marsha know about her mother and my great uncle?"

"She says she remembers him, but she was only five."

"I like Marsha. We worked together at the company. She was very upset when I was forced out."

"I'm sure she was," Nakayla said. "You might want to talk to her sometime." She looked at me. "About what we've told you."

I nodded, agreeing with what Nakayla wasn't saying more than what she was saying. We weren't going to reveal the kinship shared by Jennifer and Marsha. It wasn't our place.

Nakayla stood. "If Judith isn't busy, maybe we could get that list now. Otherwise, my email address is on my card."

Jennifer rose. "Certainly." She started around her desk, and then paused. "Do you think my grandfather was calling to tell me about Lucille and his brother?"

"Probably," Nakayla said. "He's trying to help her."

I thought of a more pressing reason. "He may have been warning you that the police might ask you for a DNA sample. He wouldn't want to leave that in a message."

"DNA?"

"Yes. They're trying to make a positive identification that the skeletal remains belong to your great uncle."

"But my grandfather's his twin. That's the best match they can get."

"Your grandfather's not cooperating," Nakayla said. "He believes Lucille is innocent and he's determined not to help build a case against her."

Jennifer looked confused. "You think he'd want to know if his brother had been killed."

"Not at the expense of creating circumstantial evidence for the prosecution."

"That's a shock. I never realized he and Lucille were that close."

"Yeah," Nakayla said. "And the police aren't happy about it."

The door from the gallery opened. Judith Crenshaw stuck her head in, her eyes wide with concern. "Excuse me. Jennifer, there's a deputy sheriff here to see you."

Nakayla mouthed one word to me. "Overcash."

If we were surprised, Deputy Overcash was apoplectic. When we followed Jennifer into the gallery, he blurted out, "What the hell are you two doing here?"

Nakayla and I kept walking. I gave him a big smile as we passed. "Why, the same thing you are. Shopping for fine art. You'll find some wonderful pieces for your mantel. That is if Herb didn't buy them all."

Before he could reply, we were out on the sidewalk.

# Chapter Eighteen

"Where's Nakayla?" Shirley looked at the open door behind me and saw only the empty hall.

"She had to run an errand," I said. "I'm meeting with Hewitt alone."

Shirley's black lipsticked lips turned down in a frown. With her heavy white makeup, she looked like a mime whose invisible dog had just been run over. "I had lunch brought in for you two. Sandwiches from the City Bakery Café." The corners of her mouth rose. "Oh, well, I guess I'll have to eat Nakayla's. Unless you want to give it to the cute guy in your office."

I stepped closer to her desk. "I thought I was the cute guy in the office."

"Yeah, right. I mean the man who was on the phone at Nakayla's desk when I stuck my head in to see what you wanted me to order. But neither of you were there." Shirley tucked her fingers under her chin and coyly batted her black-lined eyes. "So, what's his name?"

"Jason. And he's too young for you."

"Really? And is he too young for Nakayla?"

"On second thought, you're perfect for each other. Enthusiasm meets experience."

"He didn't look experienced."

The intercom buzzed. "Shirley," Hewitt said. "Which one of these sandwiches is mine?"

"The one labeled crow. Enjoy. And Sam's here. He's enthusiastic about experiencing your great wisdom. Don't disappoint him."

"Send him back."

"A brilliant decision, sir. I never would have thought of it." She looked at me. "You heard his lordship. And the sandwiches are all turkey."

I headed for the conference room.

"Wait." Shirley bent under her desk and retrieved a brown bag. "I also bought oatmeal raisin cookies. I knew if I left them with Hewitt, you'd never see them."

"Thanks. You've outdone yourself."

"I know. Not an easy task when you're perfect. Now run along before I start to like you."

Over the sandwiches and chips, I briefed Hewitt on the encounter with Mick Emory and the conversation with Jennifer Lang.

"How much of Emory is hot air?" Hewitt asked.

"Hard to say. He likes to think of himself as a badass. He's also got a real mean streak. I think that rage could erupt on the witness stand if you pushed the right buttons."

Hewitt swept the remnants of his sandwich aside and jotted notes on his legal pad. "John Lang," he murmured.

"What?"

"John Lang. I'll get him on the stand to tell about the confrontation between Jimmy and Earl Lee Emory after those garbage bid presentations in 1967. If I also have Mick Emory as a witness, then he might be really pissed after John testifies."

"What about Lucille telling the story? Surely she'd have an emotional impact on the jury."

Hewitt shook his head. "That would be hearsay. She learned about it from John. He was the eyewitness. And if I put Lucille on the stand, then Chesterson can cross-examine. I don't dare subject Lucille to that."

"So, she won't testify in her own defense?"

"Not if I can help it." He leaned back in his chair. "And the winds are shifting to make that a real possibility."

"How?"

Hewitt smiled. "The appearance of Deputy Overcash at Jennifer Lang's gallery. What role could she possibly play? She wasn't born when Jimmy disappeared. She's estranged from her father and grandfather. She knew Marsha and Lucille but isn't particularly close to them. So, what's her connection to the case?"

"Her DNA."

"Precisely. Which means what?"

I understood what boosted Hewitt's optimism. "William Lang is no longer a cooperating prosecution witness."

"Yes. Daddy must still have controlling interest in the company. And if William's backed out of his DNA sample, he may have backed out on his testimony."

"Couldn't Chesterson just be looking for backup confirmation?"

"Why? No one's denying Jennifer's relationship to her father and he's a generation closer to Jimmy. No, I think Chesterson's case is a wedge of Swiss cheese. The more he examines it, the more holes he finds."

"I mentioned the DNA possibility to Jennifer and that she was under no obligation to provide a sample."

"Good. We'll know her response soon enough."

The intercom buzzed on the phone in the middle of the table. "D.A. Chesterson's on line one," Shirley announced. "You want me to tell him you're enjoying a cookie and can't be disturbed?"

Hewitt's bushy gray eyebrows arched. "Well, well, speak of the devil. No, I'll take it. Thanks."

"I live to serve you."

Hewitt pulled the phone closer and put his index finger to his lips, signaling me to be quiet. Then with the same finger he punched the flashing line and activated the speakerphone.

"Mr. Chesterson. To what do I owe this pleasure?"

"The cause of justice, Mr. Donaldson." Chesterson's voice tried to strike a confident, yet friendly tone.

"Wonderful. I take it you're dropping all charges against my client."

Chesterson forced a laugh. "Hardly. I mean we have the murder weapon and the motive. But no one's interested in putting an eighty-five-year-old woman through the rigors of a trial."

"Especially since we don't even know whom she allegedly killed."

Silence. Hewitt wiggled his fingers at the phone, taunting the disembodied voice of Chesterson to speak.

After a few seconds, the district attorney obliged. "Oh, we will. The DNA sample we acquired this morning should be back within a week. And I'll have the preliminary report on the victim's DNA this weekend."

A flicker of surprise flashed across Hewitt's face. Then his expression turned hard. "You want to tell me the DNA source or make me wait for discovery?"

"Depends. Do you want to talk about a deal, or wait for the results and take the chance the deal or any deal will still be on the table?"

"If you're offering something, you know I have to take it to Miss Montgomery."

"Then here's what I can do. First, she confirms the identity of the victim and tells us what happened. If those circumstances are extenuating and match the physical evidence, then I'll go for leniency on the appropriate charge."

"Meaning if she claims self-defense, she walks?"

"Nice try, but no. The body in the hollow log rules that out. Either she stuffed him in there or he was desperately trying to hide, which indicates she was coming after him."

Hewitt looked at me and shook his head. Then he stared at the phone. "Sounds like the best you can do is voluntary manslaughter. That's a class D felony with active prison time."

"And maybe she serves a year. No parole board's going to go hard on her."

"When you're eighty-five, a year can be the rest of your life."

"Spare me," Chesterson snapped. "She's outlived Jimmy Lang by over forty-five years."

"If it is Jimmy Lang."

Chesterson laughed again. "Don't kid yourself, pal. You and I both know what that DNA match will show. You've got till five o'clock tomorrow afternoon before the offer expires."

"And who provided the sample?"

"Jennifer Lang. Tell your hotshot detective he just wasn't persuasive enough. And if he pressures her again, I'll charge him with intimidation and harassment."

A click, and the line went dead.

Hewitt sighed. "Well, now he's pissed me off."

"What do we do next?"

He eyed the paper bag on the table beside me. "Shirley said something about cookies."

I slid the whole bag to him. Chesterson cost me my appetite.

Hewitt pulled out a cookie as big as his fist. He studied it for a second. "Jennifer Lang. Maybe she agreed just to spite her family." He took a bite and talked as he chewed. "And why the big rush on the plea bargain, especially now that he has the DNA in play?"

"He gets a conviction. A win is a win, even if it's pled down to jaywalking. Why take a chance with an old lady and a jury?"

"I wonder."

The turning wheels of Hewitt's brain were almost audible. Whatever he was thinking, he wasn't ready to share it.

"Nakayla and I are supposed to go to the John C. Campbell Folk School tomorrow about the missing Ulmann photograph. You still want us to pursue it?"

"Yes. More than ever."

He took another bite and his eyes lost focus. Wherever his thoughts were leading, I couldn't follow. I got up and left.

Nakayla arrived at the office about thirty minutes later. She told me that after dropping Jason at Armitage Security Services for his interview, she'd gone to the veterans' hospital to see how early Jason could be discharged the next morning.

"I explained he was moving into your apartment." Nakayla sat in her customary spot on the sofa, bare feet tucked under her.

"Was that a problem?" I was in the closest armchair. Holmes and Watson.

"No. They love you there. God knows why. I said you had an appointment out of town and needed to pick Jason up by eight. They promised to complete the paperwork this afternoon and have Dr. Anderson sign off on Jason's release first thing in the morning."

"Good. Thanks. Who's getting word to Jason?"

"I saw your friend Sheila Reilly in Physical Therapy. She took it as her personal mission."

"Then it will be done. Sheila cuts through bureaucracy like an icebreaker through the Arctic."

"We should have ample time to get Jason settled. David Brose had invited us for lunch at the school, but I slid our appointment to one o'clock. We'll need to be on the road by eleven. We're still going, right?"

"Definitely." I gave her a summary of my meeting with Hewitt and the call from D.A. Chesterson.

Nakayla sat quietly for a few minutes while she processed the new developments. Finally she said, "I agree with Hewitt. Chesterson's urgency for a deal doesn't make sense if he's still got Jennifer Lang's DNA to analyze. It's like he thinks it will go against him."

The quick deadline had been bugging me since I left Hewitt's office. I thought back over Chesterson's offer and one phrase jumped out.

"First, she confirms the identity of the victim."

"What?" Nakayla asked.

"It's what Chesterson said. Lucille has to identify the victim. Why bother if he's got forensic DNA?"

"They'd want to have independent confirmation, wouldn't they?"

"Yes. But it was the way he said it. Not confirm that Jimmy Lang was the victim. Just confirm the victim's identity."

"When's he getting the report on the remains?"

"He said over the weekend."

Nakayla's half-smile brought dimples to her cheeks. "Right after the expiration of the plea bargain offer."

"Yeah. I think Hewitt suspects that Chesterson knows some-thing about that DNA report. Something he doesn't like."

"I wonder if Jennifer Lang even gave a DNA sample." Nakayla stood.

"Where are you going?"

"To give Jennifer a call."

"Chesterson told us to stay away from her."

"No. Chesterson told Hewitt to tell you to stay away from her. He never mentioned me." She walked into her office and closed the door.

Nakayla didn't want me lurking over her desk and mouthing questions. I stayed seated. She would give me the details.

Five minutes later, her door opened. Nakayla looked like she'd just drawn an inside straight and couldn't keep her poker face together.

"What?" I stood. "Am I going to have to buy dinner again?"

"Well, it depends upon how valuable you think the informa-tion is."

"Are you going to make me commit in advance?"

"No. I'll let your sense of gratitude be your guide."

"You left out the word undying."

"Jennifer Lang did agree to give Deputy Overcash a DNA sample."

"Okay." I drew out the two syllables knowing there was more to follow.

"She agreed and so Overcash went to his car to get a saliva collection kit. He should have brought it with him, but I guess he didn't want to appear presumptive. Mistake. Especially since Asheville street parking is tight and he must have been a few blocks away."

"Enter Judith Crenshaw," I said, and sat down again.

"Smart boy." Nakayla returned to her spot on the sofa. "Judith asked what was going on. When Jennifer summarized her conversation with us, Judith told Jennifer she was acting hastily. Marsha Montgomery was her friend and how did she know the case wasn't being railroaded? Why wasn't her grandfather helping identify his own brother?"

"The protective gatekeeper who challenged us turned on Overcash."

"Exactly. When Overcash returned, Jennifer told him she wanted to think about it. And Overcash overreacted. He demanded her cooperation."

I imagined the deputy's face turning red. I'd witnessed how he lost his cool when someone challenged his authority, and I'd seen enough of Judith Crenshaw to know she didn't hesitate to challenge authority.

"Did Overcash leave empty handed?"

Nakayla nodded. "For the moment. Jennifer said she'd be back in touch. She wanted to talk to her grandfather first. Overcash said he'd wait while she made the call. That's when Judith Crenshaw ordered him to leave. He did."

"Wish I'd been a fly on the wall. Did Jennifer reach her grandfather?"

"No. And she hasn't tried. She and Judith decided to talk to us first. She was getting ready to call."

"How was it left?"

"I advised her not to speak with her grandfather. Why take a chance he would make her mad and change her mind?"

"Good point. And it sounds like William definitely backed out of providing DNA. Otherwise Overcash either wouldn't have been there or gotten so angry."

Nakayla tapped her slender fingers on the sofa arm as she must have thought through the ramifications. "Did Chesterson lie to Hewitt or did he think Overcash had Jennifer's DNA?"

I shrugged. "Who knows? There's a good chance Overcash phoned him on his way to get the collection kit and said mission accomplished. When it fell apart, he wasn't so anxious to share bad news."

"I hope Chesterson lied because that pushes him farther out on a limb. Hewitt can call his bluff."

"I bet Chesterson calls Jennifer Lang directly," I said. "He won't want Hewitt to find out if he can help it."

Nakayla gave me a sly smile. "Isn't going to happen. I told Jennifer to call Overcash immediately and say she would like to help but wants to talk to her attorney first. She has an appointment Monday. That preempts the district attorney's pressure and gives Hewitt a chance to see the victim's DNA report."

I looked at my partner with amazement. "Miss Robertson, where would you like me to take you for dinner?"

"I'll think of somewhere nice, Mr. Blackman. Meanwhile I'll cover Hewitt on what we've learned."

I stood. "I'll do it."

"No, you won't. You've got a houseguest arriving tomorrow. Go get some groceries for him. Then clean your apartment and pack what you'll need to bring to my place."

"Anything else while you're giving orders?"

"Yes. I expect you to pick me up at six dressed for dinner at a fine restaurant. And bring plenty of money."

# Chapter Nineteen

"Oh, my God. Is this where you live?" Jason Fretwell pressed his nose against the side window of the front passenger's seat and stared at my apartment building.

We'd just crested the top of the ridge above Biltmore Village where the Kenilworth Inn sat on several acres of expansive lawn. Built as a grand hotel in the 1890s and rebuilt in 1913 after a devastating fire, the Kenilworth stood as a historic landmark representing Asheville's rich architectural past. Five stories high, the Tudor-revival building had nearly a hundred apartments ranging from lower-level basement to fourth floor and from studio to two bedrooms.

"This certainly is a change from the V.A. hospital," Jason said.

From the backseat of my CR-V, Nakayla tried to smother a laugh.

"What's so funny?" Jason asked.

"Nothing really," Nakayla answered. "Just that for a good part of its life, this place was a military hospital. Both World Wars. Then it was a private mental institution for a while before being converted to apartments. When my sister lived here, she called it the asylum."

Jason leaned forward and looked across me to the tall flagpole with Old Glory flapping proudly in the morning breeze at the front of the inn's stone porte-cochère. The backdrop of blue sky and white puffs of clouds provided a picture-postcard setting for the grand structure. We looped around the lawn following the blacktop to the rear. In nice weather, I parked behind, not needing to let passengers out under the shelter of the main entrance.

"Your sister lived here?" Jason asked with undisguised awe. He knew Nakayla's sister had been murdered.

"Yes. Sam took her apartment after she died. He came here straight from his hospital discharge."

From the corner of my eye, I saw Jason's face pale.

"She was killed here?" he asked.

"No. Tikima died during the course of a personal investigation. It had nothing to do with where she lived." Nakayla sighed. "But it's ironic. You're the third amputee to use the place. My sister lost an arm serving in Iraq."

"I heard she worked for Armitage Security Services," Jason said. "I hope I can follow her there as well."

I pulled into a parking space near the rear door of the wing where my fourth-floor apartment was located. "Whatever the outcome, Nathan Armitage will let you know soon enough. He won't leave you hanging. If he doesn't have something appropriate, he'll help us brainstorm the next step."

"Does he know how to reach me?"

"He has my landline number. Feel free to answer it." I pointed to the small duffel bag at his feet. "Need a hand with that?"

Jason reached his left arm across his chest and opened the passenger door. "No thanks. What I can do for myself, I need to do." He grinned. "Especially carrying my dirty laundry."

Nakayla came with us and I showed Jason my access code for opening the outside door.

"The same sequence works for all external entrances," I told him.

He followed us down the long, narrow corridor to the centrally located single elevator. The floors were the original hardwood and the walls had mounted lights every twenty feet that accentuated the sense that the hall went on forever.

"It is like a hotel," Jason remarked.

"Quite the place in its day," I said. "And quite a history. A hotel that was carved up into hospital rooms and then renovated into apartment floor plans. Because of the challenge of working around old piping and sprinkler systems, no two units are exactly the same. That's what I like about it. Lots of character and lots of characters."

Nakayla pointed at me. "Sam fits right in."

"Maybe I could get my own place here," Jason said.

"Maybe," I agreed. "This way you'll get a chance to try it."

When we reached my door, I opened it and waved Jason to enter.

"Nice." He turned in a half circle. On his right was a long granite counter that divided the open room into a compact kitchen and an ell-shaped living/dining area that wrapped around it. To his left were a leather sofa, an upholstered reading chair, and a flat-screen TV sitting on a bookshelf that I decluttered the previous afternoon. Beyond that area, the dining space had room for a small table and four chairs. Comfortable and cozy.

Along the hall to the right of the kitchen were a louvered door shielding a stacked combination of clothes washer and dryer, a second door to the bathroom, and at the end of the hall, the doorway to my bedroom.

I pointed in that direction. "Toss your bag on the bed and we'll give you the cook's tour."

We began at the most important spot in the apartment. The refrigerator. I'd stocked it with a variety of local beers.

"Didn't you buy any food?" Nakayla asked.

"Sure. Lots of frozen dinners in the freezer."

Nakayla shook her head. "Men."

I gave Jason instructions on how to use the washer/dryer so he could clean his clothes. In the bedroom I slid open the mirrored closet door where I kept my wardrobe. "We're about the same size. I took plenty of clothes with me yesterday so feel free to wear anything that fits. You may as well wash all your dirty laundry in one load." I pulled out a pair of jeans and a hiking shirt, the same outfit I'd worn to the ill-fated mushroom hunt. I'd washed out all traces of my fall into the log.

"I don't know what to say." Jason's voice broke. "You're being so kind."

"A lot of people were kind to me. Unfortunately, our country seems to be making wounded vets an ongoing industry. So, at some point you can do the same for someone else."

"I will. I promise."

I walked to my desk by the bedroom window. "Here's my computer. You don't need a password to use the Internet." I rested my hand on a black cordless phone beside the keyboard. "This is the landline and the other extension is in the kitchen."

"You'll call me if you hear something from Armitage?"

"Yes," I said. "But I'm sure he'll deal directly with you. You've got my cell number if you need me. Coverage may be spotty where Nakayla and I are going so leave a message. Otherwise, just hang loose today, walk around the grounds, and we'll catch up with each other this evening."

"For dinner," Nakayla insisted. "I'm cooking at my place. I'm not leaving you with frozen food for your first night out of the hospital."

"Sounds great," Jason said. "Don't worry about me. I'm used to spending time alone."

As a sniper, I remembered. Patient. Deliberate. Deadly.

The drive from Asheville to the John C. Campbell Folk School in Brasstown was over two hours. Much of the road was four-lane, but stretches shrank to two where it ran through the rugged Nantahala Gorge, a steep canyon with the Nantahala River, the narrow highway, and a railroad track fighting for space between the nearly vertical slopes. Where the gorge did widen, entrepreneurs had built rafting and kayak services catering to the whitewater enthusiasts who challenged the rapids.

We stopped for lunch in Murphy at a downtown restaurant with the unusual name of ShoeBooties Café. Nakayla had eaten there several years ago while investigating a fraudulent insurance claim in the area. Murphy was about eight miles from Brasstown and the folk school. We'd made good time and didn't want to arrive any earlier than fifteen minutes ahead of our one o'clock appointment. David Brose would be eating lunch till then.

I ordered a Reuben, my customary move when testing a lunch menu. If the establishment can't make a good Reuben, everything else is suspect. Nakayla went for the veggie burger.

While we waited for our food, Nakayla gave me some background on the school.

"John C. Campbell was a Mid-westerner educated in New England. At the beginning of the twentieth century, Southern Appalachia was viewed as a mission field, not for religion, but for educational and social enlightenment."

"So he wasn't a preacher."

"He studied theology but he was inspired to improve the quality of life for people in this world. He and his new bride, Olive Dame of Massachusetts, stocked a wagon as their traveling home and studied the culture of the mountain folk from Georgia to West Virginia. John researched the agricultural practices of farmers. Olive collected the old Appalachian ballads and studied the crafts that had been handed down from generation to generation."

"Sounds like they were getting more of an education themselves."

"They never lost the goal of improving life through teaching the educational basics, but they were also captivated by the tools, techniques, and artistry demonstrated by the mountaineers in their daily life. John and Olive sought to preserve and share those skills with the world.

"Unfortunately, John died in 1919 before his dream could be fully realized. Olive and a good friend, Marguerite Butler, traveled to Europe to study folk schools in Scandinavia. They came back determined to start one in Appalachia."

"How'd they come to Brasstown?"

"A local shopkeeper bought into the idea. His family donated land bordering two counties and the people of those counties pledged labor and building supplies. In 1925, the John C. Campbell Folk School began its mission."

"That's about the time Doris Ulmann began her summer treks to the mountains."

Nakayla nodded. "You can see how Olive Dame Campbell and Doris Ulmann would be a perfect match. Doris tried to preserve the mountain ways through her photography, and the school's collaborative instruction kept the old ways alive."

"Explains why Ulmann left the school a substantial part of her estate," I said.

"And maybe why John Jacob Niles was anxious to push her for a bequeathment. He knew firsthand Doris Ulmann's close relationship with Olive Dame Campbell."

"Does the school have a lot of Ulmann prints?"

"I believe she sent Olive copies of the photographs she took in the area."

"Would that include the Kingdom of the Happy Land?"

"We'll soon know." Nakayla looked up as our waitress brought our food. Then she eyed my Reuben. "Want to swap?"

I pulled the plate closer. "Don't even think about it."

The sandwich was spectacular. I chased it with caramel fudge pecan cake. We could have turned around and gone back to Asheville and the trip would have been worth it. But, duty called and we pressed on to our appointment.

The John C. Campbell Folk School spread over a beautiful green valley. Numerous outbuildings could be seen as we followed the signs to the parking lot.

"This place is big," I said.

"They offer a lot of things. Quilting, weaving, blacksmithing, woodworking, pottery, music lessons on every instrument ever played in the mountains, and classes on home crafts from cooking to soap making."

"Then I know where I'm coming for the apocalypse."

We found David Brose in a two-story stone building called the History Center. If the school was more than I was expecting, so was the curator. In a realm where most wore jeans or other heavy-duty work clothes, Brose appeared at the door in a light orange dress shirt with a multicolored tie and a suit vest with matching trousers. He sported a full mustache and neatly combed brown hair. I guessed he was about twenty years our senior.

"Nakayla," he said warmly. "Good to meet you."

Nakayla introduced me and we followed Brose up a narrow staircase to the second story. It was basically an open floor plan with a few interior walls subdividing off small sections for locked storage. The main room had walls covered with mismatched bookshelves jammed with a variety of volumes and manuscripts. A small pedestal table accommodated four chairs. Brose indicated we should take seats.

"You said on the phone you were interested in an Ulmann photograph."

"Yes," Nakayla said. "It would have been taken in the summer of 1932 and probably identified as the descendants of the Kingdom of the Happy Land."

"The freed slave commune near Flat Rock. Interesting. I don't believe I know the photograph. Can you describe it?"

Nakayla gave the most detailed description she could.

Brose got up from the chair and went into a small storage room. He returned with a sturdy box about a yard long and two-feet wide. A label on the side read 1932-1933. "Let's see what we can find."

The prints were loose inside. We carefully examined them one at a time. There were portraits of old men and women, close-ups of hands carving wood and working with looms, shots of potters and musicians, and children who looked aged beyond their years. But nothing matching the photograph stolen from Lucille Montgomery.

"Just because it's not here doesn't mean it doesn't exist." Brose closed the box. "Have you contacted the other repositories of her photographs? Berea College? Oregon University? University of Kentucky?"

"Yes," Nakayla said. "So far no luck."

"Well, don't give up. It might be in a very small collection. I'll do a little research and see what I can come up with."

Brose started to rise with the box.

"What do you know about John Jacob Niles?" I asked.

"He was Doris Ulmann's traveling companion through the Appalachians. Primarily the trips she made from 1930 to her death in 1934. He claims to have known her since 1925 but there's no real proof of that."

"I've heard him described as a leech and a gigolo."

Brose smiled. "I doubt you were in Kentucky at the time."

"This was from a letter of Julia Peterkin's and comments by Doris Ulmann's chauffeur," Nakayla said.

"Niles is a native son of Kentucky," Brose said. "He's revered there. Other places? Well, let's just say Niles never missed an opportunity to promote himself and some people say he never let the truth get in the way of casting himself in the most favorable light."

Brose got up and left the box of photographs. He walked to a shelf behind him and returned with a small, clear glass bottle. "Here's something of John Jacob Niles'. We found it under the cabin where he used to sleep when Doris Ulmann came to visit Olive Campbell. The cabin had gaps in the floorboards and Niles' empty bottles of moonshine would fall between them. Evidently he drank himself to sleep each night."

"Is moonshining one of the crafts you teach at the school?" I asked.

Brose laughed. "No. But maybe we should. There's a strong argument to be made for ensuring that one of our most famous mountain traditions is preserved."

"Let me put my question bluntly. Do you think Niles was a thief? He was the only one alive when this particular photograph was stolen."

"That's going a little too far in my opinion," Brose said. "Sometimes he might have blurred the line between songs he collected and songs he said he wrote. His most well-known one is the Christmas carol 'I Wonder As I Wander,' but the story round here is he heard the song sung by a little mountain girl over in Murphy. She charged him a quarter a verse to sing it to him so he could write it down. At times, he claims she sang only one line. There are instances of when he earlier said she gave him three verses. That's the problem with Niles. His stories changed as the people who could contradict them died off."

"Not a thief, but a long-term borrower," I said.

"That's a good way to put it," Brose agreed. "And don't get me wrong. John Jacob Niles performed a real service writing down and preserving the mountain songs as he traveled with Doris Ulmann. What can I say? He was who he was, warts and all. And we're indebted to him."

We thanked David Brose for his help and his promise to make further inquiries. But as we left the school, I felt discouraged.

"That was a strikeout. No picture and nothing to indicate John Jacob Niles had any proclivity to steal it, despite what Julia Peterkin wrote about him."

"We always knew it was a long shot," Nakayla said. "Something we had to pursue before eliminating."

We reached Murphy and turned east toward Asheville. To the south, a wall of gray clouds moved over the mountain ridges.

"Looks like the rain's coming like they forecast," Nakayla said. "We're going to have a wet ride home."

"And a slow one, especially through Nantahala Gorge."

"It's two o'clock now. We might be without cell coverage during that stretch. Think we should check in with Hewitt before we lose the signal?"

I pulled my phone from my hip and raised it to my eye line. No messages. Then the screen flashed with an incoming call. Hewitt's law office.

I turned the screen toward Nakayla. "You and Hewitt share mental telepathy?"

"Yeah. Too bad you don't have a receiver."

I accepted the call. "Sam Blackman."

"It's over." Hewitt said the simple sentence like he was describing the war in the Middle East.

"What's over?"

"Chesterson's dropping the charge. He's decided not to prosecute."

"Hold on. Let me put you on speaker." I handed the phone to Nakayla so I could keep both hands on the wheel. "Okay. Repeat what you said. Nakayla's listening."

"D.A. Chesterson threw in the towel. He's dropped the charge against Lucille."

"What about his plea-bargain deadline?" Nakayla asked.

"I turned it on him. He had till five o'clock to dismiss or I'd call a press conference."

"About what?" I asked.

"About what I suspected. Chesterson had received some preliminary findings on the victim's DNA from the Greenville, South Carolina, test lab. I have my own sources and got the same information without having to wait for Chesterson to make it available through discovery. The skeleton has genetic markers for African descent. That's why Chesterson was pushing his offer because losing the connection to Jimmy Lang, a man Lucille could have married if he were African-American, blew up his motive. That's why he demanded she confirm the identity of the victim. He knew it wasn't Jimmy Lang but he still had the gun connection to Lucille so he tossed a Hail Mary pass hoping Lucille would confess."

"Have you told Lucille?" I asked.

"Yes. She was with Marsha. Lucille broke down. She was so relieved. Marsha took the phone and thanked us for believing in her mother."

"That rifle bothers me," I said. "At some point it could still come back to Lucille."

"Well, we have the theft of the photograph," Hewitt said.

"That didn't go anywhere."

"But no one can contradict it was stolen, which means the rifle could have also been taken and returned. If Chesterson gets an ID on the skeleton and can connect it to Lucille somehow, then he's still got that problem to deal with. He won't be too anxious to repeat his folly. When he caved, he blamed Deputy

184 Mark de Castrique

Overcash for an overzealous arrest and for asserting there was unimpeachable testimony from William Lang."

"The district attorney makes the ultimate decision to prosecute," I said.

"I know," Hewitt agreed. "Which makes Chesterson even more of a weasel. He threw the deputy under the bus and then backed it over him."

"So they'll do what?" I asked.

"I hate to say this but they'll probably make a few half-hearted inquiries in the black communities of the area, but not push it beyond that. A nameless black man who could have been murdered more than fifty years ago? Nothing will come of it."

"That's not right," Nakayla said. "He deserves justice as much as if it had been Jimmy Lang."

"You're right," Hewitt said. "And maybe when the dust settles and we see the full DNA report, we can apply some pressure from outside to prompt a more thorough investigation. I'm willing to work on it."

"Thanks," Nakayla said. "And thanks for what you did for Lucille."

"I'd be lying if I said I didn't love threatening Chesterson with that press conference. Only wish I could have done it face to face." He hung up in mid-chuckle.

"Well, that eases the disappointment with the folk school trip," I said.

Nakayla patted my thigh. "I have to admit I enjoyed spending the day with you."

"Me too. We should try it again some time."

Large raindrops started splattering the windshield.

I turned the wipers on high. "Looks like we're going to be in for it."

"Just stay on the road and out of the Nantahala."

My cell rang. Nakayla still held it. She looked at the screen. "It's your apartment. Must be Jason."

"Go ahead and answer it. These aren't the conditions for driving and talking on the phone."

"This is Nakayla." She listened a moment and then broke into a broad grin. She took the phone away from her ear and punched the speaker button. "You tell him," she said.

Jason's voice vibrated with excitement. "I got the job, Sam. Starting Monday I'm an employee of Armitage Security Services."

"That's great. We'll celebrate tonight at Nakayla's. Why don't I pick you up around…?" I looked to Nakayla for the cue as to what time she'd want Jason arriving.

She mouthed, "Seven."

"Seven. I'll give you a call when I'm close and pick you up at the front entrance."

"Okay. And I've got some other interesting information for you, but it can wait till we're all together."

"All right, hotshot. See you in a couple of hours."

Nakayla ended the call. "Your battery's getting low. We'll charge it while we're in the Nantahala dead zone."

But we didn't make it into the gorge before the phone rang a third time.

"I don't think I can take any more good news," I said.

Nakayla answered. She listened, and then her face fell. "I'll tell him," she said solemnly. "He'll want to call you when we get off the road."

She pulled the phone from her ear. I saw her eyes glistening. "That was Captain. Harry Young died about an hour ago. He wanted us to know. He said the end was peaceful. He said to tell you the old man's friend finally came for the Mayor."

"Pneumonia. Well, we knew it was imminent. Still I hate to lose him."

"A hundred and five. He was living history."

The rain swept across us in sheets. We rode through the torrent in silence.

When we reached Asheville, it was after five and still raining. I went to the store with Nakayla to get the groceries she needed for dinner. She decided to fix fresh trout from the local Sunburst Farms and whatever seasonal produce looked freshest. While she examined the spring peas and arugula, I went in search of my priorities: wine and dessert.

I called Captain from Nakayla's and learned the retirement center was holding a memorial for Harry Young on Tuesday. Captain asked me if I would say a few words and I agreed. Then I helped Nakayla prepare for our dinner guest. I liked setting the table and straightening up Nakayla's small den. We were entertaining as a couple, inviting someone to dine at home. For the first time I could see it as our home.

At six thirty, Nakayla sent me for Jason. The storm had dwindled to a steady drizzle. As I crossed the French Broad River from West Asheville, I telephoned Jason and told him that I should be under the porte-cochère in about fifteen minutes. He could grab a rain slicker from my closet and wait inside the lobby door.

I came up the hill to the Kenilworth by the straightest, steepest route, avoiding the twisting switchbacks on the slick pavement. The heavy clouds brought early darkness and the front of the grand hotel became a checkerboard of glowing apartment lights. The lobby also cast illumination out onto the terrace running along the front of the building.

I hooked to the left onto the circular drive running under the porte-cochère. Jason must have seen my approach because he stepped through the lobby door and stood at the edge of the terrace. He raised his right arm and smiled.

A spark flew from the palm of the artificial hand. Jason's head snapped back and he fell like the earth had been yanked out from under him. He hit so hard I heard the crack of his skull striking the stone terrace. A split-second later the sharp report of a rifle rolled over me. The sound still echoed as I jumped from the CR-V and darted around the hood out of the line of fire.

I crawled up the steps and knelt by Jason's side. His eyes were closed and blood already flowed from a wound on the right side of his forehead. An even more ominous pool spread from the back of his head, collecting in the mortar depressions and soaking the collar of his shirt. My shirt.

His body spasmed as he struggled to breathe. I could hear rattling as his lungs filled with blood.

A older man came out of the lobby, walking a salt-and-pepper miniature Schnauzer. The dog started barking.

"Call an ambulance," I shouted. "This man's been shot. Then call the police."

He jerked the dog back inside and pulled out his cellphone.

I put my lips close to Jason's ear. "Hang on. Help's on the way."

There was no response.

And I was afraid, as afraid as I've ever been, that this wounded boy, who had endured and overcome so much, was dying right in front of me.

# Chapter Twenty

I felt a hand on my shoulder and looked up to see Asheville police detective Curt Newland looking down at me. His face was lined with worry.

"Hell of a thing," he whispered. "Feel up to telling me what you know?"

I nodded.

He sat in one of the outdoor rockers beside me. I'd gone to the far end of the terrace, away from the spot where the medics loaded Jason into the ambulance. I'd just sat there, staring out into the dark.

"Ted called me," Newland said. "Efird's with me. We're taking the case."

"Your nephews did a good job securing the scene."

Ted and Al Newland were identical twins and uniformed Asheville patrolmen. Tuck Efird was Newly's new partner, and, though a bit of a hotdog, a competent enough investigator.

"Thanks," Newland said. "They're learning. Ted told me you just loaned the victim your apartment and helped him secure a job."

"Nathan Armitage gave him the job. He was a good kid and now because of me, he's hanging on by a thread."

"How do you figure that?"

"He was wearing my clothes. We're about the same height and coloring. In the rain, he could have passed for me."

"Did you have any reason to believe your life was in danger?"

"No."

"Then blaming yourself is a waste of effort. Are you going to help us with this or sit on the sidelines?"

"You know the answer to that."

"Good. So the victim is Jason Fretwell. You know a next of kin?"

"No. Best thing is to run all that through the veterans' hospital. Jason's from somewhere near Fort Wayne, Indiana."

"Okay." Newland looked back to the porte-cochère where the ambulance had rocketed away forty-five minutes ago. "Latest word I've got is he's in surgery. He's lucky Mission Hospital is less than a mile way."

"Any prognosis?"

"He's got some big hurdles to get over. The metal hand deflected the bullet so that it struck the forehead at a survivable angle. The fall to the stone terrace split his skull. If he survives the surgery, he'll probably be put in a coma while they monitor and try to control the cranial pressure from his swelling brain. That could last a while. Then recovery is anybody's guess. He may be fine or he may suffer severe cognitive disabilities." Newland shook his head. "Why don't you show me what happened."

I rose from the rocker, but had taken only a few steps when I heard my name. Nakayla came running around the yellow crime scene tape and down the driveway. Her hair became a cascade of diamonds as the backlight of the flashing police cars transformed water drops into jewels.

I jumped from the terrace onto the lawn and pulled her tight against me.

"Oh, Sam," she whispered. "I'm so sorry. Why would anybody want to shoot Jason?"

"I don't think they did."

She stiffened and then stepped back a pace. "Then you? The shot was meant for you?"

"I was still in the car and Jason had just stepped into the light. It was raining and he was dressed in my clothes."

"But, again, why?"

"Simple. Someone doesn't like me or what I'm doing."

"Good evening, Nakayla." Detective Newland joined us. "We need to press on, Sam. You know how a trail goes cold."

He was right. Catching the shooter was the priority. My only priority.

"I want Nakayla with me," I said.

"No problem. Walk me through it. You know the drill."

The crime scene skills I'd developed as a Chief Warrant Officer for Uncle Sam rose to the surface for Uncle Newly. He and Nakayla followed me to the shelter of the porte-cochère. I walked twenty feet beyond and stopped.

"I was about here when Jason came to the edge of the terrace. He waved and then fell backwards. I heard one shot and though my windows were up, I'm pretty sure it came from the edge of the woods."

I turned toward the entrance off the public road. To my right were houses built on the edge of the ridge. To my left were hardwoods and underbrush, and, beyond them across the road, the slope fell so severely no houses could be constructed. "I would guess he fired from a thicket or even from the shoulder of the slope. I immediately ran to Jason. If the shooter drove away, I didn't hear the vehicle. He had to be lying in wait and maybe parked lower down the hillside."

"Could he have fired from a car?" Nakayla asked.

"Maybe, but the position wouldn't have been ideal. He'd want to be prone. When that Washington D.C. sniper was killing people several years ago, he rigged a shooting platform in his trunk and had a driver. I don't think our man would have tried that from a parking lot where so many residents were coming in and out."

"Did you notice whether someone had been following you on the drive over?" Newland asked.

"No. And in the rain all I saw behind me were halos of headlights."

"Hey, Newly. I think we found the slug." Newland's partner Tuck Efird stood by the stone column nearest the lobby door.

"Come on." Newland climbed the steps to the terrace.

Efird nodded to Nakayla and me, and then pointed to a hole in the masonry between two rocks about seven feet above us. "Given the ascending slope, the bullet was traveling on an upward path. When we dig it out, it'll probably be too mangled for a ballistics match."

"Sam," Newland said. "Take the position where Jason was standing when he was shot. Try to get the angle the best you remember it."

I walked to the edge of the terrace and pivoted counter-clockwise so I was head-on to my CR-V. I raised my right arm, duplicating Jason's wave.

"Okay," Newland said. "The victim was struck first in the artificial hand and then the bullet creased his forehead. We have to allow for the deflection." Newland walked up behind me and reached his arm over my shoulder. "If Jason raised his hand so it was between him and the shooter, then this is the line of fire."

His finger pointed across the length of the lawn to the dark woods at the left edge of the parking lot.

"That shot would have cleared your car, right?"

"Yes," I said. "By a good five or six feet in front of the hood."

"I think we ought to throw some light down there, Newly," Efird said. "Headlights, flashlights, as much as we can get so we don't destroy any evidence stumbling around during the search."

"We could wait for daylight," Newland said.

"That's eight more hours of potential drizzle," I said. "If you act now, you might find a depression where the guy lay in wait. I wouldn't want that washed away."

"Okay," Newland agreed. "I also think he had to be close to the fringe of the woods. Otherwise, his aim would have been more limited by the underbrush."

Efird organized four cars in a semicircle concentrating their beams on the target area. Then he and Newland stepped care-fully into the woods.

In less than two minutes, Efird called out, "I think I've found the spot. Come straight in behind me."

Nakayla and I watched Newland swing around and approach the way Efird requested. For another five minutes, they played their halogen flashlights over the scene and along the line of sight to the Kenilworth.

"Sam, you and Nakayla come in. Follow my beam." Newland flipped his light in my face and then directed it along the ground, indicating the path we should follow. He guided us to a spot right beside Efird and him.

Efird ran his beam over a section of the ground in front of us. In a few spots, the wet, dead leaves had been scraped aside to reveal black soil underneath. I guessed the shooter dug in his boots as he lay in position.

"The slight incline matches the overall rise to the terrace," Efird said. "He had a perfect angle, either resting his elbow on the ground or using a barrel-mounted bipod. If there's a matching depression, it's too faint to eyeball. The lab boys might be able to find it."

"That could give us the height of the shooter," I said.

Efird played his beam about five or six feet in front of the boot marks. "Maybe, especially if it's an elbow imprint."

"What's that?" I pointed about a foot to the left. "At the edge of your light."

Efird eased the beam over.

"Stop," I ordered. "See the twigs?" I pointed to two stems with green laurel leaves.

"I don't want to disturb the ground to get them," Efird said.

"You don't need to," I said. "There's no laurel around the immediate area. Clearly someone brought them here. And I can see the ends are cut."

"Camo," Newland said.

"That's my guess," I agreed. "He probably wove laurel in his hat to break the profile of his head. Against the backdrop of the underbrush and in this drizzle, he'd be virtually invisible."

Newland looked at the front of the inn. "The shot's probably sixty or seventy yards."

"That's my estimate," Efird said.

"Then how did he know you'd pull up to the entrance?" Newland asked me.

"I don't know that he did. If I parked my car in one of the spaces beside us, I'd walk up the drive to the front entrance. He'd have all the time in the world to shoot me in the back."

"Yes, but you didn't park. You drove up and he shot Jason coming out of the lobby. You think he would have known your car if he was planning to ambush you after you parked."

"Not necessarily. A night vision scope with high-power magnification. My little limp with my leg. Easy enough to identify me."

"How did he know you wouldn't park around back?"

"He didn't. The front lot is the first one you see driving in. He couldn't be in two places at once so he had to pick one. This vantage point offered the best route of escape."

"We need to look for signs of his flight as well." Newland turned to Efird. "Do you mind working with Al and Ted to tape off the area?"

"No problem," Efird said. "Are you taking Sam into the station for his statement?"

"No. I'd like to find a dry spot to talk before we go downtown."

"How about my apartment?" I suggested. "There's hot coffee. Efird, you're welcome to come up when you're done. I'll give you the code."

"Thanks. I might take you up on it."

Nakayla put on a pot of French roast while Newland and I sat at my dining table.

"Have you had any threats?" he asked me.

"No."

"Then who have you pissed off? And don't say no one because you're a master of annoyance."

"You know I'm working on the skeleton case. I've interviewed several people in the last few days."

Newland pulled a notepad from his jacket pocket. "Give me the details, and don't give me any crap about client privilege. The guy's still out there and he'll soon learn you're not dead. At least not yet."

I didn't argue. I gave him the whole story from the mushroom hunt to Hewitt Donaldson's news that Chesterson dropped the charges against Lucille. When I finished, Newland immediately jumped to his person of interest.

"Mick Emory," he said like the very words tasted bad. "Now there's a waste of human flesh."

"So you know him?"

"Oh, yeah. He's been caught with the occasional fenced item. And we suspect he uses the pawnshop to launder cash. Not big amounts. Walking-around money for some small time meth dealers up in the hills. Did you come on hard with him?"

"I exerted the charms of my sparkling personality."

"And Jason Fretwell was with you?"

"Yeah, he was playing the role of gun enthusiast."

"Did he exert his sparkling personality?"

I remembered Jason pointing his mechanical hand at Mick Emory and pulling an imaginary trigger. "We both played with his head a little bit."

"And then you gave him your card and told him to get in touch if he found the rifle for Jason."

"Correct. Why?"

"Maybe it came in. Maybe he made a home delivery."

I shook my head. "The guy's chicken shit. All bluster."

"You don't have to be brave to hide in the dark and shoot someone who's unarmed. That's also chicken shit."

Newland had a point, although I couldn't see how our little tiff with Emory provoked such a reaction.

"Maybe Emory didn't care which one of you he shot if he thought both of you dissed him," Newland said. "Did Jason say anything after he was hit?"

"No. He was unconscious when I reached him."

Nakayla set two cups of black coffee on the table. "He did say he had something interesting to tell Sam and me."

"When was this?" Newland asked.

"When he phoned to say he got the job. Sam also heard him."

"That's right," I agreed.

Newland took a sip of coffee and saluted Nakayla with the cup. "Excellent, thank you." He set it back on the table. "Did Jason seem anxious or excited about whatever it was?"

"Hard to say," I said. "He was excited about the new job and that he was coming to dinner. Whatever he wanted to tell us could have been mundane and still wrapped up in his overall emotion."

Newland let it go. "If the shooter did think Jason was you, who would have seen you in those clothes recently?"

"I wore them last Saturday when I found the skeleton. So, it would be the mushroom club, Donnie Nettles, now murdered, Ed Bell who owns the property, Deputy Overcash, deputies from Greenville, South Carolina—."

"Overcash," Newland interrupted. "The deputy you said Chesterson threw under the bus?"

I smiled. "Yeah, but if he was going to shoot somebody, I figure it would be the D.A."

Newland wasn't amused. "And the others you've talked with were John and William Lang, Jennifer Lang and her partner Judith Crenshaw. Anybody else?"

"Well, if you're asking for everyone, there's Lucille and Marsha Montgomery. Also David Brose, the historian at the folk school."

"Okay." Newland looked back over his notes and then closed the pad. "I'll talk to all of them. Starting with Mr. Emory. He has more guns than good sense."

"Maybe one less. There was an empty spot in a display case of Berettas, a model that might match the gun that killed Donnie Nettles."

Newland re-opened his pad and jotted a note. "Emory should have sales records."

"Did you know his father?" I asked.

"No. Not alive."

Nakayla sat down. I stared at Newland. It was an odd thing to say.

"I was a young patrolman. I was called to the pawnshop the morning Mick Emory found his father's body."

"The suicide," I said.

"That's what it looked like."

"It wasn't?"

"It was. According to the coroner's inquest. But the investigation started as a homicide. That's standard procedure. There was an old detective must have been thirty years my senior. Mark Patterson. He's long dead. Patterson complimented me on the way I secured the scene at the pawnshop. He told me to always approach a death as a homicide. A killer will look for a way to pass off murder as something else. Usually an accident or a suicide because the best way to get away with murder is never have it revealed to be a murder. I never forgot what he said."

"He was right." I suddenly became conscious of my prosthesis, damp from the rain and irritating my stump. "I lost my leg because someone tried to kill me by making the attack look like Iraqi insurgents. A murder passing for a war casualty."

"Nothing new about that," Newland said. "King David sent his loyal soldier Uriah into the front lines of battle so David could marry his widow Bathsheba. Lust, betrayal, adultery. Pick a motive. Maybe the worst is when murder passes for righteousness, soaking streets in the Middle East with the blood of innocent men, women, and children, or leaving a smoking pile of rubble and bodies where the Twin Towers of lower Manhattan once stood. You can try passing it off as something else, Sam, but it's still murder."

# Chapter Twenty-one

I woke at four when a voice from a subconscious corner of my brain refused to stay mute. Nakayla lay sleeping beside me, her breathing as regular as a metronome.

We were at her house where we came after I gave Newland my statement at the Asheville police station. I couldn't face going back to my apartment. Jason had spread his clean clothes across my bed in preparation to either hang or fold them. I would deal with them later.

The voice in my head that roused me wasn't Jason's or Nakayla's. It was Detective Newland posing a question he hadn't asked. "If you were that easy to identify, then why weren't you?" I'd argued that the shooter would have been able to spot me walking from the front parking lot to the Kenilworth. A rifle scope powerful enough to yield a perfectly placed shot to Jason's head could also provide an image magnified enough to see the quarry wasn't me. Although the shirt and slicker Jason wore were mine, they weren't that distinctive. But, the artificial hand at the end of his right sleeve was. That trumped our similar height and coloring.

If I wasn't the target, then why Jason? His involvement with the case started and ended with Mick Emory. Newland would be all over that lead. Either the shooter had made a hasty decision to fire based solely on clothing, or he knew damn well who was in his crosshairs. That meant parallel investigations, one with me as the target and the other focusing on Jason Fretwell. And if it were tied to Jason's involvement with our case, then there was some connection Nakayla and I were unaware of.

"I've got some other interesting information for you, but it can wait till we're all together." Jason's words from yesterday afternoon. From the time Nakayla and I left for the folk school to when we spoke with him at the mouth of the Nantahala Gorge, Jason had learned something of interest to both Nakayla and me.

Suddenly, I had an urgent desire to get back to my apartment. If any trace of Jason's information existed, it would be there.

I slid out of bed, felt along the floor for my prosthesis, and dressed in the guest room. I wrote Nakayla a short note asking her to call me when she got up.

The rain had stopped and the cooler air of a high-pressure system dispersed the last remnants of the clouds. Traffic consisted of a few Saturday morning delivery trucks and farmers headed to the Asheville market on Charlotte Street. In no more than fifteen minutes, I pulled into the long driveway of the Kenilworth.

Retracing the route I'd taken less than twelve hours earlier, I sped passed the site where the gunman had waited. I parked in the rear and jogged to the exterior door, still unsure as to who had been the bullet's target.

In my bedroom, Jason's duffel bag sat empty at the foot of the bed. His socks, underwear, shirts, and slacks were on the spread where he'd laid them after taking them out of the dryer. On the nightstand were the two Jack Reacher novels I brought him the previous Monday. A slip of paper marked a spot about two-thirds of the way through the top volume. The makeshift bookmark was blank, a strip torn from a sheet of computer paper.

The chair at my small desk was pulled out. Jason had sat there. When I touched the spacebar of the keyboard, the computer screen flared to life. The text on the page read,

WELCOME TO THE US ARMY SNIPER SCHOOL.

WHEN YOU VOLUNTEER TO UNDERGO THE TRAINING HERE, YOU ACCEPT ONE OF THE

MOST DEMANDING CHALLENGES THE ARMY
HAS TO OFFER. SNIPERS HAVE A PROUD HERI-
TAGE WHICH CAN BE TRACED BACK TO THE
REVOLUTIONARY WAR. UPON COMPLETION
OF YOUR TRAINING, YOU WILL BE A MEMBER
OF THAT ELITE GROUP. IT TAKES A SPECIAL
TYPE OF SOLDIER TO MEET THE CHALLENGE.
HIGH STANDARDS HAVE ALREADY BEEN SET,
NOW IT IS UP TO YOU!

"ONE SHOT—ONE KILL"

MISSION

TRAIN SELECTED SOLDIERS TO ENGAGE
POINT TARGETS WITH LONG RANGE PRECI-
SION FIRE; TRAIN SNIPER FIELD CRAFT TECH-
NIQUES; DEVELOP SNIPER DOCTRINE; AND
PROVIDE SUBJECT MATTER EXPERTISE TO
THE FORCE.

The website's URL was www.specialoperations.com/Schools/
Army_Sniper/

Jason had been looking at the information for the school at
Fort Benning where he'd received his training. I clicked the arrow
to go back to the previous screen. It was a GOOGLE search for
sniper school, Fort Benning, Georgia. One more click back and
the page switched to the Military Channel's Top Ten Snipers.
I scrolled down to number one. Marine Corps sniper Carlos
Hathcock. Nicknamed "White Feather." He served two tours of
duty in Vietnam. Ninety-three confirmed kills with unconfirmed
kills in the hundreds. He was so deadly the North Vietnamese
put a thirty-thousand dollar bounty on his head. Hathcock died
from complications of multiple sclerosis in 1999.

The fact that Jason would have been looking at these sites
wasn't unusual given his special ops training. What was eerie and

an unacceptable coincidence was his shooting occurred within a few hours at the hands of a sniper.

Nothing else showed up in the browser's history. Nothing was written on the notepad I kept by the phone. But I picked the pad up and examined the top sheet. A faint depression showed where the pressure of the adjacent ballpoint pen had made an imprint. It could have been from my writing on the previous sheet, but the letters were a childlike scrawl. Jason trying to write with his left hand.

I opened the desk drawer and found a number two pencil. I laid the point on its side and lightly ran the lead back and forth over the sheet.

A phone number appeared. 706-555-6505. I wasn't familiar with the area code. Then a word appeared under it that was a mystery unto itself. "ghost." Two more words followed. "missed mission."

I went back to the computer and called up the Web page for the sniper school. I clicked the Contact icon. The identical phone number appeared. Jason Fretwell had called someone at Fort Benning and discovered something he wanted to share with Nakayla and me. Something tied to "ghost" and "missed mission."

The time was close to five o'clock. That was early for even the military. I dialed the number and got a recording. "You have reached the U.S. Army Sniper School. Leave your name and a brief message and we will get back with you as soon as possible." The male voice was clipped and authoritative. The beep sounded and I hung up. My inquiry wasn't one I wanted to leave on a machine.

I figured the school would probably open at eight, nine at the latest. I didn't know whom Jason had talked to, but the army kept good phone logs. I debated whether to turn what I'd found over to Newland or pursue it myself. The answer was easy. I'd been a Chief Warrant Officer. I knew my way around the military bureaucracy far better than an Asheville police detective.

For the next thirty minutes, I searched the Internet using word combinations with "ghost," "sniper," and "army," but I found nothing remotely relevant. There wasn't anything more to do until I could reach someone at Fort Benning. I lay down on the sofa and fell asleep.

My cellphone rang.

"Hello," I muttered.

"Sorry," Nakayla said. "Did I wake you? You told me to call."

My head cleared quickly. "What time is it?"

"Seven thirty. What's going on?"

I summarized the notepad and Web information. "Jason made a call to Fort Benning."

"If he actually spoke to someone. Does your landline phone keep a list of outgoing calls?"

"No. Just incoming."

"Well, we can check with the phone company. You don't know if he was tracking down someone he served with?"

"No, but the fact that he was looking at the top snipers in history might be a clue."

"Who was number one?"

"A marine named Hathcock. Vietnam."

"William Lang was in Vietnam," Nakayla said.

"Yes. And that's a damn good alibi since Lucille and John Lang both said William returned there the week before Jimmy disappeared."

"Right." She thought a moment. "There's somebody else on the periphery, but I don't see how he would have fit in."

"Who?"

"Donnie Nettles. He was in Vietnam and he knew the terrain of the Kingdom of the Happy Land. He might have had a role, good or bad, in this whole mess."

Nakayla was right. We couldn't ignore even the most unlikely connection. "Okay. Can you find out a little more about him?"

"Yes. I'm heading into the office."

"Why?"

"Because that phone system does keep a log of recent calls, both in and out. Jason was there on Thursday while you and I were talking with Jennifer Lang at the gallery. Maybe he started making inquiries then."

"Shirley," I said. "She described him as the cute guy on the phone."

"Then we need to find out who he was talking to."

"And call Newland. He needs to put Jason in protective custody, coma or no coma. I'll be in as soon as I place the call to Fort Benning."

Shortly after eight, I redialed the number.

"U.S. Army Sniper School. Staff Sergeant Benfield." His voice sounded identical to the one on the recording.

"Yes, sir. This is Chief Warrant Officer Sam Blackman calling from the V.A. hospital in Asheville." I neglected to add the word "former" in front of my rank.

"I'm investigating a shooting involving a special ops sniper who was discharged just yesterday. We're trying to determine if the incident involves the army in any way."

"Yes, sir. How can I help?"

"The victim was one of your graduates. Probably came through within the past year or eighteen months. SPC Jason Fretwell."

"Fretwell? Ah, Jesus." The pain in his voice was audible.

"You know him?"

"Yeah. I mean we get thirty to forty men for each five-week course, but some of them stand out. Fretwell was top of his class. How bad is he?"

"Head wound. He's in critical condition."

The staff sergeant paused, absorbing the news. "Sir, if he was discharged, can you tell me why you think it's an army matter?"

"Fretwell was shot by a sniper."

The phone went absolutely silent.

"Staff Sergeant Benfield?"

"Sorry, sir. I hate to hear it. Fretwell was very easygoing. I can't imagine him having a run-in with someone."

"I agree. I know him. I like him very much. And I'm going to get to the bottom of it. Now I have reason to believe Fretwell called this number yesterday between ten and three."

"I was in a training session all day," Benfield said. "I can check the duty roster for who would have taken the call."

"Thank you. I'm more interested in the person Fretwell asked to speak with. Track him down and have him phone me immediately. Here's my direct line."

I gave Benfield my cell number and thanked him.

When I stood up from the sofa, I felt light-headed and realized I hadn't eaten since lunch in Murphy the previous day. I fixed a bowl of granola with milk and poured a large glass of orange juice. The old adage was true for even a pretend soldier. An army travels on its stomach.

I was shoveling the last spoonful into my mouth when my cellphone rang. I grabbed it from my belt, hoping for the callback from Fort Benning. Nakayla's number flashed on the screen.

"Hi," I said. "I haven't heard anything from the sniper school yet."

"That's not why I'm calling. I'm at the office. The phone memory shows Jason made one call Thursday while we were at the gallery."

"Let me guess. Fort Benning, Georgia."

"No. At a quarter to twelve, Jason phoned the Double G Pawnshop."

"Mick Emory? We'd just left him."

"Yes. Curious, isn't it?"

"You know what we've got to do."

"Yes. You or me?"

"I'll do it. He'll have questions even though I don't have answers." I disconnected from Nakayla, opened my contacts icon, and speed-dialed Detective Newland.

# Chapter Twenty-two

Curt Newland and his partner Tuck Efird were already en route to Mick Emory's home—a cabin outside of the Candler community about nine miles west of Asheville.

"And you have no idea why Fretwell phoned Emory?" Newland asked after I'd given him word of the call.

"No. Jason congratulated me on the way the interview had gone. He didn't mention anything he thought needed to be followed up."

"Would he have taken the initiative on his own?"

I thought about Jason's desire to work for our agency. "Possibly. He wanted to feel like he was helping us."

"Okay. Let's assume something came to his mind after you left him at your office. We'll see if Emory mentions the call unprompted. If not, we'll press him. You're sure about the time?"

"Nakayla's the one who checked the phone log."

"Then I'm confident it's accurate. I'll be back in touch. And Nakayla called earlier. We've got a guard by Jason's bedside."

"What's the latest?"

"Touch and go. He's been placed in an induced coma, but the cranial pressure's increasing. I'll keep you posted."

He hung up before I could mention the Fort Benning lead.

It was nearly nine o'clock when I reached the office. Nakayla sat in front of her computer screen, whipping through web pages like they were unwanted newspaper ads.

"Any luck?" I asked.

"A little information on Donnie Nettles. I knew he was a real estate developer, but I didn't know how successful. He worked the commercial side—office buildings and shopping centers. He was evidently careful not to over extend himself and was one of the few to survive the collapse of 2008."

"A real estate mogul who hunted mushrooms. You think he'd have been out on his yacht."

"Donnie was down-to-earth in a lot of ways. He was born in Harlan, Kentucky in 1948. His family moved here in 1960. He's listed as a member of Asheville American Legion Post Two."

"Someone from the Legion called William with the news," I said. "He and Donnie must have been in the same Post."

"Post Two's Web page has a brief bio stating Donnie was on active service in Vietnam from 1967 to 1969. He would have been nineteen in 1967, a year younger than William."

"We need to go to army records to see if they served together." I thought about the implications. "If they were buddies, I wonder if Mick Emory would have been a common enemy?"

The office line rang and she snapped up the receiver. "Blackman and Robertson." After a second, she said, "Oh, hi, David. No, you're not too early." She swiveled to face me and mouthed, "David Brose."

I gave her a thumbs-up. The historian of the John C. Campbell Folk School must have come up with something. I crossed the middle sitting room, entered my office, and sat impatiently at my desk. Waiting to take action drove me crazy. I could never have been a sniper.

My thoughts drifted to Jason Fretwell. Had his parents been notified? Were travel arrangements being made? I felt an obligation to speak to his physical therapist Sheila Reilly, but I didn't know if she was in the hospital on Saturday. She would be devastated if Jason died. Despite her gruff exterior, there was no question how much she cared about her patients.

And then there was the other end of the age spectrum. Harry Young. I pulled out a legal pad and wrote Harry Young across the top. Might as well use the time to work on my remarks for Harry's memorial service.

Before I could start, Nakayla rapped on my door. "We might have a break. David Brose thinks he's found the photograph." She slid into my extra chair.

"Can he scan or fax a copy?"

"He doesn't have it. He said after we left he started thinking about the date 1932 and the fact that Doris Ulmann was with Julia Peterkin taking photographs for *Roll, Jordan, Roll,* their book about the South Carolina lowcountry. The folk school wouldn't have received prints of those images. The excursion to the mountains for the Kingdom picture was just a day trip from Peterkin's plantation.

"So, Brose sent an email to a friend at the South Carolina Historical Society in Charleston. They have one-hundred-sixty-nine platinum prints and a copy of the deluxe edition of *Roll, Jordan, Roll.* He got a reply last night and felt it was too late to call us. But his friend said the Kingdom photograph sounded familiar and could be part of their collection. Remember, the Kingdom straddled the state line."

"Yes, which is why Deputy Overcash hurried to establish jurisdiction. What happens now?"

"Brose suggested I call his friend at ten. She'll be at the historical society then, and maybe she can email a copy of the image."

I glanced at my watch. "In forty-five minutes."

"Right. I hope we can learn something to share with Newland while he's pursuing his interviews today."

I nodded, but I wasn't enthused about the prospect. Jason Fretwell's shooting made an evil in the present much more of a priority than an eighty-year-old photograph. And now that the district attorney had dropped the charges against Lucille Montgomery, the descendants of the Kingdom of the Happy Land weren't even relevant.

Nakayla must have read my thoughts. "What's the matter? You think we're wasting our time?"

"Probably. I not only don't see a connection, I can't even imagine one."

"The tendrils of the past can be long and deadly." Her face hardened with resolve. "Just because you can't imagine it, doesn't mean it doesn't exist."

She was correct and knew that fact better than I did. An event from 1919 had claimed the life of her sister.

"I'm keeping an open mind."

Nakayla stood, shaking off the dark memory. "Better an open mind than an empty one."

She returned to her office and I picked up the legal pad. Harry Young. He'd been the connection between the murder of Nakayla's sister and that of her great-great grandfather. The tendrils of the past had reached across ninety years with deadly consequences. I jotted down notes referencing the world of Harry's boyhood and the world he lived to see. Through all the changes, Harry remained consistent in his kindness and love for others, regardless of their race or economic status. I wanted to think the world had become more like Harry. But it hadn't. Jason Fretwell clinging to life was proof enough.

I worked on my remarks, only vaguely aware of Nakayla's voice when she placed the call to the South Carolina Historical Society.

The phone rang. Nakayla was still on the first line so I answered. "Blackman and Robertson. Sam Blackman."

"What the hell do you think you're doing? Why'd you sic the law on me?"

I recognized the angry, whiny voice of Mick Emory.

"I didn't sic the law on anybody, Mr. Emory. They're investigating the shooting of my friend. I gave them the names of everyone we spoke with yesterday. Yours was one of many."

"Well, they took all the boots and pants from my closet."

Soil sample, I thought. Looking for a match to the dirt at the crime scene.

"And they're shuttin' down my business."

That was a surprise. "Why?"

"To check the ballistics on all my rifles. You know how many god-damned guns I've got?"

"You still have your guitars."

"Listen, smartass. I didn't shoot your friend and I didn't try to shoot you. You're no more to me than a pimple on my butt."

I started to lose my cool. "Oh, yeah. Then how do you explain your phone call with Jason Fretwell?"

Emory was silent a moment. "Look. I never talked to him. I was tied up with a customer and the answering machine took it. He asked me to phone him and left this number. But you two pissed me off and I didn't call him back. That's the God's truth."

"What did he want?"

"I don't know. Like I told the police, he said he had a question and would I please get in touch. He sounded friendly enough." Emory sighed. "I'm sorry he was shot. I wish I could help."

I didn't like the guy, but he sounded sincere. "All right. If I learn what Fretwell wanted to ask, I'll be in touch."

"Can you get the police off my ass?" he pleaded.

"No. They've got a murder to solve. And if I find out you're lying to me, you'll want them for protection." I hung up.

I started to phone Newland, but I had nothing to tell him other than Mick Emory was shaken by his visit. Better to let the detective do his job without me pestering him.

"Sam, can you come here?" Nakayla sounded urgent.

She was off the phone with her face close to her computer monitor.

"What is it?"

"Pull up a chair and take a look." Nakayla scooted aside to give me room.

In the middle of her screen was a black and white photograph, remarkable in image detail. Five people stood in front of a stone chimney. I recognized the landscape as virtually identical to the site of the Kingdom's last remaining vestige that Ed Bell had shown Jason and me earlier in the week.

Two African-American women stood side by side with three children in front of them. The elder woman leaned on a black cane and her hair was covered with a white kerchief. The dress covering her thin body was a simple checked print. Even though she was far from a kitchen, she wore a white apron tied at the waist.

The other woman looked to be around thirty, and though her face was lined, her smile rejuvenated her youth. Her dress was a smaller checked pattern with a rounded white collar and matching trim on three-quarter-length sleeves. Her hands rested on the shoulders of a pretty African-American girl of no more than five. Her floral print dress was sleeveless and hung loosely around her body. Her wavy black hair sported a bow made from the same fabric.

I realized the girl had to be Lucille with her mother Lucinda and grandmother Loretta. Two boys flanked her. The one on the left held her hand. The boys were a couple of inches taller than Lucille. Each wore what looked like canvas dungarees cinched at the waist with a loop of hemp rope. Matching gray shirts were tucked in place.

I leaned in closer. The bewildered expressions on the children's faces must have reflected their reaction to Doris Ulmann in her long dress standing behind the big camera. The boys' expressions were identical because their faces were identical. Identical white faces.

I turned to Nakayla. "Lucille said there were more children in the picture than this."

"Lucille lied. That's why Marsha looked confused during our interview."

I studied the photograph again. The light went off like an old-fashioned flashbulb. "Jimmy and John Lang."

"I don't know another set of twins mixed up in this."

Pieces began to fall together. "This photograph is of descendants of the Kingdom. Julia Peterkin's letter confirmed that."

"That's right," Nakayla said. "Which means the twins are also descendants of the Kingdom."

"The body in the log. It's Jimmy Lang after all."

"Yes. It explains why John Lang was so adamant about not giving a DNA sample."

"But then Lucille and Jimmy could have married."

"If Jimmy revealed his lineage, he also exposed his twin brother."

"How did they manage?"

"They were passing. It's been done. Among the offspring of Thomas Jefferson and Sally Heming, three of the children lived in white society. But after the Civil War, the southern states implemented their rule that one drop of black blood classified you as black. One ancestor of African descent assigned you to the Negro race, forfeiting all rights and privileges enjoyed by whites in a segregated society."

I shook my head with disbelief. "So, the irony is the Loving versus Virginia Supreme Court decision meant a black man who was passing could marry a black woman without recrimination."

"Without legal recrimination," Nakayla corrected. "Southern white society would still have frowned upon a union it saw as an abomination. Lucille understood that."

"And so did John Lang. He was helping Lucille because she knew the secret."

"Yes," Nakayla said. "And Lucille knew the brothers' business would be destroyed. Now all the motives are back in play with Jimmy Lang as the murder victim. We need to talk to Hewitt."

"No. We need to talk to Lucille. It's time we got some truthful answers." I stood and pointed to the screen. "Print that photo with the best quality you can."

"Where are you going?"

"I'm calling Captain. I want to know if Marsha is with her mother, and I want Captain setting protection for Lucille."

"Protection?"

"As far as John Lang thinks, Lucille is the only other one who knows the truth behind the photograph. That might be why John Lang tried to hire us in the first place. If a print of the photograph turned up, he hoped to control it."

"You think he killed his own brother?"

"What was the very first homicide?"

"Cain and Abel." Nakayla's face turned grim. "Call Captain. I'll print the picture."

# Chapter Twenty-three

"Marsha was here this morning, but she left about thirty minutes ago." Captain whispered the words at the opposite end of the hall from Lucille Montgomery's apartment.

"Do you know if Marsha's coming back this afternoon?" Nakayla asked.

"I overheard her say she'd see her mother for church tomorrow."

"How'd you manage that?" I asked.

Captain looked hurt. "Give me credit for some subterfuge. I had the copy of the morning paper with the story of the D.A.'s dismissal of the murder charge. When Marsha opened the door, I pretended to be bringing it to Lucille to make sure she'd seen it." He patted the seat of his walker. "I sat about twenty feet away. Close enough to hear them come to the door. My legs might be weak but I've still got good ears."

"Anything else we should know?"

Captain nodded. "Lucille didn't look too good. She's been under stress and it shows. She said she didn't feel like coming to the dining room for lunch and would eat in her apartment."

"Okay. Thanks, Captain."

He grabbed my arm, and then looked back and forth from Nakayla to me. "Do you think she's in danger?"

"Maybe," I said. "Let's not take any chances."

"Then I'll activate the corridor patrols. A little tougher since she's at the end of the hall, but we'll make it work."

He stepped back and saluted.

As we neared Lucille's door, Nakayla whispered, "She's been under stress but she's also grieving. No one but she and John Lang understand what the DNA report confirmed."

"She, John Lang, and us." I lifted the manila envelope I carried in my left hand. "This won't be easy. Will you take the lead?"

"Yes. That may mean I ask you to leave if she doesn't open up to both of us." Nakayla knocked on the door.

"Just a minute," came the muffled response.

We heard Lucille's footsteps shuffle closer on the other side. The door opened and Lucille gasped.

"I wasn't expecting company." She looked down as if uncertain whether she was properly attired. Her beige cotton dress was one of comfort, not style.

"May we come in?" Nakayla said. "It's urgent."

Lucille stood there, bewildered by our sudden appearance and Nakayla's request. Good manners won out and she turned aside.

"Yes, yes, certainly. But you know I've been cleared. Everything's all right."

"Please sit down, Miss Montgomery. We'll be as brief as we can."

The old woman closed the door and walked with hesitating steps to her rocker. "I should have called you. I'm grateful to you and Mr. Donaldson for what you've done."

I sat on the sofa and Nakayla took the armchair next to Lucille.

"You haven't been cleared," Nakayla said. "The murder charge was dropped for insufficient evidence but you could be charged again. Especially since Sam and I know Jimmy Lang died in that log."

Tears welled in Lucille's eyes. "No, that's not true."

Nakayla nodded to me and I pulled the print of the photograph from the manila envelope. I laid it on the coffee table and turned it to face Lucille.

The wells of tears overflowed and spread across the wrinkles of her cheeks. "Where did you find it?" She reached out, hesitant to touch it less the picture vanish.

"This is a copy we found in Charleston," Nakayla said. "You can see there aren't the number of children you claimed were in it."

"It was so long ago. I couldn't remember."

"You remember very well. Well enough to try and protect the twins, Jimmy and John Lang. Descendants of the Kingdom just like your family. Jimmy's holding your hand, isn't he?"

Lucille took in a breath, and then exhaled a long, staggered sigh.

"My Jimmy," she whispered. She closed her eyes and wiped the tears from her face with both hands.

Nakayla and I sat silently waiting for her to compose herself.

She opened her eyes and fixed them on the photograph. "Jimmy and John grew up on Peterkin's Lang Syne Plantation."

Lang Syne Plantation and Jimmy and John Lang. I should have made that connection. The boys had taken the surname of the place they lived.

"Their father had been what white folks called an octoroon," Lucille said. "One-eighth Negro. He was born on the Kingdom and a descendant of the first king, the mulatto slave owner who was said to have a white wife.

"According to my mother, their father had been killed when a cart loaded with apples he was pushing up a hillside rolled back on him. His wife was expecting and went to be with her sister who was a housemaid at Lang Syne. After the twins were born, their mother stayed on, joining her sister as one of the servants."

Lucille lifted the photograph and held it close to her eyes. "The boys were not only fair-skinned but inherited white features. Miss Julia didn't try to pass them as white, but they were given an education on the plantation and stayed in the finer quarters of the house servants."

She angled the picture first to Nakayla and then me as if we were seeing it for the first time.

"Our families stayed in touch and we would visit on occasion. Miss Julia knew their father's connection to the Kingdom, so when the photographer wanted to take this picture, Jimmy and John came with them."

"But you saw them after that?" Nakayla asked.

"Yes. Once or twice a year. My grandmother Loretta also worked for a time at Lang Syne before her husband purchased our homesite. That was back when Miss Julia and Mr. Willie were courting."

"Mr. Willie?" Nakayla repeated.

"Yes. Willie Peterkin. Miss Julia's husband."

In my mind I saw William P. Lang's nameplate on his fine desk at the paper company.

"Willie Peterkin Lang," I said.

"Yes," Lucille said. "John named his son after Mr. Willie."

"How did they cross the color line?" Nakayla asked.

Lucille gave a bittersweet smile. "It started as an accident. Jimmy had come up to visit our family. He was about seventeen. And he went into town to pick up some sugar for my grandmother. No one knew him. The plantation was its own little world in South Carolina and he'd always kept to the mountain land near the old Kingdom when he and John came to visit. Well, he passed the sidewalk test. Not on purpose. He said he was just daydreaming."

I looked at Nakayla, but she was as confused as me.

"What's the sidewalk test?" she asked.

"Yielding to the white folk. You were expected to step off into the street if a group of white men or women was too wide for everyone to pass by without changing their stride. Jimmy said four men came out of the feed store and were walking side by side. He'd been unaware of their approach until the last moment. Before he could step out of the way, the men closest to him said, "Good Day," and moved into a single file until they were clear. White men had never spoken to him as an equal before."

"When was this?" Nakayla asked.

"I guess the summer of 1944. He watched the white men move away and saw two dark-skinned black men step into the street, ceding the whole sidewalk. The white men continued walking four abreast as if the black men didn't exist. And I guess back then they didn't."

Lucille dropped the photograph on the coffee table as if that shameful period could be discarded just as easily.

"So Jimmy walked to the bus station and without hesitation took a long drink from the white water fountain. No one paid any attention. That's when he saw the possibilities open for him and his brother. He returned to Lang Syne, saved every nickel he could until he had enough to buy some property, and became the white Jimmy Lang. You know when he knew he'd pulled it off?"

"No," Nakayla said.

"The day he registered to vote."

"But the state of North Carolina made him choose between you or a better life," Nakayla argued.

"It was a choice between having his potential limited to the status of a black sharecropper or having a better life for both of us. His brother jumped at the chance, and I pushed Jimmy just as hard. But when the marriage barrier fell, Jimmy believed he didn't have to make a choice any longer."

"And you did."

"I've already told you. Laws don't change hearts. In 1967, people weren't going to accept Jimmy marrying a black woman and treat him as a legitimate business man."

Her face tensed. "Why does this even have to come out? What difference will it make?"

"Someone killed Jimmy," Nakayla said firmly. "You told us you wanted justice for him."

Lucille's lower lip quivered. "I do. Lord knows I do. But I can't see how destroying lives sets this right."

Nakayla's eyes narrowed and a tremor of anger rippled through her body. "Having African blood doesn't destroy a life, Miss Montgomery. This isn't 1967. I'm proud of who I am and what I do. The lives of John Lang, William Lang, and Jennifer Lang will not be destroyed by their genes. Any lives destroyed will be because of their actions and it isn't your responsibility to protect them. You have a responsibility to Jimmy Lang, the man who was willing to give up everything for you."

I jumped in before Lucille could respond. "And a responsibility to Jason Fretwell."

"Who?" Lucille asked.

"A young veteran who was gunned down last night while trying to help us with your case. A twenty-three-year-old kid who may never wake up from a coma."

Lucille stared at me, unable to say anything.

I ratcheted back the edge in my voice. "Miss Montgomery, has John Lang threatened you?"

"No. Of course not."

"You knew his secret. Did anyone else? His son? His granddaughter?"

"No. Just me. Not even Gladys his wife. They were married in 1946 within six months after John moved here. A legally married white couple. No one ever suspected. And John never threatened me. He was grateful."

I looked to Nakayla. She nodded for me to continue.

"Now that we know Jimmy Lang was killed on the old site of the Kingdom of the Happy Land, take me back to that day and tell me everything you remember."

"I already have."

"Then Nakayla and I want to hear it again. When did Jimmy tell you that he would pick you up at the camp on July 14th?"

"The night before. He came by and ate supper with Marsha and me."

"And why did he say he was picking you up?"

"He had something to show me."

"Show you, not tell you?"

"He said show me. Otherwise he could have just told me the night before. You know, when he made the arrangements."

I leaned back on the sofa, trying to parse extra meaning from her words. "You said something else in Mr. Donaldson's office about new beginnings."

"That's right. Jimmy said it was time for a new beginning. That we couldn't go back, but we could start over. That would be a real treasure."

I pointed to the photograph on the coffee table. "And your copy of this picture was there after he left that night before he disappeared?"

"Yes. Jimmy had walked over to it. I remember because that's when he talked about new beginnings and we couldn't go back. You know, go back to when we were children."

Nakayla smiled at me and I knew she thought we were making progress.

I pressed on. "Miss Montgomery, the stone chimney in this photograph is still standing."

"Really? After all these years?"

"Yes, ma'am. I saw it myself earlier this week. That means it would have definitely been there the day Jimmy disappeared. The day we now figure he was killed on that property."

"You think he went to look at that chimney?"

"I don't know. Do you have any idea why he'd be there?"

She shook her head. "No, sir. I would tell you if I did."

"So, let me just check that I understand the situation back then. You didn't want to marry Jimmy after the Supreme Court decision because nothing had really changed as far as discrimination, and the county trash contract was too important."

"That's correct."

"John's wife had died a little over a week before and I imagine he was still quite upset."

"Yes, sir."

"William Lang had returned to Vietnam."

"Willie took the bus to Fort Bragg the day after the funeral. He said he'd fly with one of the units being sent over. I packed him a lunch with some of the food that friends brought for the family after Gladys passed away."

"And Jimmy wanted a new beginning."

"That's what he told me."

I sat for a moment, trying to put myself in Jimmy Lang's head. What leverage did he have? What could he do to change Lucille's mind?

"Miss Montgomery, what would have happened if Jimmy had made his mixed race public?"

"What? You mean confess he'd been passing all those years?"

"Yes. What law would he have broken that was still in effect in 1967? The Civil Rights Act had passed. Voting rights were guaranteed."

"But the business."

"Yes, the business may have been the casualty of his honesty. Would you have left him if he lost the business?"

"No, certainly not."

"And then what would have been the reason not to marry him?"

She said nothing. Her eyes seemed to be looking beyond the walls.

"Jimmy loved you, Miss Montgomery. He knew what you would do once he knocked down that last obstacle."

"A new beginning," she said softly.

"Maybe. What do you think John would have done if Jimmy told him he was going to admit his racial heritage?"

"I don't know. He would have been upset for sure." She leaned forward and shook a bony finger at me. "But I know what he wouldn't have done. He wouldn't have murdered his own brother. I stake my life on that. Someone else shot my Jimmy. Someone who had something to lose more valuable than kinfolk. I think you should take a close look at that Emory family, Mr. Blackman. Jimmy told me never to turn my back on them. Never. He said they'd sooner shoot you as look at you."

"We are, Miss Montgomery. Does the name Donnie Nettles mean anything to you?"

"No, sir. Who's he?"

"Just someone who might have been familiar with the Kingdom property back then. A friend of William's."

"I've never heard of him. I don't think William ever mentioned his name."

"Thank you for your candor." I stood and took her hand. "And one last thing. This has been between the three of us. No one else has seen the photograph and, at this point, no one else will while Nakayla and I think about what you've told us."

Nakayla rose from the armchair, bent down, and kissed the elderly woman's tear-streaked cheek. "Don't worry. Things will work out for the best."

Miss Montgomery shook her head. "If things had worked out for the best, Jimmy would have grown old along with me." She looked at her lover's portrait on the table by the television. "There was no new beginning for us, only an unhappy ending."

She wept quietly.

Nakayla and I left her with what might have been.

# Chapter Twenty-four

"What do you think about Lucille's faith in John Lang?" I raised the question as we drove down the ridge from the Golden Oaks Retirement Center.

"Probably misplaced," Nakayla said. "He had everything to gain by keeping her happy. She had a five-year-old daughter and the man in her life had left. She was vulnerable."

"Do you think there was more to their relationship?"

"My gut instinct says no. If anything, they're close like siblings but both so steeped in their racial charade that their public personas mirrored their segregated society."

I thought about the intervening years since Jimmy's death. John Lang had provided Lucille with a job. He enabled his illegitimate niece Marsha to have a good career with his company. Was that altruism or guilt?

"Do you think Lucille is deluding herself?" I asked. "She refuses to accept that John could have murdered his brother?"

Nakayla turned in the passenger's seat. I glanced from the road long enough to read the sadness in her eyes.

"I think every time Lucille stared into the face of John Lang, she saw his twin. How hard would that be?" Nakayla looked away, contemplating her own question. "To grow old with the aging image of the man who should have been her life partner. I'm no psychiatrist, but I think it would be nearly impossible to accept that face as the mask of someone so evil."

"And is John Lang capable of such evil?"

"That's the question, isn't it? Did the drive and determination he had to build such a successful company include eliminating the greatest threat. His brother."

"I don't know."

"But you have a plan to find out," Nakayla said. "I could see it in your eyes when you asked Lucille what she would have done if Jimmy had revealed his true identity."

"Not a plan," I said. "But perhaps the beginning of one. Jimmy Lang's new beginning."

We headed straight for our office. I was anxious to check in with Detective Newland and still hopeful I'd receive a call from Fort Benning. I believed a request from a Chief Warrant Officer would be a priority, unless someone checked and discovered I was no longer in the military.

Nakayla offered to walk to the City Bakery Café to pick up sandwiches for lunch. While she was gone, I placed two calls. The first went to a former CID colleague now stationed in Fort Bragg, North Carolina. I asked him to run a check on Donnie Nettles, his tours of duty and anything that stood out in his record. I requested he do the same for William Lang, even though he'd been in Vietnam at the time. You can learn a lot about a man from his service record, and I might have to confront him over the possible actions of his father.

My second call went to Detective Newland. He answered on the first ring.

"Sam. What's up?"

"Nothing really. Just checking in. I had a call from Mick Emory pleading for me to get you off his ass."

"I bet. Nothing that scumbag fears more than police cars in his parking lot."

"Is he still a suspect?"

"He has no alibi and a store full of guns, scopes, and ammo. He claims he never talked to Fretwell."

"That's what he told me. He said Fretwell left a message on his answering machine."

"Well, I'm tracking down the length of the call with the phone company because Emory said he erased the message. He also can't find the bill of sale for the Beretta PX4 he told you he sold."

"Maybe he sold it to someone he shouldn't have," I said.

"Maybe. Or he used it himself and doesn't want it ever found. I'm going to let the sheriff lean on him for that in case it ties into the Nettles murder."

"Has your investigator friend made any progress?"

"He said Nettles' wife gave them a description of the stolen jewelry. They'll check the pawnshops starting with Emory's. The garage owner where Nettles left his car said he gave Nettles a lift to his American Legion Post. Nettles was getting a ride home from there."

"Does he know with whom?"

"No. They're still following it up."

"William Lang's a member. That's how he learned about Nettles' death."

"I'll mention it. And I've already given my friend Jimmy Lang's name like you asked."

"Thanks," I said. "Any leads off ballistics for Jason?"

"The slug was pretty well mangled. A few rifling marks survived. I don't know if it's enough for a match, but I didn't tell Emory that. We're pretty sure it's a thirty-aught-six, one of the most common guns in the mountains."

"Not like a Remington fourteen and a half. You talk to John and William Lang yet?"

"Yeah. Efird and I are just leaving William's house. We spoke with the old man earlier."

"And?"

"John Lang says he went straight home from the plant last night, watched PBS Newshour and the Nightly Business News, and turned in a little after eight. William went to a charity fundraiser for Mission Hospital. Some gala dinner and silent auction at the Renaissance Hotel. It lasted till ten. William won the high bid on an abstract painting by one of the artists in his daughter's gallery. He showed us the piece. The most artistic thing about it is the frame. We're headed to see the daughter now."

"When did that charity event start?" I asked.

"Seven."

I realized whoever pulled the trigger at the Kenilworth wouldn't have made it to a ritzy affair downtown at seven. "Do you think the old man could have managed it?"

Newland thought a second. "He's spry. With a bipod support for the rifle and a good scope, yeah, it's within the realm of possibility. But why Jason Fretwell?"

"I don't know. He either thought Jason was me or he shot at me in the car and hit Jason by mistake."

"And motive?"

"I have no idea."

"Then watch yourself," Newland said. "You must know something important and don't realize it."

I knew more now than I did the previous night. The Ulmann photograph revealed the Langs' secret. Had John Lang somehow known we were on the verge of that discovery? Had Brose's friend in Charleston tipped him off? The possibility of so elaborate a conspiracy stretched credulity to the absurd. But I wasn't ready to share that information with Newland. I'd made a promise to Lucille and I'd keep that promise until I had no alternative.

"Well, if you figure out what I know, Newly, please tell me."

"Only if you promise not to go it alone."

We hung up after agreeing to check with each other at the end of the day.

Nakayla returned with sandwiches and two bottles of root beer. We ate our lunch in the sitting area and I brought Nakayla up to date on my conversation with Newland.

"Do you think holding back the information about the photograph is hurting his investigation?" Nakayla asked.

"No. His line of questioning would be the same. If Mick Emory or his father had known the Langs' secret, they would have used it against them forty-five years ago. If old man Lang killed Jason, then Newland needs something concrete for a motive. They never met or even spoke with one another. If he was trying to kill me, then I'll wait till Newland has run all his interviews and has gotten his lab reports."

"Wait to do what?"

"Wait to confront him. Show him the photograph and tell him I'm going to the police. I won't be expanding the circle of knowledge because John Lang already knows the truth."

"What will that accomplish?"

I shrugged. "I'll have poked the tiger, and maybe he'll come out of the underbrush."

The office phone rang. Nakayla started to get up to answer.

"Finish your sandwich. Whoever it is can leave a message."

We heard the beep and then a voice said, "This is William Lang. I'd like to talk with—"

I didn't hear the rest of his words because I jumped from my armchair and ran for the office line. "This is Sam," I managed to say before Lang finished speaking.

"Mr. Blackman. Uh, the police were by." He suddenly sounded flustered like he was better prepared to talk to a machine. "They told me about the shooting and that your friend was severely wounded."

"Yes." I said nothing further. He'd made the call.

"I guess they came to me because of our meeting at the plant. I realize I wasn't the most gracious in my response to your questions. And I was devastated when I got that call about the murder of a friend of mine."

"Donnie Nettles. I knew him. Great guy."

"Right. He mentioned he was there when you found the skeleton. And that's the other thing. I was upset when I thought my uncle's remains had been discovered. I overreacted. With you and with Lucille Montgomery. I knew she'd been angry with my uncle, and, well, I read more into that than I should have."

"All right. If you didn't fire the shot, then you have nothing to worry about."

"I didn't. Do you have any idea why someone would try to kill that young soldier?"

"No. Not a clue."

"Did you go see Mick Emory after you asked my father and me about him?"

I wasn't about to give William Lang a play-by-play of my investigation. "Why would that matter?"

"Just thinking out loud. Emory's a pretty good shot. We've crossed paths at some of the local turkey shoots. Believe me, it doesn't take much to set him off. He's as unstable as a Mason jar full of nitroglycerin. And he doesn't like people snooping in his business. No offense, but if you grilled him about my Uncle Jimmy, he'd have taken it personally. And someone who's only a pretty good shot could have hit your friend by mistake."

"If I talked to him."

There was a long, silent pause.

"Well, that's all I wanted to say. Sorry for what happened."

"I'm sorry for what happened to your uncle."

"We've been told those remains weren't my uncle. They're from a black man."

"I'm sorry for what happened to your uncle," I repeated. "That's all I wanted to say. Goodbye, Mr. Lang." I hung up.

"What was that little game?" Nakayla asked.

"It's called poke the tiger's cub. I want to see what gets back to John and how he reacts."

"You're playing with fire."

"I know, but at least I'm taking the heat off Lucille Montgomery. John Lang will be more worried about what I might do."

The phone rang again. This time it was my cell. The number had a 706 area code. In for a penny, in for a pound. "Chief Warrant Officer Blackman."

Nakayla rolled her eyes.

"Yes, sir. This is Staff Sergeant Walker Gilchrist from the sniper school."

"Yes. You're calling about SPC Fretwell?"

I heard him swallow.

"I am, sir. It's true then? Fretwell's been shot?"

"Yes. He's hanging on, but it doesn't look good. I'm trying to fill in the background for our investigation."

"Man. I heard he lost an arm and now this. Poor Little Ghost. Can't catch a break."

The hair on my neck rose. "Little what?"

"Ghost. Little Ghost was the nickname I gave him."

Little Ghost. Who then was the Ghost? Jason must have been on a fishing expedition.

"You spoke with him yesterday?"

"Yes, sir. In fact it was about the Ghost."

"His nickname?"

"No, sir. The original. Willie P. Lang."

From the corner of my eye, I saw Nakayla stiffen. She couldn't have heard Gilchrist's end of the conversation, but my astonished expression must have alerted her something big had happened.

For her benefit, I asked, "Willie P. Lang was the Ghost?"

"Yes, sir. One of the best snipers to come through the training program. I'm second generation and my father served in Vietnam with Lang. Dad said the guy was so good that by the time you knew the Ghost was there, you were already dead. The North Vietnamese Army had a fifteen-thousand-dollar bounty on his head. Eighty-six confirmed kills."

"What did SPC Fretwell want to know?"

"If I knew where the Ghost lived now. He said he'd run across the name in Asheville, and if that Willie P. Lang was the same man, he'd like to meet him."

"What did you tell him?"

"That I'd double-check with my father, but I thought he said Lang was from North Carolina."

"Have you talked with your father?"

"Not yet. He's on a fishing trip with some buddies in Idaho. Not exactly territory with great cellphone coverage. I can call you back after I hear from him."

"That's all right. You've cleared up my questions." At this point, I didn't want to get the military involved, especially since I was impersonating an officer.

One thing still bugged me. "Fretwell was looking through a list of the top ten snipers in history. Would the Ghost be on that list?"

"Maybe. If it was just Americans. My dad said Lang could have been in the top tier, but he missed a mission. In fact, my dad went in his place and killed eight high-asset NVA officers. Those would have been Lang's and put him ahead of White Feather."

I remembered that was the name of the top sniper on the list Fretwell read on the Internet. If Lang was in that league, the shot at the Kenilworth would be little more than point-blank range.

"Thank you, Staff Sergeant Gilchrist. I appreciate your help."

"Just get the bastard, sir."

"We will."

Nakayla sat patiently, waiting for me to collect my thoughts, thoughts that were zooming around in my brain at ninety-miles-an-hour.

"William Lang was one of the military's top snipers. That was the information Jason wanted to tell us."

"And William Lang killed him?"

"I don't know. Jason heard Lang's name when I questioned Mick Emory." I flashed back to the confrontation in the pawn-shop. "In fact, he started to ask about Lang but I cut him off, afraid he would give Emory more information than I wanted."

"So, Jason tried to contact Emory later from our office," Nakayla said.

"That makes sense. And when he didn't hear back, he pressed on yesterday with a call to his former instructor at Fort Benning. The question is whether William Lang knew Jason was tracking him down. If Jason left a detailed question on Mick Emory's machine, then Emory might have informed Lang and not told the police about it."

Nakayla frowned. "What's in it for Emory? Blackmail? Why should he think one sniper trying to connect with another is blackmail material?"

"Right. If Emory's not involved, then William Lang heard it directly from Jason."

"Call Newland," Nakayla said.

"Okay. But I'm only going to ask that he obtain the records for my apartment line from the phone company so we can see Jason's outgoing calls."

"And if there's one to William Lang?"

"Then we have to figure out how he was in two places at once."

"The Kenilworth and the charity ball?"

"That would explain Jason's shooting. I was thinking about Jimmy Lang and how the Ghost could be in two places at once. The Mekong Delta and the Kingdom of the Happy Land."

"You have a plan?"

"No. But Jimmy Lang did. I'm just going to implement it."

# Chapter Twenty-five

Greed. Did the motive behind the deaths of Jimmy Lang and Jason Fretwell come down to so mundane a word? Nakayla and I reviewed everything we'd learned to date, eliminating all the usual suspects—love, jealousy, blackmail, revenge—to be left only with greed and its coverup.

My theory was constructed on a foundation of circumstantial evidence, incriminating but not conclusive. The case would have to be made by the perpetrator, which meant I had to bait a trap, and I didn't know if Detective Newland would sanction an operation that could either go wrong in its execution or taint evidence for a court of law. I also didn't relish being shot.

Nakayla and I divided up duties. She went shopping for the supplies while I made two phone calls. I reached Hewitt Donaldson at his home and asked him to research inheritance laws in North Carolina. Then I tracked down Nathan Armitage and explained the resources I wanted to borrow from Armitage Security Services. He was shaken by Jason's shooting and readily offered his assistance.

Newland called toward late afternoon reporting that the interviews with Jennifer Lang and Judith Crenshaw at the gallery yielded nothing. Neither claimed to know Jason Fretwell even existed. At the time of the shooting, Jennifer had been at the same charity event her father attended.

I suggested a followup question Newland might ask Jennifer about the charity auction, and I told him I was checking some background information through my contacts in the army that might shed light on Jason's military service. Newland interpreted that to mean I suspected someone in the army held a lethal grudge against Jason and the shooting had nothing to do with the Lang case.

Again, the detective advised me not to go it alone.

Nakayla returned with a simple, black frame the size of the Ulmann photograph, some parchment, and an inexpensive fountain pen. She also bought an oilskin large enough to double-layer wrap the frame.

Nakayla experimented staining the parchment with weak coffee for an aged look, drying it in our small microwave, and then using the fountain pen to print on it with black ink. After several attempts, we finally developed a process that would pass a cursory examination. When Hewitt phoned with his legal research, Nakayla drafted the information into a short note on the treated parchment, and we wrapped it and the newly framed photograph in the oilskin.

"When will you place the calls?" Nakayla asked.

"After I've planted it."

"Will you wait until dark?"

"No. Too dangerous. There's a chance I could be followed. If so, I'd rather deal with that in daylight. We'll leave the office in my car. You can drive and I'll get out at some point when we're confident no one's behind us. I'll walk back to the parking deck for your car. You go straight to Nathan Armitage's house. You'll be safe there. I'll join you later."

Nakayla handed me the oilskin. "Are you concerned about Lucille's judgment?"

"To be honest? Yes. But I can't think of another way to get definitive proof."

We left as planned. Nakayla headed north on Lexington, driving slowly in hopes of being able to pass through an intersection just as the light changed. We were the last car to make it across Walnut Street. Nakayla sped up, made a quick right on Woodfin, and I hopped out in half a block at Chicken Alley, a narrow lane of backdoors and dumpsters with a colorful mural of roosters painted on the corner brick wall. Cute, but not exactly a tourist thoroughfare.

Two hours later at a little after five, I pulled into the pasture on the Kingdom of the Happy Land. My errands had taken me to Nakayla's for my "Land Rover" prosthesis, to my apartment for my Kimber forty-five semi-automatic and shoulder holster, and to a hardware store for a crowbar, hammer, and chisel. As I carried the tools and oilskin package up the trail to the Kingdom's last stone chimney, Lucille's words rang in my head. "There was no new beginning for us, only an unhappy ending."

A new beginning. A real treasure. With Jimmy Lang's phrases, I could create a plausible story for Jimmy telling Lucille he would pick her up at work. A story that explained the missing Ulmann photograph, Jimmy's presence on the Kingdom of the Happy Land, and the disappearance of his pickup. Whether it was true or not didn't matter so long as no one knew anything to contradict it.

The light through the pines held the soft, magical quality of late afternoon. The stone chimney of the long-vanished cabin seemed to be washed in its golden glow. I circled the base, seeking a spot where the old mortar was widest and weakest. I wouldn't want the markings to appear fresh and show the dust of my invasive attack.

The stone mason of more than a hundred years ago had been a craftsmen. The rocks had been selected and shaped to fit tightly together like pieces of a jigsaw puzzle. Most of the mortar was behind them so the dry-stack technique weathered the elements almost as if the chimney was one solid stone. Like a rigid house of cards, dislodging the wrong rock could bring a section of the chimney tumbling down.

I raised my search higher until, at eye level, I spotted a eight-inch rock with a larger stone above it overlapping the two on either side. The perimeter edges were caked with moss that had worked its way into the narrow crevices. I used the chisel to penetrate the gap, working the blade around the stone until

I could slide it to the left, enlarging the opening on the right. I inserted the flat end of the crowbar and jiggled it back and forth while pushing deeper into the chimney. Then I pressed my weight against the crowbar's curved end, forcing it to the right and applying all the leverage to the back of the stone. It popped free like a molar extracted by a dentist.

I planned to put my oilskin into the empty hole, break up the removed stone into smaller pieces, and then reseal the space the best I could. But the hole was already deeper than the rock I dislodged. I reached in and my fingers grabbed an object about the size of a hardback novel.

Electricity ran up my spine. All of the preparation Nakayla and I made had been for naught. Jimmy Lang had beaten us to it. I suddenly had the uncanny feeling that the connection between me and the skeleton in the log had been more than just my physically crashing into his remains. I had tapped into something beyond coincidence, something that had guided and shaped my thoughts from the moment I tumbled through those mushrooms and into an unfulfilled dream from nearly half a century ago.

And this gift that I held in my hands would finally set things right.

I was superstitious enough not to want to leave the Kingdom in case someone would somehow arrive in my absence and destroy my discovery. But in this desolate location, I had no cellphone service so my only option was to drive to the main road and seek a spot with a decent signal.

I'd gone about a mile when the bars on my screen came to life. I pulled to the side of the road and speed-dialed Nakayla.

"Did it go okay?" she asked.

"It's there. The real deal."

"What?"

"Wrapped in plastic but I can feel the frame."

"Then the story you made up—"

"Wasn't fictional," I interrupted. "It's so true it's scary."

She paused a moment, thinking over the implications. "What are you going to do?"

"Go with the plan. Except now I don't need to worry about Newland. I'm not planting anything."

"Are you coming to Nathan's?"

"No. I'm going to set things in motion now."

Another pause. Nakayla wasn't happy with the accelerated timetable.

"What about Nathan's supplies?"

"I'll go without them."

"You'll do no such thing!"

Her voice was so loud I had to move the phone a few inches from my ear.

"You listen to me, Sam Blackman. Lucille lost Jimmy on that spot. I'm not going to have history repeat itself. I'm coming there."

I knew Nakayla well enough that trying to dissuade her now was pointless. She'd have to be incorporated into the plan.

"Okay. But you can help best by being in position to give me a warning. Tell Nathan there's no phone service on the site and get his suggestion. We've got about two hours till dark. Come as soon as you can. I'll make the calls, and we'll abort if I can't connect with everyone."

"Where are you?"

"I'm on the shoulder about a mile from the property's entrance."

Her voice dropped to a whisper. "I love you."

"I love you too." The words swelled up from inside my chest with a power that surprised me. "I'll be careful. I promise."

My next call went to Detective Newland, who listened patiently and then agreed to follow my advice.

The net needed to be inclusive enough to safeguard against any undiscovered motives. I'm a firm believer in the axiom that what you don't know that you don't know will get you killed.

Timing was critical so I waited in the CR-V until six-thirty when I figured it was safe to set things in motion. I placed the first call.

I reached Jennifer Lang at the gallery and prefaced my question with the rationale that her father seemed uncooperative with my investigation. I wondered if he'd ever mentioned to her that his brother might have had a favorite spot on the Kingdom property.

"My grandfather told me the case against Miss Montgomery has been dropped," Jennifer said. "The victim was a black man."

"Yes, that's correct. But I'm still looking into the theft of the Ulmann photograph. I've reason to believe your uncle took it, not for any personal gain, but for a completely innocent purpose. And he might have hidden it on the Kingdom."

"That sounds bizarre," she said. "Whatever for?"

"It's too long a story to get into over the phone. I think he was planning a surprise involving some of the legends of the place."

"Legends? Sorry. My father never mentioned anything of the kind. I first heard of the Kingdom when Marsha asked me to look for that photograph."

She sounded genuinely perplexed and I apologized for bothering her.

John Lang didn't answer his phone. That threw a monkey wrench into the whole scheme. I checked the time and realized at six forty-five he was probably at dinner. Nakayla's background check revealed he was a member of his local country club. I called information and they dialed the number directly. The woman who answered promised to have someone check the dining room and either Mr. Lang or she would call me back.

Ten minutes later, my cell rang.

"What's this about?" John Lang demanded.

"I found the photograph."

Silence. I waited for him to steer the conversation. Whatever he was thinking, he was proceeding cautiously.

"Are you sure?" he asked at last.

"Yes. Two adult women, Loretta and Lucinda. Three children, Lucille, Jimmy, and you."

I heard the wheeze of his sharp intake of breath.

"Lucille told you that?"

"No. She kept your secret. I figured it out on my own. Hewitt Donaldson told me that when he reported to Lucille that the remains were of African descent, she started sobbing. Donaldson and Marsha thought it was from relief that the charges had been dropped. You and I know it was from grief. Her worst fears had been confirmed."

"What proof is that?"

"None. But when I confronted Lucille, she couldn't deny it. I know about Lang Syne Plantation. About you and Jimmy coming with Doris Ulmann, John Jacob Niles, and Julia Peterkin to have your picture made on the site of the Kingdom. And frankly, I don't care. What I do find disturbing is that you don't care either. You don't care that your brother was murdered."

"That's not true!" His voice was a harsh, raspy whisper. Lang must have stood in some alcove in his exclusive club, a place where he never would have been allowed to join if the truth had been known. "I want justice for my brother."

"Then tell me why he was shot. Tell me why he was even at the Kingdom."

"I don't know."

"Here's what I think, Mr. Lang. Jimmy was going to bring Lucille there. A spot that held so much history for both of them. I think he was going to commit to revealing his racial heritage and eliminate the last obstacle keeping Lucille from marrying him. And I think he placed that photograph and maybe other things as symbolic treasures to be pulled from the final ruins of the Kingdom. Only someone killed him first."

"It wasn't me. And I'll be god-damned if I let you spread that rumor around."

"I haven't told anyone anything. I plan to return to the Kingdom tomorrow," I lied. "To find evidence of what I told you."

"I don't care what you find. I didn't kill my brother."

"Do your son and granddaughter know about your ancestry?"

"No. No one but Lucille. And now you."

"So they don't know that the remains belong to Jimmy?"

"No. As far as they're concerned, there's no way it could be Jimmy."

"Then I'll leave it that way for the time being. At least till I get more information. Fair enough?"

I heard a sigh of defeat.

"What choice do I have?"

"Mr. Lang, you've always had a choice. Don't kid yourself into thinking otherwise."

I hung up.

My last call went to William Peterkin Lang. He was the person I expected to have difficulty locating on a Saturday night. Fortunately, he'd phoned me at the office from his cell and I'd retained the number. He wouldn't recognize mine, which might mean he wouldn't answer an unfamiliar one. My worries were unfounded.

"Lang." He sounded annoyed by the interruption.

"Mr. Lang, this is Sam Blackman."

"Yes, Sam." His mood instantly changed, as if we were old pals. "Any luck finding who shot that poor vet?"

"No. I'm afraid the police haven't had a break yet."

"Terrible thing," he said. "Go through the hell of war and then have that happen."

"Yeah, it is. But that's not why I'm calling. I'm still looking into your uncle's death."

"Oh, is there a new suspect?"

"No. Not yet. But we might have a fresh angle. You told me you overreacted when you thought your uncle's body had been discovered and you blamed Lucille."

"Yes. And I'm not proud of jumping to conclusions."

I chose my words carefully, knowing I had to balance specula-tion with factual evidence. "Lucille told me Jimmy was supposed to pick her up the day he disappeared. He'd talked about a new start and a real treasure. I think he might have been going to surprise her with some gift. Maybe a peace offering at a special place."

"If what she's saying is true."

"Yes," I agreed. "It's not a certainty, but it's all I've got. Maybe he re-framed that Ulmann photograph of Lucille's family. Or made some arrangements for little Marsha. Maybe he was leaving, but was going to make provisions for his child."

"Maybe."

"You used to hunt with him. Did he have any favorite spots, a lake or a nice mountain view where he might have planned something special?"

There was a long pause. "Nothing comes to mind. How do you think finding it would be helpful?"

"Because I believe your uncle is dead and maybe he was killed on that spot. Maybe for the ten thousand dollars he'd taken from his bank account. Maybe for another reason. But it might have happened at that location. Before I press Lucille further, I wanted to check with you."

"Wish I could help. I really do."

"Thank you. I'll speak with her tonight and start following up tomorrow."

"Don't hesitate to call me if you think I can help," he offered.

"Thanks," I said. "But we're probably chasing ghosts. Or at least a ghost."

I ended the call. The players were primed.

And then I got the word from the Chief Warrant Officer at Fort Bragg. Donnie Nettles' role became crystal clear.

# Chapter Twenty-six

The pink tinge of the western clouds faded to gray. I lay in a depression in the shadows about twenty yards to the east of the stone chimney. The trail from the pasture rose below. Anyone climbing would have trouble peering through the murky underbrush shielding me, whereas their silhouette would stand out as long as faint vestiges of daylight remained in the sky. After full darkness, I'd have to use starlight and the abrupt silence of the night creatures to know when I was no longer alone.

"Are you all right?" The tinny sound of Nakayla's voice came through the small earpiece.

"Yes," I whispered. "At least I'm not dealing with Iraqi sand flies. I'm just anxious to get this over."

"Patience," she cautioned. "And no unnecessary chances."

"Copy that, and patiently lying by."

Within five minutes, the forest reverberated with crickets and a host of other insects that could fill a naturalist's handbook. Somewhere in the distance, an owl hooted, preparing for a night of hunting. I wished us both success.

Dusk turned to night.

Static burst in my ear. "Car approaching," Nakayla whispered. A few more seconds of static. "It's turning in."

"Can you tell the make?"

"Too far away. All I see are headlights. My guess is a sedan. Should I close in behind?"

"No. Too soon. Let's see what develops. I'll lock transmission when there's contact."

"Got it," she said. The earpiece went quiet.

A sedan would take longer to navigate the rugged road than my CR-V. Nakayla had driven me to the pasture and then returned my vehicle to the safety of her vantage point along the main highway. The approaching car would see no sign that anyone else was on the premises.

For the next five minutes, the forest returned to its nocturnal cacophony. Then brief flashes of light winked through the narrow gaps between the trees. I never saw the car, just the reflected glow of its headlights along the final stretch.

Again, the woods were swallowed in darkness. I flattened into the dry pine needles, the ground covering I'd sought because it was less noisy than the leaves of the neighboring hardwoods.

My visitor made no attempt to mask the sounds coming up the trail. Halting footsteps mixed with the swishing of brush being knocked aside. The beam of a flashlight swung between the path underfoot and the top of the knoll as if the owner was anxious to see the destination.

Stepping into the small clearing, the figure appeared stooped. The flashlight was in the left hand and a cane in the right. The back spill of the halogen beam illuminated a face marked by grim determination.

"John Lang," I whispered, and locked down the radio's transmit button.

The old man played the light over the chimney from base to top like an archaeologist who stumbled upon an ancient monolith. He leaned against the cane as if the very sight of the Kingdom's remains sapped the strength from his body.

I waited for him to make a move, to take some action that connected his presence to the death both of us knew happened here so many years ago. So far, trespassing was John Lang's only provable crime.

The chimney and surrounding area grew brighter as a cloud blew clear of the half moon. I could now see he wore a tan canvas hunting jacket over matching pants. His boots were brown leather and cut a few inches above his ankles. He had come prepared for the hike.

Like the opening of a door or turning on of a front porch light, the emerging moon broke Lang from his rooted stance and bestowed permission to come closer. He tapped one of the larger base stones with the tip of his cane, and then shifted the flashlight into the same hand so that he could place his free palm flat against the rocks. He held that position for at least a minute as if summoning courage to continue his mission.

He leaned his cane against the chimney and slowly slid his fingers across the rock surface like a blind man reading a braille tablet. His hand passed under the loose stone and I thought I'd masked its location too well for the old man's eyesight. He went beyond it, but the outer edge of the beam must have caught the deeper depression around the stone's perimeter. I could see him dig his fingernail into the moss. He transferred the flashlight into his left hand and pulled a hunting knife from a sheath beneath the canvas jacket. The blade gleamed in the light as he wedged it into the crevice and repeated the maneuvers I'd made with the chisel and crowbar. Within a few minutes, he'd extracted the stone and pulled the packet from its hiding place.

Jimmy Lang's plastic had disintegrated in my hand, so I'd soiled and stressed the oilskin before re-wrapping the original articles. John Lang was too anxious to see the contents to think about the authenticity of their protective covering. He knelt down using his cane for support, spread the oilskin like a picnic blanket, and stared at the three items his brother had planned to show Lucille.

First, he picked up the ring. The scattered refractions of the small diamond danced on the pine needles like sparkling fairies. Then he examined the Ulmann photograph, the actual print Julia Peterkin had sent Lucille's grandmother eighty years ago. Finally, he opened a manila envelope and pulled out a stack of one-hundred-dollar bills and two sheets of legal paper folded to the same size as the currency. He read the handwritten words

I'd seen a few hours earlier. Even from my hiding spot in the woods, I could see tears streaking his weathered face.

Now was the time to confront him. The evidence of Jimmy Lang's threat to him lay undeniably before him.

I lifted myself to all fours, preparing to stand and make a dramatic entrance as if I'd materialized out of thin air.

The dramatic entrance shocked John Lang almost as much as it shocked me because the dramatic entrance wasn't mine.

"You'd better give me those." William Lang gave the order in a calm, firm voice.

I froze.

John flipped up his flashlight to reveal his son standing on the path at the edge of the woods. William wore a light camo jacket and black jeans. For a second, I couldn't understand why Nakayla hadn't warned me. Then I remembered I'd locked the transmit key in the on position. She couldn't get through.

William Lang moved across the clearing with ghostly speed and silence.

The old man clutched the papers to his chest. "These belong to your uncle."

"Then destroy them." William stood over his father, holding out his hand. He snapped his fingers impatiently, demanding the document.

John Lang recovered from the startling appearance of his son. His eyes narrowed. "How did you know to come here?"

"Sam Blackman told me he'd be checking the chimney tomorrow. I didn't know why, but I suspected it was in our best interest to learn what he expected to find."

I rose to my feet and stepped behind the large trunk of a neighboring white pine. "That's a lie, William." I bellowed the words toward the woods behind me, hoping to mask my exact location.

Two beams from flashlights crisscrossed the area around me.

"Mr. Lang. I told your son I thought Jimmy might have hidden the Ulmann photograph at the site where someone killed him. There's only one reason William knew to come here."

"Are you accusing me of killing my uncle?" William shouted. "You haven't the nerve to say that to my face."

I reached inside my jacket and unsnapped the flap of my shoulder holster. Then I stepped from the shelter of the tree, hands empty and away from my sides. I walked into the clearing and stopped about four yards in front of the two men.

John Lang had gotten to his feet. He held his cane in one hand and the papers and flashlight in the other. The diamond engagement ring and framed photograph lay on the ground between father and son.

"Willie was in Vietnam." John Lang's words were half-question, half-plea for confirmation.

"That's right," William Lang snarled. "I was over ten thousand miles away. I was a hell of a shot, but not that good."

"You were more than a hell of a shot. You were lethal. A sniper known as the Ghost."

"So? That's no secret."

"And that was the problem," I said. "Jason Fretwell learned you were the same Willie P. Lang he heard about in sniper school."

"Is that the kid who was shot at your apartment?" John Lang asked. His face paled because he already knew the answer.

"Yes. The same kid who tried to reach Mick Emory because Emory first mentioned Willie P. Lang. Then Jason called Fort Benning, and finally, in a huge mistake, he called William. He wanted to impress me with his detective skills and bring me the whole package. The Ghost, the missed mission, the possibility that you killed your uncle. He had the right target, but he pulled the trigger too early. What did he say, Willie P? That he was a sniper school veteran who happened to be in Asheville? That he wanted to know about the missed mission?"

"That's a god-damned lie," William growled. "I never talked to him."

"Well, then, would you like to explain why there's a record of a ten-minute call yesterday morning made by Jason Fretwell from my apartment to Lang Paper Manufacturing? I don't think he spoke with your father."

Old man Lang shook his head slowly. "What missed mission?"

"The one that would have put your son in the record books with the most sniper kills in Vietnam. The mission he would have been on if he'd returned to his unit on time."

"They deployed early," William said.

I stepped closer, spreading my empty hands with exaggerated appeal. "Come on, Willie. Staff Sergeant Gilchrist's father knows better than that. He took your place." I looked to John. "Lucille packed Willie a lunch for the bus ride to Fort Bragg after the funeral for your wife. I figure Willie got off the bus at the next stop, probably Saluda, and returned. And a man trained in concealment would have no trouble living off the land until the time was right. Until Jimmy came to bring the items to the spot he and Lucille first met."

I looked back at William. "Your uncle told you his plan, didn't he? How he was going to ask Lucille to marry him?"

William's voice thickened with anger. "My uncle was a fool. He would have been the laughing stock of the county and our family would have been out of business. But I didn't kill him."

I shrugged. "Okay. Then help me clear up a few things. You gave Deputy Overcash unsolicited testimony that your uncle said he was concerned Lucille Montgomery would become angry when he refused to marry her. I think your words were something to the effect that she would react violently like all black women do."

"I told you I was upset when I read about the discovery of the skeleton. At that time, I thought it might be my uncle and I over-emphasized what was only a potential problem with Lucille."

"But the rifle involved in the murder had been in Lucille's possession." I made a show of scratching my head. "You see that bothers me because it's a fact. Just like the DNA proves the skeleton belonged to a man with African ancestry."

I took another step closer. We were less than five feet apart. "And I've been by Marsha's house where an anonymous caller said he saw her burying the murder weapon. Here's what I think happened. The informant wasn't a man walking his dog. You went to the house to retrieve the rifle because you'd read about the discovery of the body in the Sunday paper. You wanted it to disappear so there would be no link to the remains. In 1967, the rifle had been used to frame Lucille, but the body was never discovered. But now, the case is so cold why risk the link? Except while you waited for Marsha to leave for church, you saw her burying the Remington and decided the original plan could still work. So, you tipped the Sheriff's Department anonymously and then later called with the concern the remains could be your uncle. A ballistics test matched gun to bullet and Deputy Overcash thought two independent leads were converging while they were actually orchestrated by you."

William moistened his lips. He looked at his father. "This is absurd. Let's go, Daddy."

John Lang raised his hand. "Let him say his piece."

I nodded to the old man. "Thank you."

William scowled, appeared to consider leaving on his own, and then glanced at the photograph and ring on the oilskin.

"You didn't know that these were here," I said. "You picked your location at the edge of the clearing and shot him as he returned to his truck. The distance should have been a piece of cake for the Ghost, and this way you didn't have to look him in the eye. But accuracy with an open sight can't compete with a scope. You scored a fatal wound, but Jimmy had the stamina to run for cover. You either couldn't find him in the log or dared not stay in the vicinity in case others heard the shot."

William Lang forced a laugh. "What did I do? Wait for nearly a week for my uncle to show up?"

"Maybe. I knew snipers in Iraq who could wait days at a time in order to get the shot. And there's the problem with Jimmy's pickup. It was never found, which is why your father and others thought Jimmy simply left. But you and I know better. You drove that truck to Fort Bragg. My guess is you probably got it into the target pool. The 105 howitzers need something to shoot at. The surviving scraps of metal would be about the size of your thumbnail."

"Ridiculous," William Lang said.

"I'll find out soon enough. One thing the army does well is keep records. I'll make the inquiries tomorrow so this cloud can be lifted from your innocent head."

"You're damn right I'm innocent."

I looked at John Lang. "But you, sir, might want to ask your son why he had his daughter bid for him at a silent charity auction last night at the same time young Fretwell was shot by a sniper. Why he told her he might be late, but to make sure his name was on several bid lists for pieces she deemed worthy. The daughter with whom he's not on speaking terms. The Asheville Police are looking into that matter because no one can confirm William's presence at the event before eight thirty. Enough time to change from camo to tuxedo."

John Lang stared at his son and said nothing.

"But for me," I said, "the heart of the solution to the crime is you standing here. I told you on the phone I thought the missing photograph might be where Jimmy was killed. Given the DNA report, you no longer have any reason to think the skeleton was your uncle's. It's an African-American. Or would you be more comfortable if I said it's just an African-American? No, you're here because of one reason. DNA or not, you know that skeleton was your uncle because you killed him, just like you killed Donnie Nettles."

"Nettles?" John Lang exclaimed. "He was Willie's friend."

"Yes. His pal Donnie Nettles left Fort Bragg for Vietnam on July 17, 1967. Three days after Jimmy was killed. And who was on the transport with him? His hometown friend Willie Lang. Nettles told me Willie said his uncle disappeared while he was in Vietnam. Nettles had no reason not to believe him. But when we told him the specific date was July 14th, Nettles knew Willie was still stateside because every soldier remembers the date he's shipped out for combat. What did Nettles do? See you at the American Legion Post? Tell you we knew the specific day Jimmy disappeared and the funny thing was you were still in North Carolina? You couldn't have him spreading that around. So, you showed up at his house late at night, he let his old friend in, and made the mistake of turning his back."

"You've got no proof," William said.

"I've got all the proof I need. You're here. A descendant of the Kingdom of the Happy Land. With the army records and a DNA match to the skeleton, you're toast. Because I'm going to burn you for Jimmy Lang, I'm going to burn you for Donnie Nettles, and by God I'm going to burn you for Jason Fretwell whether he lives or dies."

The flashlight wobbled in John Lang's hand. I took my eye off William long enough to see it fall to the ground.

A blur of motion and suddenly William held a nine-millimeter Beretta in his hand. Not a compact but a full-sized weapon. He aimed it at my head. I'd made a gross miscalculation.

The muzzle flashed a split-second after the cane slashed down on William's wrist. The punch in my chest felt like a cannonball fired at point-blank range. I tumbled backwards, choosing to go for my Kimber rather than break my fall.

William shoved his father to the ground. Somewhere behind me I heard thrashing in the woods.

John Lang's flashlight had landed against the base of the chimney, shooting its beam up the length of the stone monolith. William stood alone, silhouetted against the gray rocks.

He raised the pistol again.

I fired two shots.

Only the chimney remained standing.

The world went black.

# Chapter Twenty-seven

"Sam. Oh, God, Sam."

I heard Nakayla screaming my name before my eyes could focus. I must have lost consciousness for a few seconds, maybe because the Beretta's slug knocked the air from my lungs, maybe because I forgot to breathe.

Then I saw the outline of her face, the most beautiful sight imaginable. I laid the Kimber beside me and wrapped my arms around her neck, pulling her close.

"Tell Nathan his Kevlar vest worked. Barely."

She laughed and cried at the same time.

"Do we need to get him to a hospital?"

I recognized Detective Newland's voice.

"No," I said. "It was only a nine-millimeter slug. A mere gnat bite."

"He okay?" Deputy Overcash joined the little party. Newland had worked the stakeout with the Henderson County Sheriff's Department, he for Jason Fretwell's shooting and Overcash for Jimmy Lang's murder. I'd told them to position themselves at the far side of the pasture where they wouldn't be seen.

"Yeah," Newland said. "He's laying down on the job. As usual."

"What about William?" I asked.

"Dead."

Overcash edged closer to Newland. "You want me to take the old man in, or do you want him?"

"You can have first crack. I have a feeling he knows more about his brother's death than the attack on Fretwell."

Nakayla helped me to my feet. "I don't know," I said. "Did you hear everything?"

"For the most part," Newland said. "What we couldn't make out, we can enhance in the audio lab. It helped when you stepped closer, but that was a damn risk. That gnat bite could have been more severe."

"I believe John Lang was genuinely shocked by what William said. He came here because the DNA report confirmed his fears and my phone call prompted him to think about the chimney. I'll be surprised if you discover any reason to charge him." I looked at the old man hunched beside his son's body, his face buried in his hands.

"He saved my life. William got the drop on me and went for a head shot. The confidence of an expert marksman. John knocked off his aim with his cane."

Overcash shook his head. "All because Jimmy Lang wanted to marry a black woman." His face flushed as he looked at Nakayla and realized what he said.

"No," Nakayla replied. "It was more complicated than that. Marriage would not only cost the company business but also divide up its value. Lucille would have become an heir and Marsha would have been recognized as a legitimate child. Out-of-wedlock, she had little rights, but in North Carolina, marriage between the father and mother immediately legitimized their previous offspring in common. And Jimmy himself was just passing for white."

"That was going to be Jimmy Lang's final plea to Lucille," I added. "He withdrew money, he made a will leaving his estate to Lucille and Marsha, and he wanted to either come clean with his identity or leave town with them and start over elsewhere. I guess he thought the legendary treasure in the chimney would be both romantic and persuasive. The photograph was a symbol of their shared past, the ring for his proposal, and the handwritten will and money as the promise for their future."

"And you don't think William knew about his ancestry?" Newland asked.

"No. I think Jimmy Lang told his nephew he was going to marry Lucille and he would bring her here for the proposal. The place had meaning for Lucille. That was no secret. And Jimmy knew his nephew was going back to war. I doubt he would say, oh, by the way, you're black. Though he might have been tempted given what I witnessed of William's racist attitudes. We'll never know the truth about that final conversation between uncle and nephew. It certainly left William angry enough to commit murder."

"The irony never ends, does it?" Newland said. "Marsha and Lucille were employees, now they're part owners of the company."

"That's a legal task for Hewitt Donaldson to tackle. He'll want those papers as soon as they can be released."

We all looked at the oilskin illuminated by the back spill of John Lang's flashlight. A ring, a photograph, a will, and money. A denied past and an unfulfilled future.

Hewitt, Nakayla, and I spent Sunday afternoon in a meeting with District Attorney Noel Chesterson. He was all smiles, assuring us he would hold a press conference to personally attest that the fatal shooting of William P. Lang had been an act of self-defense. I restrained myself from ripping open my shirt to show him the grapefruit-size bruise in the center of my chest, evidence enough that Lang tried to kill me.

But, the meeting wasn't about me. Hewitt pressed Chesterson for a quick closure of the investigation, citing all that Lucille Montgomery had gone through and that she deserved to take possession of what Jimmy Lang clearly intended her to have so many years ago. Chesterson promised his full cooperation as soon as his office received the final report from the M.E. and the Sheriff's Department. In the meantime, a very happy Deputy Overcash provided us with photo-copies and photographs.

Monday morning, Hewitt, Nakayla, and I called on Lucille Montgomery. Marsha admitted us into the apartment. Her mother wasn't in her customary spot in the rocking chair. She sat at one end of the sofa, and, from the depression in the cushion next to her, I deduced Marsha had been sitting beside her. The elderly woman was obviously going through a tough time, and I wondered if Hewitt Donaldson's insistence that we see her had been a mistake.

He gave a slight bow before speaking. "Miss Montgomery, do you mind if I sit next to you?"

"You are welcome to sit anywhere you like, sir."

Hewitt sat and rested a large manila envelope on his lap. "I'm sorry that we've confirmed Jimmy Lang was the victim Sam discovered."

She nodded and stared straight ahead. "And that he was killed by the hand of his own nephew."

"Yes, ma'am. That's also a grievous burden for everyone to bear."

Lucille turned her head to look at Hewitt. "How is John faring?"

"I'm afraid not well. He had no idea what his son had done."

"I lost my Jimmy, but I didn't lose who he was."

"No, ma'am. One thing we do know, Jimmy Lang was true to his word." Hewitt lifted the envelope and unfastened the clasp. "He was committed to you, Miss Montgomery." He pulled the sheets of paper free. "You and Marsha. Here's what Sam found in the old chimney, the chimney from the Ulmann photograph. This is the treasure Jimmy planned to give you."

He handed her an eight-by-ten picture of the modest diamond ring. To Deputy Overcash's credit, he'd removed it from an evidence sleeve and placed it on a pale blue cloth.

Lucille smiled, though her lower lip trembled. "I wonder where he got that?"

Marsha stepped closer and Lucille handed her the photo. Hewitt passed Lucille three pages clipped together, photo-copies of Jimmy's handwritten will. "We'll go over this later, but Jimmy wrote that you and Marsha were to be the heirs of his estate. He also acknowledged Marsha as his daughter. That wouldn't have been an issue if you married, but he wanted to insure Marsha's wellbeing in case you still refused him."

Lucille briefly glanced at the document before rubbing her fingers over the text. It was the familiarity of the handwriting that attracted her attention, not the meaning of the words.

"What does Mother do with that now? There's no estate."

"I believe you have a clear claim to half of Lang Paper Manufacturing."

"But John built that company," Lucille said.

"He's in no shape to run it. There's no reason it too should be sacrificed."

Mother and daughter looked at each other.

"Jennifer," Marsha said. "We need Jennifer to come back."

I smiled. A new family was being created before my eyes.

"The missing Ulmann photograph was also in the chimney," Hewitt said. "It's safely under lock and key with the sheriff. And then there's the money," he added. "The ten thousand dollars Jimmy withdrew. The sheriff will give it and everything else to you as soon as the case is closed."

"The money should go to you," Lucille said. "If it's sufficient to cover your fee."

Hewitt shook his head. "No. We were working for John Lang. That money belongs to you."

Lucille frowned. "But will he pay you?"

"He's Jimmy's twin, isn't he?"

Lucille reached over and clasped Hewitt's hand. "Yes. And like Jimmy, and like you, Mr. Donaldson, John's a man of his word."

The sky was gray with small patches of blue peeking through the thinnest parts of the cloudy shroud. Beams of sunlight broke through, and I thought of Jason Fretwell. Earlier that morning I'd been at his bedside. The doctors were confident it was safe to start bringing him out of the medically induced coma.

I grabbed Captain's arm and helped him guide his walker up the slope through the open cemetery gate. Nakayla walked on the other side of him.

Harry Young's casket was already in place atop the knoll of the historic Newton Academy Cemetery. The small graveyard was little more than two acres and lay less than a mile from my apartment. I never knew it existed.

We passed markers so eroded by time that the epitaphs were no longer legible. Some had been supplemented by newer marble stones, particularly those of the Revolutionary War veterans. Small flags graced the graves of all war veterans in anticipation of Memorial Day now less than a week away.

We might be witnessing the last grave to be dug on this quiet hill. At a hundred and five, Harry Young might be the final descendant whose immediate family had been interred here. A trustee for the foundation overseeing the care of the cemetery agreed to have Harry laid to rest beside his father, a man who died in 1919.

The chaplain who conducted the ecumenical Christian service at Golden Oaks Retirement Center stood beside the simple wooden casket, watching our approach. His Bible was already open.

"Thank you for bringing me," Captain said. "This spot is perfect for the Mayor." He chuckled. "Harry will definitely be the new kid on this block."

We stopped across the open grave from the chaplain. Just the four of us. The men from the attending funeral home stood farther away, yielding the space to us, Harry's designated loved ones. And we were.

The chaplain began slowly reading the Twenty-Third Psalm. "The Lord is my shepherd, I shall not want."

My mind drifted from the familiar words as I thought about all that Harry had seen and experienced in his lifetime. My eyes caught sight of a row of Confederate battle flags marking the stones of unknown Confederate dead. "CSA 1861-1865" was all that summarized their lives.

"Thou preparest a table before me in the presence of mine enemies."

A few yards below them, a row of U.S. flags marked the graves of unknown Union soldiers. Nameless enemies sharing the same hillside. Forever.

Maybe here is where the ironies end.

Loving versus Virginia. The very name summarized another conflict—the power of love versus the power of the state.

"And I shall dwell in the house of the Lord forever."

Harry Young was in the house. So were Jimmy Lang and Donnie Nettles.

The chaplain closed the Bible.

Captain saluted.

# Acknowledgments

I am grateful to the many people who offered their expertise, encouragement, and, in some cases, their names for the creation of this novel.

The Kingdom of the Happy Land existed in the North Carolina mountains as described. The story of the commune of former slaves and the slave owner who led them to their refuge was first told to me by the late Louise Bailey, friend and keeper of our mountains' history. Ed Bell, whose family owns the site of the Kingdom, was invaluable for showing me the actual location and for being a character in the book. I'm indebted to Henry Harkey for his research of North Carolina inheritance laws and to Judge Fritz Mercer for sharing courtroom procedures and appearing as a fictional version of himself. Arborist Jack McNeary provided facts regarding the hollow log, and Sheriff Chipp Bailey enabled me to learn about the forensic evaluation of gunshot wounds. My brother Craig de Castrique and the Asheville Mushroom Club offered suggestions for Sam's fungi quest.

Historian and folklorist David Brose gave me access to hundreds of Doris Ulmann photographs housed at the John C. Campbell Folk School and he shared stories about the travels of Doris Ulmann and John Jacob Niles to the area. Thanks to David for also spending time with Sam and Nakayla. All other characters are fictional and any resemblance to actual persons is coincidental.

Readers might be interested in several books used for reference: A Devil and a Good Woman, Too—The Lives of Julia Peterkin by Susan Millar Williams; and The Life and Photography of Doris Ulmann by Philip Walker Jacobs. I'm grateful to Blue Ridge Community College for access to Sadie Smathers Patton's 1957 limited edition monograph, The Kingdom of the Happy Land.

While the existence of the Kingdom and the photographic treks of Doris Ulmann and John Jacob Niles were real events, the linking of the two is an invention for the story.

Creation of a novel is not done in isolation. Thanks to Jessica Tribble, Annette Rogers, Robert Rosenwald and the entire staff of Poisoned Pen Press, and to my editor Barbara Peters and agent Linda Allen. Also thanks to my wife Linda, daughters Lindsay and Melissa, and son-in-law Pete for reviewing the manuscript.

Finally, I'm grateful to the booksellers and librarians who recommend my stories to their patrons, and to you, the reader, for spending your time with Sam and Nakayla in the mountains of North Carolina.

Mark de Castrique
January 2013
Charlotte, North Carolina

To receive a free catalog of Poisoned Pen Press titles, please contact us in one of the following ways:

Phone: 1-800-421-3976
Facsimile: 1-480-949-1707
Email: info@poisonedpenpress.com
Website: www.poisonedpenpress.com

Poisoned Pen Press
6962 E. First Ave. Ste 103
Scottsdale, AZ 85251